Also by KJ Charles

The Doomsday Books
The Secret Lives of Country Gentlemen
A Nobleman's Guide to Seducing a Scoundrel

All of Us Murderers

KJ CHARLES

Copyright © 2025 by Web Alchemy, Ltd.
Cover and internal design © 2025 by Sourcebooks
Cover art by Marcela Bolívar
Internal design by Tara Jaggers/Sourcebooks

Sourcebooks, Poisoned Pen Press, and the colophon
are registered trademarks of Sourcebooks.

All rights reserved. No part of this book may be reproduced in any form or by
any electronic or mechanical means including information storage and retrieval
systems—except in the case of brief quotations embodied in critical articles
or reviews—without permission in writing from its publisher, Sourcebooks.

No part of this book may be used or reproduced in any manner for the
purpose of training artificial intelligence technologies or systems.

The characters and events portrayed in this book are fictitious
or are used fictitiously. Any similarity to real persons, living or
dead, is purely coincidental and not intended by the author.

All brand names and product names used in this book are trademarks,
registered trademarks, or trade names of their respective holders.
Sourcebooks is not associated with any product or vendor in this book.

Published by Poisoned Pen Press, an imprint of Sourcebooks
1935 Brookdale RD, Naperville, IL 60563-2773
(630) 961-3900
sourcebooks.com

Cataloging-in-Publication Data is on file with the Library of Congress.

The authorized representative in the EEA is Dorling Kindersley
Verlag GmbH. Arnulfstr. 124, 80636 Munich, Germany

Manufactured in the UK by Clays and distributed by
Dorling Kindersley Limited, London
001-355374-Oct/25
10 9 8 7 6 5 4 3 2 1

For Zachary Holmes Spence

*a wonderful, generous soul and a
reader of impeccable discernment.*

*May you never be trapped in a sinister
Gothic mansion (or if you are, may there
always be a mysterious hottie to help out)*

*With love
KJ x*

content warnings

This book contains ableism towards a character with ADHD, and references to sexual abuse (not shown on page).

For a detailed list of content warnings, please visit https://kjcharleswriter.com/content-warnings

one

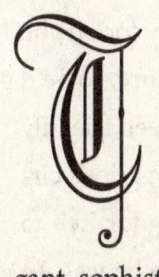HE GATES WERE BEAUTIFULLY wrought iron, elegantly monogrammed with interlocking *W*s. The motor-car's headlights illuminated the black paint, the curlicues and details gleaming gold. It was an elegant, sophisticated gate. It was also twelve feet high if you counted the spikes, and it stood in a very solid brick wall that matched its height.

Zebedee Wyckham contemplated the gate and the towering wall, its top dimly picked out by the waning moon. He considered the bleak moorland through which they had been driving on the roughest possible track for hours without seeing evidence of human life. Then he asked the chauffeur, "Lackaday House, yes? Not Dartmoor Prison?"

"Lackaday House," the man said, unsmiling.

"Right."

Zeb had not been to Lackaday House before. Its owner was his cousin Wynn Wyckham, but Wynn was over two decades his senior, and the Wyckhams were not a close or a loving family. Zeb had met him exactly twice, both times as a child under orders to keep his mouth shut; he'd barely thought of the fellow since.

Then, six months ago, he'd had a letter, quite out of the blue, asking him to come for a visit. Since Zeb wouldn't cross the street to see any of the relatives he knew, he had snorted at the idea of crossing the country for one he didn't. Nevertheless, it had been a kindly gesture, so he'd replied, and Wynn had kept pressing. He'd been friendly and pleasant, which made a nice change, and various circumstances had arisen that made it appealing for Zeb to be somewhere else, and long story short, here he was. In cold, dark Dartmoor at the arse end of November, staring at a firmly closed gate.

He couldn't help feeling he'd misjudged this.

"It's extremely secure," he remarked. "Is there much danger of burglars here?"

The chauffeur looked round at him with an expression of utter contempt. He was a heavy-set man, in his fifties but obviously powerful, with a rat-trap mouth, so the expression was very effective. "No."

Zeb had spent the last two hours in silence, since the noise of the motor and the wind and the road surface had made conversation impossible. He'd also been sitting as close to still as he could, which was to say fidgeting relentlessly and hoping it wasn't annoying his driver too much, and the combination of enforced immobility and enforced taciturnity was building up under his skin. He really wanted to talk.

He'd been told often enough he should realise when people didn't want to listen. He locked his jaw, concentrating on the feel of the rosary in his pocket, sliding the string of smooth beads round and round between finger and thumb while his foot tapped compulsively. He needed to be out of this blasted car. Maybe he could get out and walk the rest of the way down the drive, once they opened the gates. If they ever opened the gates.

"Gosh, this is taking a while," he said. "It is rather cold to sit here, isn't it? And it must be trying for you to wait like this every time. Unless it's not every time?"

The chauffeur didn't even answer. Zeb's toes twitched violently in his shoes.

A man finally turned up to unlock the gates and haul them open. The procedure took several minutes and was accompanied by a deeply unpleasant screeching of metal on stone. The sound would drive Zeb mad if he were the gatekeeper.

Maybe they didn't open the gates often. Maybe the gatekeeper was already mad and didn't mind. Maybe they wanted it to be noisy so that nobody could escape the grounds in secret.

Zeb grinned to himself, recognising his imaginings as the sort that Gothic heroines frequently thought and dismissed at the start of a book. Specifically, it was very much what Clara thought and dismissed at the beginning of Walter Wyckham's Gothic classic *Clara Lackaday*, which was why she entered the brooding walls that would become her prison instead of legging it for the horizon in chapter one. The more fool Clara.

The gates were finally pulled wide. The chauffeur got the motor going again, its bangs and growls an unwelcome intrusion into Dartmoor's clean, quiet air, and they chugged along. Behind them, the gate screamed protest once more before shutting with a resoundingly final clang.

They drove on up the drive. After a few moments, Zeb said, "Where's the house?"

"Not there yet, are we?" the chauffeur said contemptuously.

"Well, that's why I asked. It seems an awfully long way. Are the grounds very extensive?"

The chauffeur ignored that as well. Zeb suspected they were unlikely to become friends.

Along with the motor's headlamps, the sliver of moon

gave just enough light to indicate that the grounds were as bleak as the moors outside. Zeb saw a few shapes which might be outbuildings, but oddly shaped ones if so. Eventually there were trees, and then Zeb saw Lackaday House at last.

It was huge, dark, towering against the night sky, a great octagonal tower topped by a cupola dominating its centre. Zeb thought he could make out crenellations and flying buttresses, perhaps because he knew they were there from photographs. He would have placed it in the year 1500 or so as a glowering relic of medieval religion and aristocratic pride, if he hadn't known his entirely common grandfather had built the thing a mere century ago.

"That's very Gothic," he said, and was ignored once more.

The motor pulled up in front of the house. The chauffeur sat unmoving and unspeaking, so Zeb said, "Well, thank you" and got out.

The relief was overwhelming. He shook his arms out, rolled his shoulder, jiggled his ankles to kick out the infuriating accumulation of fidgets, and then realised the chauffeur was still sitting there, very possibly watching him in the wing mirror, and clearly had no intention of getting his luggage out.

Zeb considered that, then went to retrieve his suitcases

from the back himself. He was starting to feel rather unsettled. It was a matter of course in big houses like this that the staff did things like taking bags or opening doors for guests, but the chauffeur didn't seem to feel that was his responsibility, and there was no indication that anyone had even noticed their arrival.

He turned to the chauffeur, who took that opportunity to drive off without a word, leaving him in a cloud of stinking smoke.

"Bye, then," Zeb said after him, and hoisted his suitcases towards the stairs and the front door.

As he did so, the door opened, spilling light down the stone steps. Zeb looked up, hoping for Cousin Wynn, or at least a butler, and saw a woman.

She was young, and very lovely, with dark hair spilling in loose curls over her shoulders. She wore a simple long white shift, possibly a nightgown, and appeared to be barefoot. He'd never seen a woman in such deshabille outside a painting. As he gaped, she clasped both hands to her generously exposed bosom and ran down the steps, fleeing past him into the dark gardens with a sob.

"Uh, hello?" Zeb said after her, too late. "Excuse me?"

She disappeared into the darkness, a dim white wraith fading to nothing. Zeb gazed at her retreat, bathed in the light from the house. That darkened with dramatic suddenness, and he turned to see that a tall man was silhouetted in the doorway.

"Oh," Zeb said, blinking at the light. "Good evening. Do you know that a woman just ran into the gardens crying?"

The man didn't reply. He stepped back and gestured towards the inside of the house, indicating that Zeb should come in.

Zeb looked at him, and back into the gardens. "No, but a young lady has legged it into the darkness, very much not dressed for the weather, and she seemed quite upset. I think someone should go after her."

"Please enter the house. The cold is getting in."

Zeb opened his mouth to ask if his interlocutor had somehow not heard him. The words never made it out because they were swamped by an impossible, overwhelming recognition that sent a shudder all along his spine. The tall silhouette. The deep, cool baritone voice.

He dropped his bags, ran four steps up the stairs, and saw a familiar face emerge from the darkness. Patrician nose, light hazel eyes, straw-coloured hair, its reddish tint made flame by the gaslight.

Gideon. It was actually, impossibly, Gideon. Zeb's heart lurched joyously in the fraction of a second before his brain caught up and his stomach plunged. The combined experience was unpleasant.

"What the—?"

"Ah, Mr. Zebedee," Gideon said over him. "You may remember me: Gideon Grey. I'm Mr. Wynn Wyckham's confidential secretary. I trust you had a pleasant journey."

Gideon didn't sound like he trusted it in the least. He sounded like he wished Zeb had driven into a ditch.

Zeb bit back *What the bloody hell are you doing here?* Mixing in his circles, one learned to take people's cues on one's previous acquaintance. "Good evening. How nice to meet you again," he managed, though his mind was scrambling. *Gideon. Here.*

Gideon gave it about two seconds. "Are you going to come in? Or just stand there?"

Right, yes, coming in was the thing to do. Zeb moved forward, realised he needed his bags, went back down again, and remembered. "No, but there was a woman. The young lady—"

"Miss Wyckham will come to no harm. Leave the bags. I'll have them taken up."

"Miss who?"

"Miss Jessamine Wyckham," Gideon said, with some exasperation. "That was your cousin Jessamine."

"My *what*?"

"Cousin!" Gideon snapped. "Just come into the house, will you? Sir," he added, more secretarially. "I would like to shut the door."

"But—"

"It is cold," Gideon said through his teeth. "If you come in, you can go up. You are the last to arrive, and dinner will be served in half an hour."

This was a bad dream. In fact, yes, of course it was a dream. Zeb didn't have a cousin Jessamine, and Gideon could not possibly be here calling him *sir*, therefore he was dozing in the motor-car and would wake up at any minute. Zeb prodded at that thought for a second in a hopeful sort of way. No waking occurred.

"Thank you," he said, because some sort of reply was needed. "When you say 'last'..."

"Get *in*."

Zeb grabbed his bags and got in, finding himself in a huge hall. Gideon shut the door with the kind of deliberate care that was more pointed than a slam. "Alfred will show you to your room. Take the luggage, please, Alfred."

A footman approached, with a truculent look reminiscent of the chauffeur. He hoisted the suitcases. Gideon added, "The rest of your family will be gathered in the drawing room, which is there, down the—"

"My family?" Zeb said. "You mean Wynn, yes?"

"And Mr. Bram Wyckham—"

"Bram?" Zeb yelped. "Bram is in this house? Right now? At the same time as me?"

"Mr. Bram Wyckham, Mrs. Wyckham, and Mr. Hawley Wyckham."

"Sweet baby Jesus!"

Gideon inclined his head. The gaslight was by no means excessively bright, and the positioning of the lamps cast dramatic shadows. His eyes and cheeks were hollower than they used to be, Zeb thought. He looked drawn, older, almost cadaverous.

And he'd said Bram was here, so this wasn't a dream. It was quite clearly a nightmare. "Tell me you're not serious," Zeb said.

Gideon gave him an expressionless look. Zeb wished he could detect sympathy in it. "Please follow Alfred, Mr. Zebedee. Mr. Wynn prefers punctuality at meals."

Zeb's allotted room was on the first floor of the west wing, towards the back of the house. It was reasonably sized, with a canopied bed, leaded windows, a heavily-framed oil painting of a man that Zeb didn't want to look at, and a Tudorish sort of air it was three centuries away from deserving.

Zeb didn't care about historical accuracy at this moment. He was more concerned with getting dressed, and also whether he could fashion a makeshift rope from bedsheets and escape.

Bram was bad enough. Elise made everything worse. Bram, Elise, *and Hawley*...well, if Cousin Wynn had planned this as a delightful family reunion, he had a shock coming.

And, worse than all that put together, Gideon. How could Gideon be here, working as Wynn's secretary? How was Zeb supposed to spend a fortnight with Gideon calling him *Mr. Zebedee* and looking at him with such cold dislike?

Obviously Gideon still hated him. That was more of a blow than Zeb might have expected. He had woken up for a year knowing that Gideon hated him, of course, that he'd ruined the best thing in his life out of his own damn fool stupidity, but he'd known it from a distance: their paths hadn't crossed since they'd parted. Now he was faced with Gideon hating him in person, and it hurt as much as it ever had.

Gideon ought not hate him. It was quite reasonable he did, in the circumstances, but he ought not. In a better-ordered world, his light eyes would have warmed as they used to, and his lips would have twitched in the little smile that utterly changed his serious face, and the stiffness of his shoulders would have relaxed, and Zeb would have run up the stairs and caught his hands...

That should have happened. And he shouldn't have that drawn, unhappy look, as though he hadn't laughed in a year; as though all the old stiff reserve had come back and calcified him. As though Zeb had ruined, not just what they'd had, but Gideon himself.

He sat on the bed, head in hands. He didn't want to have hurt Gideon; he also very much didn't want to spend a fortnight having the fact he had done so rubbed into his own face. Perhaps that was cowardly and he deserved the punishment, except he couldn't imagine Gideon enjoying the next fortnight either. Why the devil was he here? *How* was he here?

Distantly, Zeb heard a gong. It didn't register for a moment, then he realised with a jolt he was supposed to be downstairs.

At least he'd got everything done but his tie. He went to do that, and winced at what the mirror showed him.

He'd meant to get his dinner things cleaned and pressed for this visit, but there had been all the kerfuffle with work, and various tasks had come up that he couldn't even remember now but which had seemed more urgent at the time, and the fact was, he hadn't got round to it. The neglect showed. His dinner jacket was decidedly grubby and creased after a few excessive nights a couple of years ago, followed by an unspecified period stuffed into the bottom of his wardrobe; the disgraceful state of his black trousers suggested very accurately that he'd spent some time kneeling in them; and his white waistcoat lacked snowy spotlessness in the same way that London's streets lacked a patina of gold.

In fact, he looked an utter scruff. He usually did, in part because of his shambolic inability to get things cleaned and pressed, rather more because he simply didn't care. His father had frequently expressed that cleanliness was next to godliness, and, as with many things, Zeb wasn't inclined to follow in his footsteps. Left to himself, he would live in old tweed, older shoes, and a general state of baggy comfort. If only people would leave him to himself.

But he *had* wanted to sort out his dinner things for this visit, and at this moment, the failure felt crushing.

He batted ineffectually at the unruly curls he might have smoothed with pomade if he'd had any. He'd intended to buy some when he got his hair cut, which he also hadn't got round to. Bram was going to love this.

Zeb got the tie dealt with in the speckled mirror while, to one side, the portrait contemplated him with a sneer. "You can sod off," Zeb told it, and wondered whether it would be rude to take it down and turn its face to the wall.

Stop dallying. Get on.

Zeb took a deep breath, and headed out of the room to find himself in a long, empty corridor. The dim gaslight revealed it was papered in dark red with an aggressively repetitive decoration of swerving, bloated lines, and hung with dark paintings of grim old men and empty moors. At least they distracted the eye from the wallpaper. Doors stretched off in both directions.

It would be very easy to have no idea where to go at this point, and end up helplessly baffled and miserably late for dinner. It was what he'd usually do, in fact, which was why Zeb had made himself consciously note the way to his room. Now, if he could just remember what that was.

He checked his bedroom door to be sure he could identify it on his return (three from the end, and opposite a painting of a man in a Georgian wig who looked like his father but with syphilis), and headed off with reasonable confidence that he had to take the first right turn and then a left. He did so, but decided after about ten feet he'd been wrong: he didn't recognise this corridor at all. Hell's bells. He doubled back, took the next right in an exploratory way, and decided that was wrong too. He turned back to retrace his steps, trying to quash the rising fear that he'd got turned around somehow, came round a corner, and almost walked into Gideon.

"Oh," Zeb said.

Gideon's jaw was set. "May I show you the way downstairs?"

"Gideon—"

"*Mr. Grey,*" Gideon said, low and savage. "Remember that. You're not losing me another job."

Zeb's stomach tensed so hard it hurt. "What are you doing here?"

"I assumed you'd get lost. Clearly, I was right."

He stalked off on that. Zeb hurried to catch up. Gideon had longer legs and a fast pace; Zeb was one of nature's amblers.

"I meant, why are you *here*?" he demanded as they stormed along the dark corridor. "Here with my cousin? How did you get this job?"

"Not off my references from Cubitt's; I can assure you of that."

He sped up, leaving Zeb entirely behind, and led the way to a door that opened on to the landing at the top of the main hall.

Zeb had been too distracted to pay attention when he had entered the house. He now saw it was impressively sized, with a very high ceiling, a couple of huge windows, and a neck-breaker of a stone staircase leading down to the flagstoned floor. It was distinctly cold. He hurried after Gideon, but couldn't quite catch him before they reached the drawing room, and his assembled family.

Everyone turned to look at him as he tumbled in at Gideon's heels. There was a silence. Finally Bram said, through tight lips, "Zebedee. You're late."

"Charmed to see you too," Zeb retorted.

He regretted it as soon as the words were out. He

always did, but his determination to be the bigger man and rise above his brother's sneers never survived contact with the blighter. He swung away before it got worse, giving his sister-in-law the obligatory bow. "Good evening, Elise. Ah—" He glanced between the two men he didn't know.

The shorter of them stepped forward, smiling, and shook Zeb's hand warmly. "Zebedee. How delightful to meet you after so long. I am your Cousin Wynn."

Wynn was cheerful, plump, and entirely bald but for a fringe of grey hair. He blinked in a friendly way through owlish spectacles. Zeb knew him to be in the region of fifty; he looked older.

"It's lovely to be here," he lied. "Very good to meet you, Wynn. Well, to meet you again, I suppose, since we have met, but I was rather young then—"

Bram muttered something not quite under his breath, in which Zeb made out the word 'wittering'. He stopped talking.

Wynn was smiling, though. "Yes, it has been twenty years or more, hasn't it? We must not let so long go by again. Thank you for coming, Zebedee."

"Zeb, please. I go by Zeb."

"Really? What an ungainly shortening of an elegant name. Still, that's young men for you, eh, Dash? Do you know Colonel Dash?"

He indicated the other unknown man, who looked to be in his mid-forties, with a ramrod-straight back and a heavy moustache. He and Zeb shook hands as Wynn said, "Wyckham Dash, our second cousin. Dash, this is Zebedee. Zeb."

Dash gave a confident smile. "Pleased to meet you. Call me Dash. Too many Wyckhams in here."

That was inarguable. Zeb crossed his fingers as unobtrusively as possible, turned to the final member of the company, and said, "Good evening, Hawley."

"Zeb, dear boy," Hawley drawled. He was much the best-looking of the younger generation, with dramatically swept back dark blond hair and striking green eyes, and sported a goatee that suited him tiresomely well. He wore an emerald velvet jacket in lieu of the conventional black (or, in Zeb's case, blackish) evening dress the other men sported; it made him look like the artist he was. He held a glass of sherry, presumably because Cousin Wynn didn't stock absinthe.

Hawley was assessing Zeb in his turn. "It's been a while, hasn't it? Now, when was it I last saw you?"

He knew very well where: a very specific sort of gentleman's club. Hawley had been there because he liked to be acquainted with London's scenes of vice; Zeb had been there because he was a member. It was a little tease, a little taunt, a little flick of the cat's claw.

"The Café Royal, I think. You were with a party," Zeb said. That was actually the last time but one he'd seen the fellow, and it had been brief, what with Hawley's party getting themselves thrown out for drunken and disorderly behaviour.

"The Café Royal?" Elise repeated in her clear, bell-like voice. "Goodness, Hawley. How strangely predictable of you. So very bourgeois."

"It can hardly be strangely predictable, dear Elise," Hawley returned, with a wolfish smile. "You muddle your metaphors."

"That wasn't a metaphor," Zeb said, and got glares from everyone involved: Hawley for the correction, Bram for inserting himself in a conversation with his wife, Elise for existing, probably. She'd never been pleased about that.

Wynn beamed around them. "How marvellous it is to have the whole family together like this. I don't know if it has happened before."

Zeb was fairly sure it had not, since the spectrum of Wyckham family relationships ran from indifference to loathing. He said, "It's very kind of you to host us all."

"Be so good as to speak on your own behalf," Bram said. "I don't require you to offer gratitude for me. Wynn is, as always, a most thoughtful host."

"Do pour yourself a sherry, Zebedee," Wynn said. "If

you care to smoke after dinner, there are cigarettes in the boxes around the house: please do help yourself, but I ask that my guests do not smoke in here or the dining room. I have a quite irrational aversion to the smell. I will just send to see if Jessamine will join us. Do please enjoy catching up with each other."

Zeb was fairly sure they'd already managed all the courteous interaction of which a group of Wyckhams was likely to be capable. He went to look at the paintings on the walls as a pretext for not talking to anyone, slipping his hand into his pocket as he did so, and realised he'd forgotten to transfer the rosary from his other jacket. Blast.

There were several rather good pictures, including a Turner seascape and two portraits of a woman in her thirties, one of which had the sensuality of John Singer Sargent's best work. In fact, Zeb realised as he examined them, it *was* a Sargent, and the other one was John Everett Millais. That must have cost a few bob to commission, and he wondered who the woman was. Wynn had never married, so far as he knew, but Lackaday House's previous owner, his father, had died around 1880—

"For goodness' sake, must you?" Bram snapped in his ear.

Zeb jumped, startled. "What?"

"Fiddling and fidgeting. It is intolerable."

Zeb had no idea what he was talking about for a second, and then realised he'd picked up a box of matches from the table in front of him and had been playing with it, pushing the drawer in and out. He hadn't noticed himself doing it; he never did. "Sorry," he said automatically, and then could have kicked himself. He had no need to apologise to Bram, for anything, ever.

At the door, Wynn clapped his hands. "Well! We are all here except Jessamine, and we will not wait for her. Let us go through."

two

HEY FILED THROUGH TO a grand dining hall with a table that would seat thirty. Their party of seven looked decidedly meagre clustered at one end, particularly since there was an eighth place set. Wynn nodded at the dour footman. "Miss Jessamine may not be joining us tonight. Leave the setting in case she changes her mind, but we will begin."

"Is that the young lady I saw as I arrived?" Zeb asked.

"That's right. Your cousin, or first cousin once removed, though we need not split hairs. As it were." He chuckled.

"I'm sorry, I don't understand." Zeb could feel several people looking daggers at him, but he didn't trust anyone here to explain matters discreetly at a convenient juncture. "I wasn't aware I had a young lady cousin. Is she your daughter, Hawley?"

Bram made an explosive noise which Zeb connected too late to the footman who was serving out soup, as if the staff wouldn't know exactly what was going on.

Hawley had no interest in manners or discretion, but his lip curled anyway. "Of course she is not my daughter. The girl is barely ten years my junior."

"She's eighteen, and you're thirty-five if you're a day," Elise pointed out. "I know you like to consider yourself an enfant terrible, but you're really getting a *little* past that, don't you think?"

"Thirty-four. And I'm quite sure a woman's thirtieth birthday comes before a man's fortieth." Hawley delivered that with a smirk.

"That makes no mathematical sense at all," Bram said.

Hawley clearly felt his aphorism should have received more applause. "How you can presume to comment on Art with your cloddish literality—"

Zeb felt a pang of sympathy for Wynn, unwittingly inviting this mess to his dining table, and for Gideon, not even a Wyckham but stuck here listening to them. "I still don't understand," he said, hoping to pull the conversation back on track. "Who is she?"

"It's a sad story," Wynn said. "You know I had a sister, Laura. Well, not quite a sister. She was our grandfather's daughter by his fifth wife, born after his death."

Zeb worked that out. "So, she was your aunt? My aunt too, I suppose."

"Indeed, but she and I were born in the same year. My father took full charge of her, and Laura and I were brought up as siblings."

"Why did your father take charge of her?" Zeb asked. "What happened to her mother? Oh, was that the housemaid?"

Bram harrumphed with annoyance. "Kindly don't dredge up family history."

"We're talking about family history. And I'm sure Walter Wyckham's last wife was his housemaid: I remember Father complaining about it."

"Yes, he was nearly eighty when love's young dream struck him in the servants' quarters. Senility is a marvellous thing," Hawley remarked.

"So why did—"

"There is no need to pry," Bram said over him. "For heaven's sake, hold your tongue."

"Not at all," Wynn said. "There is no mystery about it: simply, Laura's mother was of low birth and weak mind, not fit to live independently. Laura and I were inseparable growing up, but at sixteen she had a love affair. The passion of youth. My father had her removed from the house when the consequences of her error became visible. He took her away, and he told me she was dead."

Wynn stopped there. Zeb could see his throat working for a moment before he went on. "He told me that cruel lie, and he gave her a small allowance to live on with her daughter so long as she did not contact me. Thus he kept us apart, until just a few weeks before his death. He said she had brought shame to the family, that she and her mother were a stain on our name. Well, let him think that. He died at last, I became master here, and my Laura returned to her home. She is there, look."

Zeb turned to follow his gesture, and was relieved to see he meant a painting. It showed the same woman as in the other paintings. She was elegantly dressed and wore a distinctly smug smile.

Wynn gazed at the portrait for a moment, eyes focused on the past, then sighed. "Our reunion was too short. All Walter's children were to die before fifty, and Laura was no exception to that. She died only a handful of years after her return."

"What a shame," Elise said, with glacial insincerity.

"It's a very sad story," Zeb added, because he felt rather bad for Wynn, his voice throbbing with feeling while nobody around the table cared. "I'm still not sure about the young lady?"

Wynn nodded. "Laura's daughter, your cousin Georgina, had come with her, of course, and we put her into what I believed to be an excellent school. But it proved sadly lax. The girls were allowed a great deal too much freedom, and as a consequence, a plausible rogue was able to insinuate himself into her trust." He glanced at Elise. "I wouldn't wish to insult a lady by speaking of matters that would defile unsullied ears."

Someone in the room inhaled, a tiny indrawn breath that was all too audible. Elise wore a smile as bright and sparkling as her diamonds but without their authenticity. "How very kind, dear Wynn," she said, her voice a musical chime.

"Very kind indeed," Hawley added. "But you need not mind Elise. I dare say she'll survive a touch of impropriety."

Bram's nostrils flared. Elise's expression didn't falter. Wynn said, "Then I shall not scruple. This villain, whose identity I was never able to discover, took ruthless advantage of Georgina, and she bore a child, though she was just a girl herself still. She was...troubled, afterwards, and took her own life. The child she bore is Jessamine."

"That's terrible," Zeb said. "I am most awfully sorry. I had no idea about this."

"None of us did," Hawley said. "It seems Wynn kept this offshoot of the family tree entirely secret, even from Bram. That must have come as a shock."

"To you all, I dare say," Elise said. "Naturally you would all be distressed at the spawning of illegitimate children."

Bram's jaw twitched. Hawley's mouth hardened to a sneer. Zeb couldn't help glancing down at Gideon. He was eating his soup with the expression of someone who wasn't listening and might not have been there at all.

"I kept her secret, yes," Wynn said, ignoring the byplay. "I kept her safe. My Laura's daughter had her innocence abused in my care, and I determined that I would not fail Jessamine as I had Georgina. I have had her brought up in the most careful circumstances, protected both from predators and from those who would scorn her birth."

"You are generous, sir," Bram said. "It is inevitable that the stain of her origins will attach to her, but I hope all of us will treat her with the pity her unfortunate situation must demand."

"I am glad you are so thoughtful," Wynn said. "But I want more for her than pity. Yes, her birth is stained. I intend to remedy that."

"How?" Zeb asked.

"By marriage, of course. Finding her a husband."

That gave the table pause. Zeb realised he'd forgotten all about his soup, and it must be getting cold. He sipped it. It was probably mulligatawny, but regrettably underseasoned.

"Well, that is very thoughtful," Bram said. "Some decent young fellow who will overlook her origins: an artisan or clerk, perhaps. You intend to give her a sum to marry on, I suppose? Of course, we have discussed the needs of the house—"

"Indeed we have, very often," Wynn said composedly. "And this brings me to the reason for this gathering. I summoned you all together with the intention of discussing the disposition of my fortune."

"Indeed," Bram said. "Yes, indeed."

"I am unmarried, childless, and Walter Wyckham's legacy rests heavy on my shoulders. He, of course, was generous to his younger sons in his will." He glanced between Zeb, whose father had received a tidy sum and stewarded it well, and Hawley, whose father had blown the lot on the horses. "I do not intend to divide my fortune. Lackaday House is not cheap to maintain, and with the world going downhill as it is, its inheritor will need every penny. Bram has persuaded me that I should keep the estate—house and money—intact."

"I'm quite sure he has," Hawley said viciously.

"The necessity is clear to any man of moderate acumen," Bram said. "With the rising cost of living, it is imperative the property should not be fragmented."

"And that's up to you, is it? Up to you, and going to you?"

"It is Wynn's decision. But I am the next of Walter's grandchildren," Bram said. "Naturally, I follow Wynn in the line of succession."

"We're not monarchs," Hawley retorted. "And *you* may believe that inheritance goes by 'winner takes all'—"

"The winner will take all," Wynn said. "The estate will be kept in one piece, no matter to whom I bequeath it."

"Of course," Elise said. "And you have named Bram as your heir. That has been understood for years."

"But I never made a formal arrangement," Wynn returned. "And I have recently concluded that I should reconsider."

Bram was going a rather unhealthy shade of red. "What is this? We have discussed this, Wynn, often. You told me I was to inherit. I am the *eldest*."

"You care greatly about that," Wynn said. "But why should I exclude Zebedee simply because he is younger?"

Elise gave a cold smile. "Perhaps because Bram has shown his dedication to Lackaday House for years, whereas Zebedee is quite useless."

"Marital support, Elise?" Hawley drawled. "You must be worried. Wynn, do I take it from my presence here that I am in this newly opened field?"

Wynn gave him a look that was hard to read. "I was not fond of your father. He was a nasty, spiteful boy who became a vicious man. But I must ask myself, is it fair to judge you on that basis?"

Bram was looking rather red around the neck. "Of course it is. This is absurd. You chose me as your inheritor years ago, with the well-being of the house and its future in mind—"

"Did I, though?" Wynn asked. "Did I really consider each of you on your merits, or was I swayed by your father's arguments in your favour, and my dislike of Hawley's father? Can that be right?"

"Of course it was right. Hawley is as debauched as his father, and Zebedee an idle wastrel. The circumstances demand frankness," Bram added over both men's strong protests. "We are talking of Lackaday House's future. Hawley's appalling career speaks for itself, and I regret to say that Zebedee has recently been dismissed from yet another post in disgrace. He is incapable of holding a position of trust."

The fraternal treachery was jaw-dropping, even from Bram. "That is utterly unfair. I was not dismissed for any wrongdoing," Zeb protested.

"I had the news from Purefoy. Do you claim he lied?"

"If he said it was for wrongdoing, yes!"

"What were you sacked for, then?" Bram demanded.

"Well, gross incompetence," Zeb had to admit. He didn't want to look at Gideon, to see his face at the news of yet another dismissal, another failure. "But—"

"Quite," Bram said heavily. "Quite. Look at the state of you. You are a scarecrow. You cannot hold a position, even as a mere clerk with no prospect of advancement—"

"Can we just recall why I have old clothes and no prospects?" Zeb said furiously. "Why I'm a mere clerk?"

"Oh, not this again," Elise said, light and deadly. "Do stop complaining."

"You had every chance to make something of yourself, and you have failed. Whereas what Hawley has made of himself is..." Bram raised a scornful brow.

"I am an Artist," Hawley said. "I have made my name—the family name—as a creator, not a pettifogging, spiteful critic who sneers at other men's work because he has no talent of his own."

"You are a dauber of paint, at best. Your latest exhibition—"

"*You* killed that!" Hawley shouted. "You and your damned patronising review and your clique of damned patronising friends with their hidebound, tedious, classical views. You will not keep your stranglehold on Art forever."

"Art, art, art," Elise said with disdain. "Goodness, you do go on about it."

"Your artistic judgement extends to deciding whether a painting matches your dress," Hawley snarled. "And whence this sudden loyalty to your husband? I don't recall you demonstrating much of that before!"

Zeb had no fondness for his family, but this display was intolerable. He looked away from Bram's red face and

Hawley's glittering eyes and Elise's anger, to the other end of the party.

Colonel Dash seemed, if anything, amused, mouth curved under his heavy moustache. Gideon's mouth was twisted in a sneer, and his eyes snapped to Zeb's as though he felt him watching, with a look of such contemptuous disdain it struck him like a physical shock.

He recoiled just as Wynn put an end to the accelerating family row by slamming his hand on the table.

"That is enough! Stop it at once. At once, all of you! Dear me." He mopped his brow. "I understand feelings run high, and I must forgive it, in the circumstances. I dare say I carry much of the blame for leaving matters undecided so long."

"They *are* decided!" Bram shouted. "I am your heir!"

Wynn carried on as if he hadn't heard. "But I have Lackaday House to consider, and my unfortunate Jessamine in need of safe harbour. I have thought long and hard about how to proceed. This visit from you all will resolve the matter."

"Resolve it how?" Elise demanded.

Wynn looked around the table. "It is very simple. One of you shall marry Jessamine, and have my fortune with her."

"What?" Colonel Dash barked. Bram gaped. Hawley gave a wolfish smile. Elise said, "But you promised it to Bram!"

"What if she doesn't want to marry any of us?" Zeb asked.

"You have all been invited to stay so you can get to know her and she you. If she does not wish to marry any of you after that, I shall not force her, but I am determined the estate will remain in the family. Jessamine will choose one of you, or she may decline, in which case I shall make my choice among you all. Whichever it is, that man will have every penny."

"But—!" Bram, Elise, Hawley, and Zeb all said, at different but urgent pitches.

Wynn lifted a hand commandingly for silence. From the door, the burly footman marched forward. The master of Lackaday House looked around at the table and said, "Has everyone had enough soup?"

three

EB GOT UP EARLY the next morning and set out to escape the house without so much as stopping for a cup of tea. He needed to get out and walk. Fresh air and movement would give him a chance to think.

The rest of the evening had not gone well. Wynn had decreed that they would not discuss his proposal further, and so everyone had made the sort of excruciating small talk you might expect when two brothers hated one another, and a cousin had notoriously had an affair with one brother's wife, and the other brother had been exposed as a feckless wastrel, and Hawley existed, and a stranger was avidly watching the whole thing, and so was Gideon.

At least the conversation hadn't included the barely

grown woman who was to be auctioned off with the house. Presumably that would be a pleasure for the evening to come.

He let himself out of the front door without seeing anyone. He wasn't accustomed to the houses of the wealthy, not having been wealthy in a decade, but Lackaday House seemed rather lacking in the servant department. Maybe nobody wanted to work in a faux-Gothic mansion miles from anywhere. A big, echoing, empty faux-Gothic mansion, which last night had been so quiet that every creak of a board had sounded like a footstep, a cry, a sob.

He'd had a horrible night's sleep in the peace and quiet of the countryside, and he wanted to go home to London, where it was never peaceful or quiet, rather than stay in a house with more or less every single person in the entire world he didn't want to be in a house with.

At least he was alone for now. The grounds were extensive but odd: not kept in the way one would expect, with formal gardens or elegant planting. There were trees and bushes aplenty around the house, but he couldn't see any evidence of flower beds to liven it up come spring, or of anything to relieve the impression of forested medieval gloom. It made for an aesthetic whole that suited the house's Gothic atmosphere, which was wonderful if you liked that sort of thing. If it was Zeb's, he'd plant flowers.

He walked on, not troubling to note where he was going. It scarcely mattered, thanks to the huge wall that he knew surrounded the grounds. If he walked directly away from the house for a mile in any direction, he'd bump into the wall, and conversely, it couldn't be too hard to find his way back to the centre. Not that he much wanted to go back for more sneers about how he was a worthless layabout. He would have liked to throw those words in his brother's teeth and was exasperated that he couldn't.

His wandering had taken him along a tree-lined path. It opened onto a much more moor-like area: a plain of orange, grey, and green grasses. In the distance stood Stonehenge.

That demanded investigation, so he set off towards it. The stone circle loomed impressively as he approached, standing alone on its plain, at least if you had your back to the house. Zeb could almost believe that he was alone in a solitary wilderness with an ancient monument, rather than looking at an absurd folly in an enclosed garden with his family nearby.

It was quite good as follies went, he had to admit. The circle was tidily complete, rather than half-fallen as with the real thing, but the stones looked suitably weathered and lichen-covered, and the central altar-stone was just the right size and height for a nubile young lady in a white nightdress to be subjected to dark deeds with a sickle.

A scene of exactly that sort had been the dramatic

climax of Walter Wyckham's *The Stone Circle*, a Gothic melodrama about a cult of murderous druids. Unless Zeb was thinking of Walter Wyckham's *The Monastery*, a Gothic melodrama about a cult of murderous monks. It was one of the two: his grandfather had been imaginatively drawn to hooded lunatics inflicting torture on young, beautiful, helpless people.

Walter Wyckham had been a highly popular novelist once, his perverse imagination striking a chord with a lot of readers, including Zeb in his misspent youth. In retrospect, the books seemed very much a product of the author's personal peculiarities and obsessions. Zeb was glad for many reasons that the old buzzard had died two decades before his own birth, but one of those was that he would not have wanted to shake Walter's hand: it would probably have been sticky.

The thought of sticky hands led him to remember a recent afternoon playing animal alphabet blocks with a friend's children. He was trying to list creatures that began with *PT*, and stuck on *ptarmigan*, when someone said, "Zeb."

The voice came from right behind him. Zeb let out a yelp of fright and whipped round, heart thudding, to see Gideon.

"What the *blazes*," he said. "Where the devil did you spring from?"

"Just behind you," Gideon said. "You were wandering along in a brown study, as always—" He cut that off hard.

Zeb held back a wince. It had been an ongoing protest of Gideon's that Zeb was liable to amble carelessly under the wheels of an omnibus one day. That had, of course, been when Gideon would have preferred him not to fall under an omnibus.

Gideon's jaw set. He went on, "I followed you. I thought we should speak."

He did not look as though he was anticipating that the conversation would be enjoyable. Zeb felt his heart sink. He attempted to hold himself a little better, straightening his shoulders, casually leaning back against the altar stone. "Right, yes, we should. I—ugh!"

He snatched his hand up from where he'd rested it on top of the altar, right in a pool of cold and viscous liquid. *Well done, Zeb, suave as ever.* He wiped his hand on his trousers without thinking, still less looking, and saw Gideon notice. He didn't react or comment, but Zeb felt disapproval anyway because Gideon took more care of his clothes, as he took more care of everything. "Sorry. All right. I'm here."

"Aren't you just. Listen. I took this job because I couldn't find another. I've been out of work for nearly a year, with that damned business following me around."

"A *year*? But you're so good—"

"Not that good," Gideon said shortly. "Not good enough to overcome dismissal on the spot for the grossest misconduct, and no reference from Cubitt's, and the endless damned gossip."

"Oh God." Zeb had assumed Gideon had found something else easily, because work had always come easily to him. He'd thought he'd lost him a job, which was bad enough. To have lost him his career—"Oh God, I'm so sorry. I had no idea."

"I'm not asking for your sympathy," Gideon bit out. "I'm telling you I was unemployed for a great deal longer than I could afford. I would not have taken a post with a member of your family if I had had any option at all. But I didn't have an option, so I took it, and I will not lose another job because of you. Understand?"

"I don't want you to. Why would I?"

"I don't know," Gideon said. "Why did you make me lose the last one?"

Zeb couldn't find an answer, not with the fuzz of panic shortening his breath and jangling his nerves. Gideon's face was tense. He'd have a muscle ticcing in his neck, Zeb knew: he'd kissed it and soothed it, before.

"I haven't come to make trouble for you," he insisted. It sounded pathetically weak. "How could I? I had no idea you were here." Something dawned on him. "But you're Wynn's secretary. You must surely have known I was coming."

"I've been anticipating this delightful reunion for several weeks, yes. I've heard all about your letters to Wynn. He seems thrilled to have you, and I'm sure you're thrilled to be here—"

"Are you joking? Have you noticed who else is here?"

Gideon's jaw hardened. "Given what's on offer, I dare say you can put up with the company."

"What's on offer?" Zeb asked blankly.

"Oh, for God's sake. I don't care if you want to crawl for this inheritance. Marry the girl, I don't give a damn. I doubt either of you will enjoy your bargain, but it's not my affair. All I care about is that you don't say or do something that will ruin my life a second time. Is that too much to ask?"

He sounded purely furious, and it took Zeb's breath entirely away for a second. "Wait. I did not come here snouting for an inheritance. I didn't even know this Jessamine girl existed till last night, and I don't want to marry her, or anyone."

"I'm sure you can force yourself to it, in the circumstances."

"Well, I'm not going to," Zeb snapped, on a sudden wave of anger that made his skin feel hot and tight. "And I've no intention of speaking about you to Wynn or anyone else, or talking to you any more than I have to, so you needn't worry. We can just ignore each other until I leave. That will suit me very well."

He turned on his heel and walked off, upset and hurt. Who the devil did Gideon think he was, throwing around accusations? Did he not know Zeb better than that? They'd been together for nine months! And yes, Zeb had ruined everything, but he hadn't done it because he was scheming or acquisitive: the very opposite.

Gideon might believe he was callous or careless or culpably stupid. He had no right to think him a villain who would marry a schoolgirl for money.

Or, Zeb thought as he trudged on and cooled down, maybe he did. After all, he knew Zeb's employment history and financial situation better than anyone but Zeb himself. And here Zeb was, sacked again, every inch the feckless wastrel Bram called him, in line for a house and fortune if he could win Jessamine's hand. No wonder Gideon was suspicious.

And, come to that, no wonder he was afraid of Zeb costing him another job. It would only take one indiscretion, one foolish incriminating remark, and Zeb knew damned well he could be indiscreet. He blurted things out without thinking, acted without consideration. He'd spoiled everything that way. He didn't want to do it again.

Zeb walked on, thinking about Gideon, and the anger in his voice, and of his face the evening before Zeb ruined his life. He thought about that last for some time, and then he reached a decision.

He couldn't stay here, being reminded daily of what he'd thrown away, knowing the man he'd loved hated him, and constantly fretting that he might do something bloody stupid, which always seemed more likely to happen if he worried about it. So he was going to leave. And if that showed Gideon that he wasn't interested in the inheritance, and he realised Zeb was truly sorry for the harm he'd done, then he'd probably feel extremely bad about what he'd said, which would serve him right.

So Zeb would go and talk to Wynn right away and let him know. But after breakfast, because he was starving.

He headed back to the house on that determination, made an excellent breakfast—the eggs and sausages were probably local and put London to shame—and went to find his cousin.

That wasn't entirely easy. The resentful footman, the only servant he managed to track down, denied all knowledge of his master's whereabouts. Zeb wandered the ground floor, hoping not to encounter any of his other relatives, and eventually found himself in a library.

It was double height, with a spiral stair up to a balcony that ran around the entire room. The ceiling was painted dark blue and dotted with what looked like accurate constellations to his inexpert eye; the chairs were all deep and upholstered with dark green leather that looked blissfully comfortable; the oak shelves were laden with books. Zeb turned on the spot till he felt dizzy.

He was a bookworm of the worst kind, entirely capable of losing himself in a book while gongs sounded, bells rang, and people bellowed his name. His father had used to demand why he couldn't apply himself like that to his schoolwork, which Zeb had always felt missed the point to a baffling degree. There was nothing like an absorbing book; this was a room made for them, and it could be all his if he married Jessamine and inherited the house. For a moment, that actually seemed like a reasonable course of action.

There was only one painting in the room, since most of the wall space was far more usefully occupied with bookshelves. It was a portrait of a man, with a face that Zeb recognised from the frontispiece engraving of several editions, not to mention the picture hanging in his room. It was his grandfather.

Walter Wyckham was portrayed at his desk, with a manuscript in front of him and a globe to one side, turned to display the West Indies. He looked about seventy, bald like Wynn with a fringe of white hair round the sides, his face clean-shaven. He wore a smile that might have been intended to give him a look of benevolence, but Zeb couldn't see it that way. He saw insatiable hunger in the twinkling little eyes, malicious pleasure in the curve of the lips, cruelty in the curved fingers that clutched the quill.

If Zeb were to inherit this house, he'd burn this picture before he so much as unpacked.

He plunged into an examination of the shelves rather than contemplate his grandfather further, and saw with a thrill that they held real books, not ones bought by the yard. There were plenty of reference works and histories and whatnot, but it was mostly novels. So many novels. All of Dickens, all of Trollope, all of Collins and Eliot and Mrs. Braddon and G.W.M. Reynolds, and that led him on to a remarkable selection of bound penny dreadfuls, and then a magnificent array of Gothic novels. Multiple editions of Walter Wyckham, of course. Mrs. Radcliffe, Maria Edgeworth, Clara Reeve, *The Monk, Melmoth.* A copy of Horace Walpole's *The Castle of Otranto* that proved to be an autographed first edition: he held it with reverent care in case the pages somehow fell apart in his hands.

There was even an entire section of William Beckford, which was impressive because Zeb had thought the man had only written one book. The shelves held copies of *Vathek* in French and English, plus a couple of satirical novels that looked rather deadly, travel memoirs and letters ditto, and an album full of sketches and images of Beckford's great, doomed edifice, Fonthill Abbey. He took that last carefully to the desk and leafed through it with fascination.

"Hello?" A hand waved between him and the page.

Zeb blinked. He'd been deeply absorbed, and it took him a disconcerting moment to pull his thoughts from spires and echoing halls and Mr. Beckford's nightmare-dream, and fully register that there was someone next to him.

"Hello," the voice said again. It was light, female, unfamiliar. "Goodness, you were concentrating, weren't you? What are you doing?"

Zeb looked up and saw the young lady who had run from the house in her shift last night. She looked decidedly more respectable now, with her dark hair pinned up and a proper dress on, albeit one that looked to Zeb rather like a schoolgirl's frock. He was no aficionado of women's fashions, though, and she was very pretty despite the dress: nothing like Elise's cool elegant beauty, but she had a heart-shaped face, a charming smile, and sparkling eyes. He couldn't see much Wyckham in her features, but that could only be a good thing. She looked like the heroine, Zeb thought, and smiled back.

"You must be my cousin Jessamine. I'm Zeb. Zeb Wyckham. Well, obviously Wyckham, we all are, aren't we, except Dash. Although his name is Wyckham Dash, isn't it, so he's definitely—anyway, good morning."

"Good morning!" She clasped her hands together and looked at him with big eyes. "I'm very happy to meet you. I'm not precisely your cousin, you know."

"Well, you're some number removed, but I was never much good at mathematics," Zeb said, eliciting a peal of laughter. "I'd be honoured to be your Cousin Zeb, if you'd care for that."

"I would like it very much, Cousin Zeb. Is it never Zebedee?"

"Never. Is it always Jessamine?"

"Always," she said, mimicking his firm tone, and they exchanged smiles. This was already the most pleasant interaction he'd ever had with a relative.

"But what are you doing?" she asked, looking at the desk. "Is that a building plan? Are you an architect?"

"It is a plan, but not mine. I was just taking a look around Cousin Wynn's shelves and came across this. It's all sorts of pictures of Fonthill Abbey. That was a magnificent house built by William Beckford, who was a terribly rich man." He was talking to her as if she were a child, he realised, and he wasn't sure why, except his own ineptitude with women. Well, that and her expression of saucer-eyed interest, which made her look very young indeed. "Beckford wrote a Gothic novel, *Vathek*. I don't know if you've read it?"

She shook her head. "Novels like Great-grandfather's?"

"Like Walter Wyckham, yes, though Beckford only wrote the one. This was Fonthill." He leafed back to the famous print of Beckford's magnificent, selfish fantasy in stone.

"Oh." She clasped her hands again. "How utterly beautiful. But how haunting. And that picture, as though it was drawn in a storm. It looks like a place where terrible things were done."

Define 'terrible', Zeb thought, since rumour had it Beckford had harboured a harem of attractive young men in his Wiltshire isolation. That sounded like fun, at least for Mr. Beckford. Probably less so for the harem. "Well, he was a very odd fellow. According to a note in here, he only ever had guests to dinner once in the whole time he lived there, and that was a party made up of Lord Nelson, Lady Hamilton, and Sir William Hamilton. *That* must have been awkward."

"Must it?" she said. "I'm afraid I don't know them."

Wynn had said he'd tried to give the girl a sheltered upbringing. If she hadn't heard of the complicated private life of England's Hero, he'd clearly succeeded. Not that Zeb could see the point of sheltering a girl from talk of mistresses and adultery, and then introducing her to Hawley, Bram, and Elise, but here they were.

"I don't suppose he had much time for parties," he said. "Fonthill fell down shortly after it was finished."

"Oh. Is it a ruin now? I love ruins. The ancient sadness of them—the knowledge one is treading through history. To imagine the medieval monks at their prayers, in their splendid isolation—"

"There weren't any monks at Fonthill, and it wasn't medieval," Zeb pointed out. "It was just a pastiche, like this place. I do think the Georgian obsession with faked Gothic architecture—"

"This house is not faked!"

"Well, no, it's a real house, and a very impressive one of its kind, I didn't mean otherwise. Just rather newer than its architecture suggests."

"It is not *faked*," Jessamine repeated, ignoring his efforts. "And it isn't new!"

"Well, it depends how you look at the matter," Zeb tried. "I realise it's more than a century old. I only meant that it's not as old as it appears."

"The land is old."

"Well, yes, Dartmoor—"

"The site of the house," Jessamine said. "Walter Wyckham built Lackaday House on the site of a monastery that was torn down."

"Oh, really? Was that in the Reformation?"

"It was razed to the ground because of the corruption of the monks."

"Well, that was the point of the Reformation."

"I mean, it was a place of great cruelty," Jessamine said. "Cruelty and secrets, presided over by evil men, until the people of Dartmoor tore it down because no such acts of darkness should be concealed in a house of God."

"Gosh," Zeb said, nonplussed by the sharp left turn into melodrama. "Odd site to pick for a house, then. Or not for Walter, I suppose. Actually, this sounds awfully like *The Monastery*. Dark deeds in the cloisters."

"Like—?"

"*The Monastery*, by Walter Wyckham. You've not read our grandfather's books?"

"No, none. There is one about a monastery? Oh, I must read it!" Jessamine clasped her hands enthusiastically. "Is it here?"

"There's a shelf of Walter Wyckham books, but I'm not sure I'd start with that one. It's a bit, uh—it caused something of a scandal at the time. Well, quite a large scandal. Actually, he never published another book, and became a social pariah."

"Really? Why?"

The Monastery was Walter Wyckham's last and oddest work, written against the current of his increasingly proper era. It was stuffed with torture, distorted religion, and sexual depravity thinly veiled by the kind of allusion that made it, if anything, more disturbing. Zeb was bang alongside sexual depravity in his reading matter as a rule, but *The Monastery* felt like an unpleasant intimacy with an unpleasant mind. He classified it (from experience) as the kind of book that led one to toss oneself off to heated imaginings and feel thoroughly ashamed afterwards.

"It's honestly rather nasty," he said. "And awfully long too. He wrote better ones. I'd try *Clara Lackaday* first to see if you like his style. That's his first, with a heroine trapped in a great walled Gothic house, and terrible things happen. Or *Coldstone Abbey*. That one has a marvellous villain, a sinister secretary who secretly orchestrates a lot of murders." He gave a moment's thought to Gideon last night, his face cadaverous in the gaslight, and had to repress a grin. "Or there's *The Stone Circle*, about a pack of druids killing people. They're all quite terrifying."

"I like the sound of *The Monastery*." Jessamine looked determined. Oh well, it would do her no harm. If she was as ignorant as she seemed, the dubious parts would go over her head; if not, the book wasn't the issue.

"Just don't read them before bed or you'll have nightmares," Zeb said. "*The Stone Circle* scared the absolute daylights out of me, and there's a scene with spiders in *Coldstone Abbey* that gives me the horrors even to think of."

"Spiders?"

"Don't talk to me about spiders," Zeb said wholeheartedly. He hated and feared the things with a passion that was frankly embarrassing in a grown man. One of Gideon's most marvellous traits had been the nonchalance with which he'd removed the creeping horrors—

Gideon. Zeb was supposed to be leaving because of Gideon, not reading about Beckford or chatting to cousins. He stood before he could get distracted again. "I'm very pleased to have made your acquaintance, Jessamine, but I was actually looking for Wynn before I came in here. Could you point me in his direction?"

four

THE LIBRARY WAS IN the east wing; Wynn's study turned out to be in the west. Jessamine escorted Zeb there and left him at the door.

His cousin was seated at a desk, with Gideon at a second smaller table. Behind him was another painting of a woman from the dining room, in a familiar style. "Is that Laura again?" Zeb asked.

Wynn looked behind him as though he had to check. "The portrait? Yes. I commissioned Alma-Tadema in, what, '81."

Zeb knew enough about the financial side of the art world to know what that meant: Alma-Tadema's prices were sky-high. He had to applaud Wynn's loyalty to his disgraced sister-aunt. "It's very fine."

"Thank you, Zebedee. Or rather, Zeb." Wynn put

a certain amount of relish on the single syllable and its ending. "Zeb-b. I see Jessamine brought you here; I hope you two are getting along?"

"We met in the library," Zeb said. He could feel Gideon's gaze, and tensed his muscles so as not to look. "She told me about the house. Was it really built on the site of a monastery?"

"So I understand. There are...certain legends associated with the site."

"I bet there are, if Walter had anything to do with it," Zeb said. "I'd call this a pretty inconvenient place for any sort of establishment, religious or domestic, but I dare say nefarious rites and perverse sexual crimes are best done in isolation. Where are the ruins?"

"Ruins?" Wynn said. He sounded slightly off-balance. Zeb's conversational style could have that effect on people.

"There must be some, surely? It's not as if anyone's used the land for anything else, and Walter Wyckham wouldn't have demolished a real medieval ruin when he could have held moonlit dinner parties in it, or wandered around looking plangent and melancholy. Do I mean plangent?"

Gideon coughed in a strangled sort of way. Zeb realised he was digressing. "Anyway, I didn't come to ask about that. Actually, I came to say I'm going to leave." He saw Gideon's jolt out of the corner of his eye but didn't look. "I'd like to go today if you can spare the motor."

"Leave?" Wynn demanded. "But you have only just arrived. We have had no time to get to know each other."

"No, well, that is a shame," Zeb said. "But I think I should go because—"

"Wait. I think this is a private conversation. Leave us please, Grey." Wynn waited for Gideon to shut the door behind him. "Now, go on, Zebedee."

Zeb took a deep breath. "Wynn, I cannot believe this scheme to marry Jessamine to one of us is right. She's awfully young. She hasn't had any opportunity to develop her own character, or taste, or to make a wide acquaintance. And tying the inheritance to her hand is surely guaranteeing a proposal for the wrong reasons."

"The reasons are that I want Lackaday House to stay in the Wyckham family, and my Laura's grandchild to make a match from which her unfortunate birth would otherwise disqualify her. I thought I made that clear."

"But you're asking her to marry a man she doesn't know."

"Hence I invited you all to stay for this fortnight. She will know you by then."

Zeb scrubbed at his face with the heels of his hands. The hard thing here was that Wynn wasn't being entirely unreasonable in principle. Old-fashioned, certainly, but few people would dispute his motives. "I see you are acting with the best intentions," he said. "But she is a charming young lady, and surely, in this day and age, her birth is not such a millstone as all that. Why not settle a reasonable sum on her and let her choose her own path?"

"She is my Laura's grandchild. I want her to be mistress of Lackaday House."

"Then why don't you just leave it to her?"

"Because it must go to a Wyckham," Wynn said, as though Zeb were a slow child. "It is Walter Wyckham's legacy. Jessamine will marry a Wyckham, and she and her husband will be my heirs together. That is how I will right the wrongs of the past."

"Marry which Wyckham, though?" Zeb demanded. "Colonel Dash, if you're counting him, could be her father. Bram is married already. And Hawley is not a man I would want my sister to marry, if I had one."

"Why not?"

Hawley was dissolute, decadent, and impatient of convention. That might sound very thrilling on paper, but in practice made him a nasty, self-centred, sneering piece of work, not caring who he hurt. Zeb's social circles intersected with Hawley's enough that he was aware of a string of affairs that never ended happily. Well, look at Elise.

"He takes after his father," he said. "Sorry, but he does.

What is Jessamine, eighteen? Hawley doesn't treat women well at the best of times; he'll walk all over a schoolgirl."

"You think so? Is there not a chance that innocence will conquer the rake where worldly experience could not?"

"That's tripe out of books. He'll ruin her life."

Wynn raised a brow. "And that leaves only yourself."

"No, because I'm not going to marry her," Zeb said. "She seems delightful, but I'm not a player in this game. Count me out."

Wynn had grey-blue eyes. They were, Zeb discovered, quite piercing. "Not a player. Why not?"

"Because I don't want to marry her!"

"But why not? She is young, charming, beautiful. Any man would want her."

Zeb regularly attended a club well-stocked with men who really wouldn't. "It's not personal. I simply don't care to marry a stranger for the sake of an inheritance."

"If you got to know her, she would not be a stranger. Zeb, you have told me very eloquently what is wrong with the other candidates. Why do you want to remove Jessamine's best hope? You are the youngest, I dare say the most attractive to a girl's eye. Would she not be better off with you than anyone else? Do you want to deprive her of that option? What is your true objection to Jessamine? Her birth?"

"I don't have any objection to her except that she's far too young."

"She is ten years your junior. When you are forty she will be thirty; that is not a gap to concern anyone."

"Yes, but—" Zeb could feel Wynn's logic closing in on him. He struck out in another direction. "Anyway, all this seems a bit hard on Bram."

"I beg your pardon?"

"Bram. You've allowed him to live in the expectation for a long time, and Elise too. Perhaps you have a reason to change that. But if he hasn't done anything to deserve being disinherited—" The irony of what he was saying occurred to him forcibly. "The point is, I don't like this and I should rather not be involved."

Wynn leaned back, interlacing his fingers. "Do you think Elise would do well as mistress of Lackaday House?"

"I should call her aesthetically perfect. She's the very model of Lady Ravendark in *Coldstone Abbey*, all icy beauty and hauteur."

"Ha!" Wynn looked genuinely pleased. "You've read Walter's books? Yes, quite. Lady Ravendark comes to a sorry end, doesn't she? Pushed down the stairs by her own husband because she is carrying another man's child. What is it he says? 'The house of my father will live on through my son. *But not his.*' And then he pushes her. What a moment."

"And then her lover shuts Lord Ravendark into the family vault and leaves him to go mad in the dark with his ancestors' corpses, since he cares so much about the family line."

"And thus the noble house comes to ruin because of a woman's infidelities," Wynn concluded. "An excellent analogy, Zeb. It quite expresses my own concerns as to Elise."

Zeb had the sudden plunging sensation of a man who'd put his foot in it. "Hold on. I didn't mean—"

"I understand your meaning perfectly."

"I only meant that she has a very assured manner and she's very lovely. And this is none of my business, any of it. You can leave your money as you please, and I dare say you'll be with us another thirty years anyway, so it's hardly pressing. You might even marry: Walter did at your age. All I'm saying is that I don't want to be part of your plans. Could I be driven to the station?"

Wynn sighed. "If you will not give my dear Jessamine a chance, I cannot make you. But I do want you to stay, all the same. I should like to get to know you properly. And who knows, perhaps you and your brother might reconcile, after a decade's estrangement. Perhaps you may discover you have been wrong about Hawley's character. Perhaps you will find yourself becoming fond of Jessamine as a cousin if not a lover. She will need a family soon enough."

"Er, why?"

Wynn grimaced. "You said I had another thirty years. I regret that is not the case."

He sounded meaningful, though he looked hale enough. "Is something wrong?" Zeb asked. "Are you not well?"

"You might say that. I think we spoke of the Wyckham curse last night?"

"Curse?"

"The fact that, since Walter, not one Wyckham has lived to be fifty. Not a child, a sibling, or a wife."

"Haven't they?" Zeb said. "Well, I suppose Walter's wives couldn't have, considering the rate he got through them. And his children died earlier than one might hope—"

"And their wives too. Your parents, mine, Hawley's. Every one of them dead before fifty."

"I thought Hawley's mother ran away," Zeb said. "I would have in her shoes."

"Dead."

"Oh. Well, that's very sad, but Walter got to nearly eighty. That surely balances out."

"More than you know. I take it your father never told you the story."

"He probably told Bram," Zeb said, perhaps a little sourly.

Wynn leaned back in his chair. "Walter was, of course,

a successful man of business as well as an author. The tale goes that one of his workers died, and this man's mother, who also worked for Walter, cursed him in vengeance. He was at that time just turned forty-nine, and already planning a grand celebration for his half century; she foretold with strange imprecations that he would be dead before he was fifty. So Walter sold his wives' and his children's futures in exchange for his own."

Zeb had had several things to say about that tale, but the last sentence struck it all from his mind. "He did what?"

"He made a bargain. He would grow old, but no wife or child of his should do the same. He married immediately, in the hope of children to exchange for his own longevity, and some say he murdered his first wife when it became apparent the marriage would not be fruitful." He smiled. "Superstition does slander the dead."

"Wait. What do you mean, bargain? With whom? Are we talking about a deal with the devil?"

"Such is the story."

"Oh, for goodness' sake," Zeb said. "The old buzzard sat around with skulls and pentagrams or what-have-you, chanting Latin and selling souls? How absolutely typical of this family. Although, where is this story from? It can't be Walter: he'd hardly tell people. 'By the way, I sacrificed your soul to Satan, hope you don't mind'—"

"It is no laughing matter!"

"Oh, it's ridiculous," Zeb said. "I'll take your word Walter did something like that, and one might well look askance at the number of wives he got through, but really, what a lot of nonsense."

"The facts speak for themselves. Walter lived to seventy-eight. No other Wyckham since his bargain has reached fifty."

"It happens! People get ill. Childbirth is dangerous. There are accidents. Your father, uh—"

"He drowned in the mire, out walking one misty winter's day. He stepped off the path, and the treacherous ground pulled him under. A long, slow, agonising death, crying out for help that never came. He was forty-seven."

That was rather more detail than Zeb had wanted. "Yes, fine—not fine, I'm very sorry to hear it—but the point is, he had an accident. My father had a cancer. Hawley's father was killed in a brawl in a public house. These things happen, especially if you're Hawley's father; I'm amazed it took him so long to get his head kicked in. It's a matter of chance."

"Chance? Then consider this piece of chance: I had my forty-ninth birthday in June. A few weeks later, I saw my doctor. He gave me less than a year."

Zeb's jaw dropped. Wynn nodded slowly. "I have never mentioned the Wyckham curse to him; he would mock as you did. And yet he told me in so many words that I will not see my fiftieth birthday."

"Good God," Zeb said blankly. "Really? Good God. I am so very sorry, Wynn. I had no idea. You are seeking help? Have you had a second opinion?"

"There is nothing to be done. Man's allotted span is three score years and ten, the Good Book tells us, but not for Wyckhams. Not for Walter's wives or children, and it seems not for his grandchildren either. Unless we take Walter's route, eh?"

"Wynn, stop this. You can't just sit down and wait to die because of superstition."

"It is not superstition that will kill me." Wynn patted his heart. "Don't worry about me, dear boy. I shall face my fate in my own way. And that information was for you alone, hmm? Don't tell Jessamine. Don't tell *anyone*. I want your word on that."

"But—"

"I mean it. I don't want it put about, especially now, with the inheritance unresolved. I have only told you this so you understand that I am not asking lightly when I beg that you will stay."

"Yes, but—"

"I want to order my affairs as best I can," Wynn said. "I want to be sure of Jessamine, and Lackaday House, and of the hands they will both go into. But I have very little time left to me, so I ask you once more, Zebedee, as a dying man. Promise me to stay for this fortnight and to consider my offer with an open mind. I will not resent whatever decision you make, but please, give me this time. Call it a meaningless comfort to a superstitious old fool, if you choose. But you can help me face the end knowing I have done my best. I would be grateful for that."

Zeb felt his shoulders sag, but there was no choice at all. "Yes. Of course I will."

All of that had swallowed the morning. Luncheon at Lackaday House proved to be an exceedingly informal affair, with cold chicken, bread, and cheese. Elise did not take luncheon; Bram attended in angry, offended silence that reminded Zeb of too many meals with their father. Hawley made it down late, his heavy lids suggesting he'd been up half the night with two prostitutes and a bottle of brandy.

"Morning, bright eyes," Zeb said. Jessamine giggled.

Hawley gave a lazy grin. He was a very handsome man in his louche way; he looked like he'd give you an extremely good time, and also the clap. "Sarcasm so early, Zeb? Please. And *you* must be my new cousin, Jessamine." He gave her a very slow up-and-down, well balanced to seem fascinated rather than intrusive. "Ah, yes. Yes, I see."

"See what?" Zeb asked, hoping he wouldn't have to do something chivalrous. Hawley was bigger than him.

"How I would paint you," Hawley replied to Jessamine, holding her gaze.

Bram gave a very audible snort. "You mean, with splashes and daubs of the sickly shades you favour? Jessamine's likeness deserves to *be* a likeness, not an upended palette."

"For a man who looks at so much art, you don't *see*," Hawley said, with the passionate intensity he always adopted for discussion of Art, capital A. "You have a very limited vision of portraiture."

"If by that you mean I have standards—something of which nobody could accuse you—"

"On the contrary. I have superb taste." Hawley sent an admiring glance at Jessamine, who was watching round-eyed. "You see what you are told to see, Bram, and order other people to see the same things. *I* see Beauty."

It was going to be like that, then. Zeb had neither the skill nor the desire to compete with Hawley in the matter of seducing young women, but he didn't want to sit here watching him charm the girl and make Bram look like a smug prick, although that was admittedly not hard. He wondered if Elise would take a hand, and which of the men she'd want to spite more.

He looked away, and saw Gideon watching the show.

He was seated at the end of the table, eating in silence as he had last night. His expression was neutral, but Zeb would have put money that it hid contempt, and he couldn't blame the man. Gideon had a good face for contempt, too, with deep-set, pale blue eyes, and that authoritative nose, which radiated disapproval all by itself. If this house was really on the site of an ancient evil monastery, Gideon would have been perfectly cast as the sinister abbot with who knew what crimes lurking under his cassock. It was hard to believe, looking at him now, that he ever smiled.

That was dismally wrong. He was a serious man, but Zeb knew, none better, how much his eyes could warm and crinkle at the edges, how his face could light up with amusement or desire or love—

"Cousin Zeb!" Jessamine said, possibly not for the first time.

"You are being addressed," Bram snapped, adding, "Oaf."

"Uh—right. Sorry, Jessamine, I was miles away. What was that?"

"I found the book, Cousin Zeb," Jessamine announced. "I read the first chapter. It's awfully strange, isn't it? I'm not sure I like it, but I want to read on."

"What book is that, my dear?" Bram asked in an indulgent sort of way.

"*The Monastery.* By Walter Wyckham."

"You gave her that, Zebedee?" Bram said, brows gathering like thunderclouds. "What absurd irresponsibility!"

"It's Cousin Wynn's copy, from the library," Zeb protested. "I'm not sure I'd start with that one, but I read them at her age."

"You are not a young lady."

"It is my great-grandfather's book," Jessamine said. "And I want to read it. I *must* read it."

That sounded a bit fervent. Young people were exhausting, Zeb thought with the wisdom of twenty-eight. "I went to the stone circle earlier," he remarked to the table, changing the subject without shame. "I'd like to take a walk around the grounds and see all the follies after lunch. Would anyone care to join me?"

"Oh, I will show you!" Jessamine exclaimed.

"I cannot resist such a tour guide," Hawley said, laughing at her in a charming sort of way. "Bram knows the grounds already, of course, having spent so much time here making himself pleasant to Wynn. I dare say you will want to attend your wife this afternoon, Bram: I suppose she has the head-ache? She so often does."

Bram's face darkened. Zeb put in hastily, "I'd love a

tour. Do you know, Jessamine, are there any remnants of this monastery the house was built on?"

"Of the what?" Bram demanded, diverted. "Monastery? Here? Nonsense."

"It is not," Jessamine said. "Cousin Wynn told me. It was a place of terrible crimes—"

The ensuing conversation, or argument, about Lackaday House's alleged monastic origins went on for some time. Zeb fixed his eyes on his plate, rotated his ankles under the table as if flexing his feet was a substitute for escape, and wished one could eat lunch with fingers in one's ears.

"It is *not*!" Jessamine shouted, the volume making him look up.

"Of course it is," Bram said.

She was clearly upset, with reddening cheeks and sparkling eyes. "It is *not* imagination," she said fiercely. "We have seen it. *I* have seen it."

"Miss Jessamine, Mr. Wynn prefers you not to discuss this subject," Gideon said quietly. "He asked that you respect that."

"But it's true! He knows it is true, and so do you!"

"Really?" Hawley said. "You've seen a ghost, Grey?"

He sounded mocking. Jessamine said, "Don't laugh," in a low, almost savage tone.

"Don't fire up, sweet cousin," Hawley told her.

"Although you do look remarkably well when you're angry; I wish more women had that gift. I'm sure Bram does too, given dear Elise's temper. But I am not laughing at you, believe me. I don't know what you have seen, but I quite believe that the earth could have bubbles, just as water does. There are more things in heaven and earth than are dreamed of in our philosophy."

"How original," Bram muttered.

"You *sounded* sceptical," Jessamine said.

"Did I? Perhaps it is simply that Mr. Grey does not strike me as a man to whom visions would be given," Hawley said, with a touch of sneer. "I associate such things with the airy, artistic, imaginative soul, not the administrative one. I quite believe you have that temperament, Jessamine; I venture to say I do too. If there are spirits to be seen, I hope I shall see them. Perhaps we might go ghost-hunting together."

Gideon said, sharply, "Don't—" and stopped as abruptly.

"Don't?" Hawley said. "No, what was that you started to say, Grey? Don't *what*?"

"I beg your pardon." Gideon's mouth was tight.

Hawley's lips curled. "You fascinate me. I must know now. What did you see?"

"Mr. Wynn does not want this subject spoken of."

Hawley's nostrils flared. He never liked refusals. "I asked you a question, Grey. You will answer me."

"He doesn't work for you," Zeb said. Maybe Gideon hated him and always would; Zeb still wasn't going to sit here while Hawley picked on him. "Ask Wynn about it, if you're so interested. It's a lovely day out there. Who's coming for this walk?"

five

IN THE END IT was Bram, Zeb, Jessamine, and Hawley. A real family outing.

Hawley took Jessamine's arm and smoked while he walked, unpleasantly perfumed tobacco that produced a cloying stench. Bram trudged on Jessamine's other side, clearly determined not to let the painter exert his charm without interference. Zeb trailed along behind because it had been his idea, and he did actually want to get a sense of the grounds, not to mention a leg stretch.

The grounds were impressive in their way, and he appreciated them more in the fast-fading afternoon sun than he had this morning, even if he was in an equally unsettled mood. It was very flat here, and the high walls that encircled them gave the place a rather prisonlike feel when in sight, but then, everything about the architecture here was odd.

The follies certainly were. The Roman temple was carved with white bas-reliefs in the usual way, until Zeb looked closely at them and saw they depicted the rape of Lucretia, the rape of the Sabine women, the rape of Leda by the swan, the rape of Ganymede by the eagle, and various other iterations of the subject. Bram and Hawley must have noticed that, as an art critic and an artist, but neither mentioned it. Zeb said, "This is rather a theme," and was comprehensively ignored.

The Egyptian pyramid was quite small-scale, and thus not terribly impressive. There was a door to enter it, but Jessamine warned them they would need to crawl inside and bring lights, and everyone declined. A stone sort of hut in the woods was called Wayland's Smithy but lacked other interest, while a Japanese temple constructed in brick and stone put Bram and Hawley into temporary allegiance as they muttered about philistine parodies. Zeb felt similarly about the family crypt, resembling as it did a miniature medieval cathedral. He attempted to find an adjective suitable for a mind that had decreed the family's eternal resting place would be indistinguishable from its garden decorations and came up with 'odd'.

The tour took some time, since the estate was two miles in diameter and the follies were dotted around three-quarters of it: the area behind the house was reserved to the kitchen garden, stable, garage, and useful outbuildings.

"The acetylene gas plant is there," Bram explained as they walked. "Wynn had it installed on my advice some eight years ago, since we are far too distant for a regular gas supply. You will doubtless have noticed the excellent quality of the light."

"It seems awfully dim to me," Zeb said.

"Cousin Wynn prefers darker shades," Jessamine said. "He finds the gaslight too glaring. Really, I think he wishes he had not had the plant put in at all. It smells dreadfully at the back with the stuff they use to produce the gas, and it is so much less poetic than candlelight."

"But so much brighter, cleaner, and safer," Bram said, in a tone of jovial instruction that would have enraged the calmest soul. "Rather more appropriate for the twentieth century, not to mention more economical once the cost of the plant is taken into account."

"Safer?" Hawley said. "I thought acetylene was known for being explosive."

"No more than any gas, if sensible precautions are taken, and less likely to cause a fire than oil or candles. It is by far the most practical option."

"Ah, your relentless practicality," Hawley sneered. "Has it never occurred to you that Lackaday House does not welcome the practical? It is a creation of dreams, an atmosphere caught and clothed in stone."

Jessamine clasped her hands admiringly. Bram made a noise of disgust. Zeb thought longingly of being elsewhere.

The last stop in their circuit was the stone circle. Zeb strolled up to the altar stone, drawn to see what he'd put his hand in earlier. The surface was roughly hewn, as though by hand axes: doubtless his grandfather had specifically ordered it that way for ancient effect. The top was stained reddish brown and looked rather damp. He rubbed at it with a fingertip.

"What on earth are you doing?" Bram snapped.

"Just looking. It's stained."

"It's lichen, you fool."

"Looks like a stain to me." Hawley raised a brow. "And quite a sinister one, with that hue, on a sacrificial altar."

"Once again, I remind you this is the twentieth century," Bram said.

"Yes, you are repetitive," Hawley agreed. "The atmosphere of this place is quite extraordinary. Jessamine, do tell us, what is this ghost? What did you see?"

"Oh, for goodness' sake, don't start that again," Zeb said.

Jessamine shot him a glare, then turned back to Hawley. "I saw a shape. A grey shape, with a hood, its face hidden. Like a monk."

"Of course you did. Naturally your imagination created

such a phantom with this tale of monasteries and ruins," Bram said. "I really don't know where that can have come from; I have never heard of any such thing."

"Perhaps you don't know all the history because it isn't your house," Hawley said.

"And I didn't know anything about it at the time," Jessamine added. "I had not lived here long when I saw it. It was a shape in the corridor, in a long hooded robe. I thought it was—I don't know, a servant, perhaps. I called out and it turned, and it looked at me."

She paused there, her mouth working. Zeb said, "What happened?"

"It had—I cannot say. It had no face, no eyes, and it *looked*." Her voice was a whisper that brought up the hairs on his neck.

"Looked without eyes?" Bram said in a jocular tone that fell flat.

"Yes. A gaze without eyes," Jessamine said with terrible simplicity. "It stared at me, and reached out—towards me—and I felt so dreadfully cold and dark and *alone*, and then it was gone. And—and I ran to find Wynn because I was afraid, and he told me I had imagined it, but I had not. So I spoke to Mr. Grey. And he went looking in the corridors, and the next morning he looked as though he had not slept, and he will not speak of it at all. He refuses." The words were tumbling out now. "And that was when I told Wynn I wanted to know, and I would not be put off. And he said there had been a monastery here once, and told me a little of the house's history, and he asked me not to mention it again, but I must. I *must*."

Zeb contemplated her: tense face, knotted fingers, quick breath. He glanced at his brother and cousin.

"Well," Bram said, nonplussed.

"That is a remarkable story," Hawley put in. "Quite remarkable. I should very much like to know more. Where is it that you saw this apparition?"

"In the corridors of the west wing, on the first floor."

Zeb's room was in that area, not greatly to his surprise. Hawley said, "I shall keep my eyes open. Is there a particular time—"

"Stop this," Bram said. "At once. Stop encouraging her when you know perfectly well this is nonsense."

"It is not!" Jessamine flared.

"I don't doubt you think you saw something," Bram assured her. "My dear child, there are no such things as ghosts. You heard some old tale, and fancy did the rest."

"I told you, I had not heard anything at all about monks, so how should I have imagined one?"

"And Grey should know better than to play on a sensitive young person's fears," Bram said, ignoring her. "I think extremely poorly of that, and I shall speak severely to him."

"On what authority?" Zeb demanded.

Bram ignored him too. "You have distressed yourself in a foolish and unnecessary manner, Jessamine. You need not be ashamed," he added kindly, as she made a strangled noise that sounded to Zeb a lot more like fury, "but you must learn to regulate your imagination better. We need not tell Wynn we discussed this. I should not wish such a tale to be attached to my property."

"But it will not be your property," Hawley said with a smile. "It will go to Jessamine's husband, and that won't be you. Will it?"

"I meant any property I owned," Bram said, reddening. "And *you* should behave with a little more humility, rather than taking your victory for granted."

"Victory?" Jessamine said.

"I take nothing for granted," Hawley said. "I would not be such a fool as to presume myself acceptable to the loveliest and most intriguing young lady I have seen in an age. She may prefer Dash, if she likes the military mind and doesn't object to a *touch* of rheumatism. Or even Zeb here." He glanced at Zeb and raised his eyebrows, indicating that there was no accounting for taste. "But you, dear Bram, are married, so she will not be choosing you under any circumstances. Will she?"

"Oh, I cannot—*no!*" Jessamine exclaimed, and was off before anyone could react, sprinting away. She had a remarkable turn of speed, given her frock. Hawley gave a hunting cry, snatched off his hat, and set off in her wake.

"For God's sake, Zebedee," Bram said. "Why aren't you going after her?"

"Are you joking? Look at her go. She could try out for the thousand-yard dash at the next Olympics, whereas if Hawley's run for anything more than an omnibus in the last decade I'll be amazed. In the unlikely event he catches her, he'll be too busy coughing up a lung to woo her."

"True," Bram admitted. "But you need to put yourself forward more instead of being so lumpish. The girl is romantic: she wants to be courted. Why are you not making more effort? I must say, your habit of expecting everything to fall into your lap without bestirring yourself—"

"Excuse me?" Zeb said. "First, I didn't ask for marital advice, and second, if I wanted marital advice I wouldn't ask you for it, and third, I'm not going to marry her, so—"

"Of course you will not, if you are so defeatist."

"I *mean*, I don't want to. I told Wynn as much this morning. This whole business is absurd."

Bram was examining his face. "You agree his course of action is incorrect? That he should return to his previous intention?"

"I don't care. It's none of my business."

"For God's sake, will you exert yourself for once in

your life!" Bram snapped. "Do you mean to let Hawley have it all? To let that lecher marry a mere child, an innocent, because you cannot bestir yourself to pluck a fortune that is dangled before you?"

"I am not obliged to marry the girl to protect her from other people's damn fool decisions."

"You are the damned fool here. You could be rich!"

"Why do you care?" Zeb demanded. "What possible right do you have to speak as if you give a damn for my prosperity?"

"That is unfair," Bram said, red creeping up his neck. "Legally, I was not obliged—"

"Oh, go to the devil."

"It was left to my discretion!"

"You played a dirty trick on me and you know it."

"Listen, will you?" Bram said. "I can emphasise to Wynn that Hawley is despicable, and grossly unfit to marry a young girl. You can present yourself well to Jessamine with a little effort. Together we can ensure she chooses you, and that Wynn supports the choice."

His brother, offering to support and help him because he cared about Zeb's future, just like a big brother should. Zeb folded his arms. "All right, what's the idea?"

"An alliance," Bram said. "You are idle, irresponsible, and incapable of applying yourself, in no way fit to manage an estate. But Wynn respects my judgement, even if this girl has wormed her way into his favour. So we will present a united front to Wynn. I will inherit and steward Lackaday House, and you will marry the girl, supported by a generous allowance from the estate. Thus Wynn's house and his charge will both be in good hands, and that wretch Hawley may take himself off back to his stinking stews. What do you say?"

Zeb couldn't say anything at all for a moment, in the sheer breathlessness of hurt and outrage. "You are proposing that you and I split an inheritance? That I stake my future on being your pensioner? *You* are proposing that to *me*? Are you *joking*?"

"I am perfectly willing—"

"Rubbish." Zeb was quivering with anger old and new. "Absolute rubbish. I don't know if the worst part of it is that you think I'm stupid enough to believe you, or that you believe it yourself while it's coming out of your mouth. You puffed-up hypocritical fraud."

Bram's face reddened even more. "I can make or break you in Wynn's eyes. If you and I work together, we can secure this. Go against me, and I will ensure he doesn't entrust the house or the fortune to you, even if you get your hands on Jessamine. And since you can scarcely afford a wife—"

"You are in no position to talk about people who can't afford their wives!"

"Mind your tongue. All I need do is speak to Wynn and you will be out on your ear tomorrow," Bram snarled.

"Please do. I'd be delighted to leave."

"Spare me the cant, Zebedee. And drop this pretence of disinterest. You aren't interested in a fortune, when you have no home or job or prospects to return to? Ha. I see what it is: you are trying to claim the moral high ground, angling for the inheritance as blatantly as Hawley. Well, I won't have it. I won't be pushed out of the way by your plotting."

He turned on that and marched off. Zeb banged his fist on a standing stone, in lieu of his brother's nose. There were a number of things he would have liked to say—heated denials, a recap of the reasons he had to resent Bram, or simply five minutes' analysis of his brother's personality and appearance. Mostly, however, he just wanted to leave.

But he wouldn't be doing that, since he'd let Wynn talk him into staying, so he should probably make the best of things.

With that in mind, he took a brisk walk to the wall and back, for health, or at least to let his annoyance reduce to a simmer, and then returned to the house. He brought his satchel, pen, and paper down to the library, in the hope that none of his relatives would choose that room to sit in. Bram, a critic by trade, only read books in order to pronounce a public verdict on them, and Zeb doubted that Hawley had ever read a book in his adult life. He wasn't interested in other people.

It was blissfully empty and he settled down at the desk. The chair was placed with its back to the many-paned window, letting him see the door, but he nevertheless built a quick wall of books in case anyone came in, so he could snatch his papers out of the way before they were observed.

It didn't take him long to find his place. He'd spent much of the journey here thinking through what he needed to do, and itching to do it, and he was soon entirely lost in his work.

"Zeb!"

The voice cut through his absorption. Zeb hated being disturbed from deep thought; it had all the unappealing qualities of being woken from deep sleep, and nobody ever apologised for doing it. In fact, they generally seemed to behave as if Zeb had wronged them by cruelly forcing them to ask for his attention twice.

He blinked dizzily at his papers now, swimming up from the depths to reorient himself: *library, Lackaday House, Gideon—*

Gideon?

"What the—"

Gideon was standing right by him, looking tense, or

possibly annoyed. Zeb swept his papers up, ruffled and embarrassed. "I didn't hear you come in. Will you please cough or something?"

"I did cough."

"Cough louder."

"Pay more attention."

"I *was* paying attention," Zeb snapped. "I was working. I can't help it if you sneak up—"

"I *walked* up. I can't help it if you don't listen."

"I don't listen when I'm concentrating, as you very well know! That's what concentration is!"

It was an all too familiar argument, which had used to be affectionate. Zeb tended to alternate between wildly skittering thoughts—Gideon had called them 'quicksilver'—and deep absorption in a subject to the exclusion of all else, whereas Gideon could apply himself an appropriate amount to the thing he was meant to be doing. Zeb had no idea how Gideon could do it so easily. Gideon had no idea why Zeb couldn't.

He didn't want to think about that, or talk about it either.

"Was there something?" he asked. "I assume you're not just here for a chat. Oh, actually, I should probably warn you, you're going to be assailed by my relatives. Bram intends to tell you off for filling Jessamine's head with ghost stories."

Gideon blinked. "I haven't done that."

"Well, she is convinced you saw a ghostly monk and is telling everyone so. Bram disapproves of the very mention of ghosts, but Hawley is going to bother you about it in order to impress Jessamine by pretending to believe her, and that will doubtless put you between a rock and a hard place. My advice is to say something provocative about modern art and leg it while they're shouting."

Gideon's lips twitched. It was just for a second, and Zeb could see him suppress it, but it was there, and with that tiny near-smile Zeb's heart hurt all over again, as if it was a year ago, the wound still fresh.

Just memory, he reminded himself. Just echoes of past feelings. It didn't matter any more.

"Noted," Gideon said, and then added, almost reluctantly, "Thank you."

"My pleasure. Did you want me? That is, you came to find me. Was there a reason for that, is what I meant."

"Uh. Yes. Yes, there is. You told Wynn you wanted to leave."

"I did. I do."

"Good," Gideon said briskly. "Are you packed? I can order the motor now."

"Did Wynn say to do that?"

"He doesn't have to give me step-by-step instructions. You want to leave, I want you to leave, so—"

"No, but I said I *wouldn't* leave," Zeb said. "Wynn and I discussed it and I agreed to stay."

Gideon's face hardened visibly. "Of course you did."

"There's no *of course* about it. I'd very much rather not be here, but he asked me in terms I couldn't refuse."

"Of course. So you'll just have to stay here, looking nobly above the undignified scramble for inheritance? Very effective."

"What the devil are you talking about?" Zeb demanded. "Gideon, this is me. You know perfectly well—"

"I know your work ethic perfectly well; I was your supervisor long enough," Gideon snarled, low-voiced and furious. "I dare say never having to lift a finger again would suit you no worse than it would suit most people. Just stop playacting, for God's sake. If I have to sit here watching you woo your damned cousin, you could at least be honest about what you're doing!"

"I'm not!" Zeb yelped. "I don't want any part of this, and I'm not wooing Jessamine and—are you *jealous*?"

Gideon's pale skin had always been treacherous. The colour flamed in his cheeks now, an ugly red. "Go to hell," he said thickly. "Go to hell, Zeb."

He walked out on that. Zeb stared after him.

six

ZEB COULDN'T REGAIN HIS concentration after that. He wasn't sure if he should go after Gideon and try to make things better somehow, or go back to Wynn and beg to be absolved from his promise, or what on earth he could do except take a vow of silence, because every time he opened his mouth he made things worse.

He'd have liked to get out for a proper walk, but the light was already dimming. Instead, he flipped through a few books, failed to settle on one, and went up to his room early, with a vague idea of not being so late for dinner this time. It was six in the evening by now, and pitch dark. The gaslight was low, with an irritating faint flicker that gave Zeb a mildly seasick feeling, unless that was the wallpaper. It was very quiet indeed, as though nobody else was staying in the corridor, or the wing, or the house.

Not that Zeb wanted to find himself closer to his relatives. If they had bedrooms in the other wing, that suited him very well. But the silence of the halls felt strange all the same.

He was more certain of his way to his room now, and found it with only one wrong turning. He came down the corridor, aware of his footsteps on the floorboards, with a rather library feeling of making too much noise. The portraits watched him as he passed.

His room had had a fire lit against the winter chill: this house was cold to the bone. The gaslight was burning low and Zeb fiddled with it to see if he could get it a bit brighter, but failed.

He couldn't stop the flickering either. It sent shadows jumping across the ceiling and up the walls, and over Walter Wyckham's leering face in that ghastly portrait, as though his painted expression were changing. Zeb attempted to ignore it as he dressed, failed, made a noise of annoyance, and took the damn thing off the wall. He didn't want Walter Wyckham staring at him in his drawers.

The room felt slightly less oppressive without Walter's presence. Zeb started the laborious business of shirt studs, and then the light flickered so dramatically, he feared the gas plant was failing and he'd find himself in the dark.

At that moment, he heard footsteps in the corridor, approaching his room. A human presence seemed welcome right now, even given the assortment of humans available, and he stepped to the door without thinking, pulled it wide, and looked out.

There was nobody in the corridor. Zeb looked up and down. Nobody there.

He shrugged, stepped back in, and started to pull the door closed. As he did, the footsteps went past the door.

What the blazes.

He looked out again, and this time, he heard the footsteps going by the other way. They echoed on the wooden floor of the completely empty corridor.

"What—?" he said aloud, and the gaslight dropped almost to nothing as if in response. It was very dark and, he realised, very cold.

Zeb stepped back into his room and shut the door. He stood there for a moment, concentrating on his breathing. *Don't rush off. Take a moment. Breathe.*

Outside the door, the footsteps passed once more, this time fading into the distance. A moment later, the gaslight brightened perceptibly. Zeb exhaled, and relaxed his hands, which he seemed to have balled into fists.

It was just noises. Probably squirrels—they got into old houses and made an astonishing racket. Or someone was on the floor above and the sound carried oddly. Or even something to do with the gas pipes and not footsteps at all. That was probably it, actually, and that would be why the two had coincided.

Zeb straightened his back and returned to his shirt studs, and if his fingers were a little unsteady, nobody else needed to know.

When he came down for dinner that evening, Gideon was already there, sherry in hand, face tense. Zeb didn't try to speak to him, or want to speak to anyone else. He wandered around the room instead and pretended to reexamine the pictures. He kept one hand in his pocket, running the rosary beads through his fingers, pressing the sharp corners of the crucifix against his thumb.

Elise was as elegant and poised as ever. She had decided to be charming tonight, and she was very charming indeed, speaking to Jessamine with a warm kindness that couldn't be faulted, yet made the younger woman look like a gauche schoolgirl. Bram watched with a fixed smile.

Colonel Dash had attached himself to the women. He was a fine figure of a man: upright, with decided charm. He'd doubtless been a lady-killer in his youth, and he wasn't bad in his forties.

Hawley arrived not much later, with a slightly blurred air that suggested the sherry wasn't his first of the evening. He didn't look quite as smug as previously. Possibly he hadn't enjoyed thundering along after Jessamine and being reminded he was no longer a spry youth, if he'd ever been a spry youth. Zeb imagined he'd mostly dodged games lessons in favour of smoking in the bushes.

He beckoned Zeb with a jerk of the chin. Zeb sidled up with his sherry. "Enjoying yourself?"

"Hardly, dear boy. Are you?"

Zeb shrugged. Hawley gave him a sideways look. "You and I would benefit from a conversation, Zebby. I will find you later. Ah, our genial host."

Wynn arrived, and the party made the sort of scintillating conversation you got when nobody had done anything all day. If this was what the next fortnight held, they'd all die of boredom. Zeb wasn't worried: the odds were there would be a screaming row within twenty-four hours.

They moved through to the dining table, where everything went in a perfectly civilised manner through the first course. Bram held forth about international politics; Colonel Dash made intelligent interventions. Zeb kept his mouth shut, except to eat his vegetable soup. It was oversalted.

The conversation rambled on as that was removed

and replaced by a chicken fricassee. Bram looked a bit waxen as that was served. He was something of a gourmet, reviewing the occasional restaurant along with plays and exhibitions, since apparently the British newspaper-reading public had a bottomless appetite for his thoughts. He had doubtless expected a much more generous and varied table, not to mention better cooking.

Elise took only a spoonful of the fricassee. "Not eating?" Hawley said. "Very wise. It does become harder to keep one's figure." He glinted at Jessamine. "That is a long way in your future. Never, if you continue your exercises."

"Do you exercise, dear?" Elise asked Jessamine, ignoring Hawley. "That is a very suitable recreation for girls; it is so sad when we leave that behind for other pursuits. What do you like best to play at? Lawn tennis or lacrosse?"

"She runs," Hawley replied, as Jessamine scowled like the schoolgirl she probably didn't want to be any more. "And gloriously. Like a nymph, an Ariadne."

"Atalanta," Bram said. "Ariadne was the weaver. The spider," he added, with a nasty glance at Zeb.

"Atalanta, then," Hawley snapped. "She is remarkably fleet of foot. I should love to paint you in motion." He let his eyes go out of focus and waved a palm in a significant way. "A canvas of movement, of speed, a transient moment of beauty held for eternity. I can see it.

'Jessamine, Running.'" He gave her his most charming smile. "Will you let me capture you in flight?"

Jessamine's eyes and mouth rounded. Elise's face barely moved, yet she still managed to give a very strong impression of a cat about to hack up a hairball, and who could blame her. Gideon's expression was blank in the very specific way he had when his opinions would be a sackable offence.

"I dare say you might paint Jessamine, if she cares to be painted," Wynn said.

"Within the bounds of decency, I trust," Dash added. "No wish to offend you, Hawley, but I read the reviews of your exhibition. Sounded rather too modern for me."

"The human form has been considered a suitable subject for art for centuries," Hawley observed, still smiling. "I hope you will judge my work on its merits, not on the sneers of those false moralists who conceal their own rottenness with a facade of outrage at others."

Bram swelled with fury. "To judge your work on its merits, Hawley—"

"Let's not talk about art," Zeb said loudly.

"Don't interrupt! You have been told a hundred times—"

"Let's *not* talk about art," Elise said. "It's hardly a subject in which Jessamine can join. Have you ever been to an exhibition, my dear?"

Jessamine flushed. "No."

"Oh, so many pleasures await you in London. The galleries, the theatres, the fashions. You really must let me take you shopping."

"Are you going to London?" Zeb asked.

"We have suggested she come and stay with us," Elise said as Jessamine opened her mouth to reply. "There is so much for her to learn. New experiences, new friends—why, she has a whole new world awaiting her. There is nothing so delightful as to be a pretty girl in London, and I should love to have a little cousin to spoil." She glittered at Jessamine. "When you are dressed, you will be very much in demand."

By a lot of men who weren't Hawley, Zeb, or Dash. Zeb tipped his mental hat to Elise's strategy. Hawley's expression soured like milk.

"We can discuss that after the end of this month," Wynn said. "After all, her fiancé might wish to take her to London."

"I trust he will," Elise said, eyes flicking between Zeb and Hawley. "I trust she will demand to see all the sights and meet all the best people. Have you ever been to the theatre, my dear?"

"The pantomime. And Shakespeare," Jessamine admitted, with downcast gaze.

Elise laughed musically. "We can do rather better than that. Modern plays are so marvellous."

"'Modern plays'," Hawley repeated mockingly. "What do you have in mind, George Bernard Shaw? I dare say *Candida* will still be playing next year. Personally, I preferred *How He Lied to Her Husband*. Didn't you, Bram?"

That froze the entire company, as well it might. Bram's face went an ugly shade of crimson. Elise's expression didn't alter but her eyes were lethal.

"I prefer musical comedy," Zeb announced loudly, since nobody else was going to save them. "I must have seen *The Toreador* three times."

"You would," Bram spat, turning his ire on the easier target. "The amount of childish rubbish spewed onto the London stage to exploit the lowest common denominators of human nature—"

"You mean, things people like," Zeb said, knowing he was being drawn in even as he said it, but unable to help himself.

"Facile pap and nonsense, consumed uncritically by the mob."

"What's facile is judging a musical revue by the same criteria you use for an Ibsen drama. It makes as much sense as condemning an iced bun for not being a chateaubriand."

"That is to say, one is a different and lesser object," Bram said triumphantly.

"What about ghost stories?" Hawley put in, with his astonishing knack for making things worse. "I suppose you include those in your condemnation of popular entertainment? Mere childish rubbish?"

"Ghost stories are not rubbishy," Jessamine said clearly. "They are true. I told you they are true. This house is haunted."

"Jessamine," Wynn said. "I asked you—"

"But we should talk of it. Cousin, we must. You know I have seen it. So has Mr. Grey. Tell them."

Everyone looked at Gideon, whose mouth tightened. "I don't wish to speak of this, Miss Jessamine."

"*Tell* them. Am I a liar? Is it just my imagination? *Is* it?"

"I really cannot discuss this," Gideon said. The tension in his voice was audible.

"You mean, you can't deny it," Jessamine said. "Because you have seen it, and so have I, and Cousin Wynn, so have you."

That got everyone looking at Wynn. His round, cheery face dropped a little. He didn't reply for a moment, and then he let out a long sigh. "Yes. I have."

"Oh, come, Wynn," Bram said.

"Don't." Wynn held up a hand. "Don't, please, tell me I was seeing things or accuse me of having too much imagination. I am a grown man. I have lived in this house all my life. I have seen one after another family member fall prey to despair, sinking into the silence of dread, and I know, too well, why that is. I *know*."

He sounded frighteningly sincere. Zeb glanced around the table and said, "You saw what Jessamine described to us? A monk-like figure with a featureless face?"

"Zebedee!" Bram snapped.

"I don't wish to—" Wynn broke off. "If you will have it, yes. Yes, I have, but this is not a subject for discussion. I don't want to see it, or for any of you to see it. Although, in the circumstances…" He shook his head.

"What circumstances?" Dash said.

Wynn raised his eyes. "Guilt. Shame. Sin. That is what brings it, and once it is seen, retribution always follows."

Dash's lips parted. Elise's cheekbones were red. Bram said, "Really, Wynn, this is—Well, it strikes me as rather poor taste."

"Taste?" Jessamine demanded. "What has taste to do with anything? This is not a—a review, where you decide if something is worthy to exist or not! It is *true*!"

There was a ringing silence, which Zeb broke with, "No, it's not."

She turned on him, eyes bright with fury. Wynn said, "Zeb, I fear—"

"I've read the book."

"What?" Bram said.

"This is literally *The Monastery*. Honestly, have none

of you except Wynn read our grandfather?" A glance around the table answered that question. "The protagonist of volume one is condemned to the monastery in male disguise by her husband and murdered by evil monks. Then the rest of the book is her ghost hounding all the various villains to their doom. She wears a monk's robe and has an eyeless glare. A joke's a joke, but I have to agree, this is poor taste."

Jessamine was gaping at him. Elise's lips curled maliciously upwards. Bram said, "Ha!"

Wynn was shaking his head. "You are right about the book." He didn't sound caught out or embarrassed in the slightest. "I quite see what you must have thought. But you have it the wrong way round, Zeb. I have not taken a ghost story from *The Monastery*. Walter Wyckham thought up *The Monastery* based on the ghost."

Zeb just looked at him. Wynn gave a weary smile. "Consult the family records if you wish. It has been seen before, many times. My father's death. Walter's. Laura's. Even poor Georgina. Truly, she died of her shame."

"But," Zeb said.

"I hope and pray none of you see it, but if you do, *don't look at its face*. Turn away and you may, perhaps, be spared. Now, we will speak of this no further; no good will come of discussing it. I shall ring for the plates to be cleared. I believe there is chocolate pudding to come."

Zeb staggered out after the meal to get some fresh air and met Hawley on the steps, with the inevitable cigarette. In the cold, his breath plumed smoke as much as Hawley's exhalations.

"Ah, Zeb. Gasper?"

Zeb glanced warily at the cigarette case he offered. "Not if it's those god-awful perfumed things. Where did you pick them up, a brothel?"

"Wynn's filled his cigarette boxes with them. You get used to it."

"Thanks, I won't. Must you render every meal hideous by sniping at Bram and Elise?"

"Why should I not?"

"It's a bit much to call a man a cuckold if it was you who cuckolded him."

"On the contrary. I can be absolutely sure that my accusation is true."

"Well, at least you ought to lay off Elise for committing adultery," Zeb countered. "That's damned hypocritical."

"Why? I never made vows to Bram, and I never forced her to break the ones she made. She degraded herself of her own free will. Should I pretend otherwise?"

Zeb contemplated the dim oval of his face in the darkness. "You know, Hawley, if you despise married women for having affairs with you, you should stop having affairs with married women. Just give it a rest, will you? I would like to get through the next couple of weeks with a minimum of unpleasantness, so if you could kindly avoid making every evening as awful as you made this one—"

"You expect me to sit silently while Elise manoeuvres? Watch her dangle London in front of Jessamine like a bribe? I think not, Zebby. Any more than I intend to watch you act out your performance of virtuous indifference. *Oh, no, I will not marry for money, I'm too noble. Give it all to Jessamine*," he mocked in a high-pitched whine that Zeb had to infer was an imitation of himself. "Absurd."

"It's not a performance. I don't want any part of this medieval nonsense."

"Oh, give it a rest. Have you another job yet?"

"What has that to do with it? No."

"No," Hawley repeated. "Sacked again, and that's what, the third time in four years? Can't keep a job, not a penny to your name, and a house and a fortune waiting to be snapped up if you can bring yourself to tolerate cunny rather than cock for ten minutes. But of course you don't want the money, no indeed. Do you expect me to believe that?"

"I don't care if you believe me, and my affairs are none of your business."

"But they are," Hawley said, puffing on his foul

cigarette. "They are very much my business if you intend to enrich yourself at my expense. Let me be blunt. I am having the girl, and the inheritance with her. If you make grounds with Jessamine, I will not hesitate to let her, and Wynn—and Bram, come to that—know exactly how you spend your leisure hours and who with. I doubt either Jessamine or Wynn's favour will survive the information that you are one of London's more dedicated sodomites. Wouldn't Bram feel vindicated then? Wouldn't dear Elise make hay with it?"

"Go to hell, Hawley," Zeb said. "Be damned to you. You had absolutely no need to say that. What have I ever done to you?"

"Nothing at all, dear boy. I have no desire to reveal your sordid secrets to the world, and no quarrel with you other than the prospect of you getting in my way. But I really must oblige you to give up any thoughts of winning Jessamine or Lackaday House. No more manoeuvring, Zebby, or I will be forced to act."

He puffed once more on his cigarette, tossed it away, a little orange shooting star in the darkness, and went back to the house without farewell. Zeb stood alone, his cheeks burning, needing the sting of cold.

He had always known Hawley was a shit. One could hardly fail to notice. But he hadn't particularly been a shit to Zeb before. When their social circles overlapped, as occasionally happened, they'd nod at one another civilly enough, or exchange a few mildly barbed words and move on. Zeb had come to regard that as a relationship in its way, just as one might get used to a snarling dog when you passed it every day, so that it came as a surprise when the cur finally went for your throat.

He stood outside, seething and miserable, until it was too cold to be tolerated and he had to retreat inside. The grandfather clock in the hall chimed ten as he came into the hall.

There were voices audible in the drawing room. Zeb skirted it; he had no desire to speak to anyone present. Not Bram or Elise; certainly not bloody Hawley; not Jessamine, whose friendliness he'd now have to repel if he didn't want Hawley to carry out his threat. Not the excessively military Dash; not Wynn, whose damn fool ideas had let him in for this ghastly event, and absolutely not Gideon, who hated him.

Sod the lot of them. He had brought *The Riddle of the Sands* and *The Phoenix and the Carpet* with him and was looking forward to both. An hour in bed with a book would be a great deal more pleasant than anything else on offer.

He headed up the stairs, noting that the light from the gas lamps was very low and flickering again. He wasn't quite groping his way along the corridors, but the dark red of the wallpaper, the dark wood of the floor covered by dark rugs, the dark rectangles of paintings, and the long, dark, windowless stretches of corridors made for an extremely uninviting journey. It was exactly the sort of dimly lit empty maze in which one might see a ghost.

He turned the corner and saw a ghost.

There was an indistinct grey cowled shape at the far end of the corridor. The lights flickered again. It was extremely cold. There was a *monk*.

It turned to face him. Slowly, slowly, it lifted its hooded head, and under the hood he saw only darkness.

Zeb knew a terrified impulse to hide his face from it, but the emotion that actually seized control was anger. "Oi!" he shouted. "Who the sod are you?"

The monk turned and whisked around the corner, its robes swishing on the floor. Zeb sprinted after it, but he skidded on a loose rug that felt like it had been greased, losing his balance, and had to windmill his arms to right himself. He swore, turned the corner—

It wasn't there.

Nobody was there. He hadn't heard a door open or shut, but the corridor was empty, as if the monk had vanished in the few seconds it had taken him to catch up.

He looked around, baffled and annoyed. "All right, very funny. You can come out now."

Silence. Absolute silence. He stood still, waiting for the giggle or the breath or the creak. None came.

Bastard. He marched down the corridor, trying all the doors on the left, then working his way back up. They all opened onto empty rooms. There was nobody here.

He could, he supposed, head back downstairs and make a fuss. That was probably what they wanted him to do, whoever *they* were. Wynn or Jessamine, he supposed—but no, that wasn't right, he'd heard them both in the drawing room as he'd passed. Bram couldn't move that fast. Elise wouldn't wear a cassock unless monasteries were hiring couturiers. Hawley didn't need to play ghost when he had a perfectly satisfactory game of blackmailer going on.

Gideon? Would Gideon really dress up in a cassock to scare him? Did he want Zeb to leave that badly, enough to do something so childish and unkind?

Zeb didn't want to think about that. He took stock of his position, summarised it as utterly miserable, and went to bed.

seven

E GOT UP EARLY again the next morning, tempting though it was to hide in bed for the rest of the fortnight. "Face the day," he told himself sourly. It was what Gideon had used to tell him as he got out of bed on time in the morning, brisk and ready for work. Zeb had not been so inclined then, and didn't want to now.

But here he was, and his desire to be outside just about outweighed his desire to stay in bed staring at the ceiling and feeling miserable, so he headed out for another turn around the grounds. He felt rather too aware of the twelve-foot boundary wall as he walked, even though he mostly couldn't see it. If he was going to stay, he'd need to get out onto the moor and take advantage of the beautiful scenery and miles of land unpopulated by Wyckhams.

He *was* going to stay; he'd made a promise so he had to take the consequences. But he hadn't promised to allow himself to be made a fool of by people capering around in costumes. He'd considered his situation thoroughly as he lay in bed last night, cold and angry and listening for noises that might be footsteps, and the conclusion he had reached was, *Sod this for a game of tin soldiers.*

He stomped around the follies, marched through the wood past Wayland's Smithy, and was coming up to the stone circle in a bad mood he couldn't shake when he saw a man approaching from the other direction. Tall, lean, looking as ill-tempered as Zeb felt: who else could it possibly be.

"Hey," he snapped. "I want a word with you."

"Mr. Zebedee?" Gideon said, with cold disdain.

His damn fool name on Gideon's lips, and Zeb's resentment and misery and anger boiled over with the abruptness of a pot of milk on the stove. "Fuck you."

Gideon's head went back. "Excuse me?"

"You heard. I don't know what I have done to merit this treatment," Zeb said. "Well, I do, but for Christ's sake, I didn't do it on purpose. I'm sorry I got you sacked; I got myself sacked too, so it's not as though the whole thing was a spree for me. I'm sorry I wasn't who you wanted me to be a year ago, I'm extremely sorry my presence here upsets you now, and I'm sure we'd both prefer it if I was anywhere else, but I'm not. And with all that said, I am sick to the back teeth of your insults and accusations and spite. I don't deserve it, I'm not going to put up with it any more, and, frankly, I thought better of you than childish practical jokes!"

Gideon had looked like he was ready to fire back, but at that last his brows went up. "What do you mean, jokes?"

Zeb glowered up at him. "Capering around in a sheet to frighten people is pretty low stuff, and if you had read *The Monastery* you might grasp quite how poor the taste of this whole farrago is."

"I have no idea what you're talking about."

"You, dressed up in a robe, prancing round the corridor last night when I went to bed!"

"I did no such thing. Robe?"

"Robe, hood, faceless monk of the kind you and Wynn and Jessamine have been making sinister allusions to. It's embarrassing. You really can't need a job that badly."

"I need this job extremely badly," Gideon bit out. "But my duties do not involve dressing up as the family ghost to scare you, and I didn't."

"Well, if it wasn't you, who was it?"

"How should I know? When was this?"

"Just after ten."

"I was playing billiards with your brother and Colonel Dash from quarter to ten until past the half hour," Gideon said. "I had an eye on the clock, as anyone would in those circumstances. I didn't leave the room for the duration of the game. Ask your brother."

Bram had many poor qualities—most of them, really—but he wouldn't collude on a practical joke, if only because of his inflated sense of personal dignity. If Gideon had been playing billiards with Bram, he hadn't been upstairs making a mock of Zeb, and Zeb felt a knot in his chest relax with a sudden lurch that made him realise just how tight it had been.

"Oh," he said. "Right. Well—sorry. I thought I heard everyone else downstairs. Sorry."

"Everyone else *was* downstairs. The only people missing were you and Hawley."

"I don't suppose it was him: he'd hardly need to bother playing ghosts in the circumstances. You should probably know he's blackmailing me about being queer."

"*What?*" Gideon yelped.

Zeb should probably have led up to that a bit more, he realised. "He's threatening to tell Wynn my sordid secrets if I don't step out of the running for the inheritance, and since he won't believe I'm not *in* the running, this is going to get nasty. I don't think he knows that you were the person I got sacked from Cubitt's with—in fact, I'm sure he doesn't, or he'd have taunted you about it. But I felt I should warn you."

Gideon looked as though he was struggling to breathe. "I literally cannot lose this job. I can't. If your damned cousin is going to tell Wynn everything—Mother of God, are you *trying* to ruin my life?"

"I didn't ask him to blackmail me! For God's sake, why would I want you to lose your job again? I still feel guilty about the last time!"

"Perhaps because you don't want me here while you're courting your cousin."

"I am not courting my blasted cousin! I don't want the Wyckham fortune at all, still less with Jessamine attached!"

"Of course not, why would you? When you're unemployed again, and on your uppers—"

"I'm not on my uppers at all. I'm doing very well."

"You don't *look* like you're doing well. You look like a tramp."

"I have always looked like a tramp, employed or not," Zeb pointed out. "I don't want the damned money, I have said so repeatedly, and I don't see why the idea is so hard to grasp!"

Gideon leaned back, face sceptical. "Because it's a hundred and fifty thousand pounds."

Zeb's jaw actually dropped: he could feel himself gaping. He closed it hastily. "*How* much? Good Lord. I had no idea. I knew he was rich but a hundred and fifty thousand? Really? Why the blazes doesn't he redecorate the place? I don't know what one could do with Lackaday House short of knocking it down and starting again, but probably one of those interiors people would have ideas. Or he could just live somewhere else. *I'd* live somewhere else."

"As you could," Gideon said. "Anywhere you like, if you marry the girl."

Zeb could feel the tug of it. A hundred and fifty thousand was an obscene sum. It was fur coat money, yacht money, Monte Carlo money. Money that would make your whole world a place of pleasure and ease. Money you'd do anything to have.

Obscene.

"It's a lot, I grant you," he said. "But as somebody, possibly Jesus, said, what does it profit a man if he gains a cartload of cash but loses his soul?"

"It profits him a hundred and fifty thousand pounds. Many people would put their souls to one side for that."

And Gideon thought Zeb was one of them. Hurt surged through him. "For God's sake, Gideon. What did I ever do to make you think I'm greedy? Irresponsible, thoughtless, careless, I'll admit all of that. But greedy? Really?"

Gideon opened his mouth, but whatever he might have said didn't come. The silence stretched out for a few eternal seconds.

"No," he said at last. "I would never have said you were greedy. I would never have thought you would stab anyone in the back for an inheritance, still less marry a schoolgirl for one. I can't reconcile the man I knew with your presence here."

"You could reconcile it very easily if you listened to me!" Zeb yelped. "I'm not *doing* those things!"

"But," Gideon began, and stopped there with an arrested look.

Zeb tried to wait for him to speak, jamming his hands in his pockets in an effort to hold back, but the words bubbled out. "Look, I'm sorry. I hate this. I wish we weren't on these terms. I'm sorry I thought you did something horrible to me, and I wish you didn't believe I'm doing horrible things now. I can't bear that we're like this, actually. Would you walk?"

"Walk?"

"Walk and talk. Since we're both stuck in this blasted house, maybe we could make things less bad if we talk to one another rather than shouting and storming off. If you want to make them less bad, of course. You might not. Up to you."

Gideon looked slightly off-balance, maybe a little wary, but something had changed in his face. "Uh—we could walk."

"Thank you. Can we go outside the grounds?"

"Not easily. The only exit is the front gate, which is kept locked."

"No back door and the front gate always locked?" Zeb asked as they set off. "I dare say Walter Wyckham might have worried about his privacy when he built this damn fool place, or been half mad, whichever, but why does Wynn live like this?"

"I understand there was an incident a few years ago. An escaped convict made his way inside the walls and was in the grounds for five days before he was identified and caught."

"You're joking." Zeb felt slightly dizzy, walking along with Gideon, having a conversation. It wasn't a conversation about anything they needed to talk about, but it was still an exchange of words which they were both trying to make work, and that was something.

"Not at all. He hid in one of the follies and stole food from the kitchens during the day. He was caught when he attacked a maid."

"Good God. How awful. I see why Wynn doesn't want people wandering in unobserved, then, but it's still rather prisonesque. Not to mention, in the middle of nowhere, a twelve-foot wall surely looks more like a temptation than a deterrent."

"In what possible way?" Gideon demanded.

"If you've built a huge wall, there must be *something*

behind it that's worth the effort of scaling it. That's what I'd think. If I were a burglar, of course."

"That is an extremely Zeb-like response," Gideon said, and there was a smile in his voice that Zeb hadn't heard in a very long time. "I find it remarkably off-putting, myself. I'm not even sure what your grandfather was trying to keep out. Bad reviews?"

"Well, they can be hurtful," Zeb said. "And he was more or less thrown out of good society for *The Monastery*, which served him right. But I would imagine his other profession had more to do with it."

"What do you mean? What else did he do?"

"He was a slaver."

Gideon was silent for a second. "I don't think I knew that. Did you tell me, before?"

"I didn't know before. I never troubled to ask where Father's money came from. But yes, Walter Wyckham, my grandfather, was a slave owner and trader. An active one, not just an investor: he owned four ships and two plantations, and he *ran* them. He visited his properties several times and came up with ideas to increase revenues. He wrote books about cruel evildoers receiving their just punishment while he was travelling back and forth across the oceans to wring more profit out of the people he kept in hell. That's the money that built this house. The wages of sin, in the most literal manner imaginable."

Gideon was staring at him. Zeb shrugged irritably. "If you're going to tell me how many great houses were built or rebuilt or filled with wonderful art on the profits of slavery, I already know. Bram and Hawley don't agree on much, but they would both tell you that Art justifies suffering. The existence of a beautiful building filled with beautiful things is worth any number of nameless, unimportant lives lost on a plantation or down a mine. Our wealth might have come from regrettable origins, but that's all in the past and there's no point making a fuss."

"You don't agree?"

"If people want to achieve greatness through suffering, it should be their own damn suffering," Zeb said. "And even if I did believe art justifies inflicting pain and misery on people, which I do not, Lackaday House is trite, cliched, and horrible. I'm not suggesting it would be all right if the house was beautiful," he added. "Just that this ludicrous Gothic rubbish is whatever the opposite of icing on the cake is. The shit on the shoe."

"Right," Gideon said. "I see. How did you learn this?"

"A chap—gentleman of colour, from abroad—paid a call on me a few months back, asking if I could give him any access to family papers since Wynn and Bram had both refused him. He was trying to make a full account of what had been done in the Wyckham plantations, for posterity, because he says the British prefer to remember the part where we abolished slavery, rather than all the enslaving we did first. I couldn't help, but I asked him to stay for tea and he told me all about it. About my family history, which was his own too, because his family, grandparents and great-grandparents, had been enslaved in Walter Wyckham's plantations."

"Oh my God."

"Quite. We talked for a long time. Or, rather, he talked; I didn't have much to say. There is something really quite awkward about sitting there with a teacup as a man tells you how your grandfather enslaved and tortured and murdered his relatives. *Our* relatives, actually, because of course Walter inflicted himself on various women while he was there and left a number of children. Jerome—that's his name—is actually my first cousin. His mother was Walter's daughter. As cousins go, he's infinitely preferable to Hawley."

"I expect so. Dear God."

"He was astonishingly decent about it," Zeb said. "I'd have punched me in the face as proxy for Walter, but he just wanted to tell a Wyckham what we did. To look one of us in the eye and say, *That was wrong*."

"And you heard him out."

"It was the least I could do. Literally: I sat there like a pudding while he laid out why my grandfather should have been hanged from the nearest lamppost and buried with a stake through his heart. He didn't say that last part. That was a conclusion I reached myself."

"Right."

"Anyway," Zeb said on an exhalation. "Were we talking about that for any reason?"

"The big wall," Gideon said, because he always remembered these things. "Why Walter built it."

"Ugh. Yes. I sometimes wonder if all those English country gentlemen who built themselves big houses with long sightlines and high walls did it because they were afraid of people coming across the seas for vengeance. I hope they were terrified. I hope that fear haunted Walter's dreams every night of his rotten, stinking life. Oh, that will be the Wyckham curse, of course."

"Sorry?"

"Supposedly an old woman who 'worked' for Walter cursed him to die at fifty, and he fell for it hook, line, and sinker. I bet that was a slave of his. At least she made him sweat."

"And now you don't want the inheritance," Gideon said slowly. "Is this why?"

"Of course it is. I wouldn't touch it with a barge pole."

Gideon grabbed his arm, stopping as he did so, so that he pulled Zeb round. They faced each other under the lowering sky. "Do you mean that? Truly?"

"Were you not listening?"

"But you *came* here for the inheritance!"

"I came here because Wynn invited me for a relaxing fortnight in the country," Zeb said. "I thought I was going to get to know a family member who was less awful than the rest. Hah. It serves me right, agreeing to live and eat off Wyckham money. I should have turned down the invitation on that basis, and then I wouldn't be in the worst house party since that one where they hosted the guests in an underground room and secretly bricked them in."

Gideon was searching Zeb's face, his light eyes intense. Zeb shifted under the scrutiny. "What is it?"

"Wynn told me you knew he intended to disinherit Bram and were expecting to be confirmed in his place. He said you and he had been corresponding, that you needed the money urgently. And after your conversation yesterday, he said he expected you to propose to Jessamine within the week."

"But he can't possibly have thought that," Zeb said blankly. "I specifically told him I *wouldn't* marry her. As for the inheritance, I had no idea it was up for grabs until dinner the first night. I did tell him that it would be convenient for me to visit because I had lost my job and a friend could take my room—"

"You can't afford your room?"

"Of course I can, but I've a pal coming down from Scotland for a couple of weeks, so we thought he could save on the cost of a hotel, and I could have my rent covered while I'm away. I dare say Wynn misunderstood that, and I will freely admit I told him I've been short of cash; I used that as an excuse not to come earlier. Maybe he got things confused. But he's simply wrong about Jessamine."

They started walking again, trudging along through rank, damp grass. Zeb didn't care. He was walking with Gideon, and Gideon was actually listening to him, and he didn't intend to stop for a little discomfort. He'd walk through a lake if he had to.

Gideon had a small frown on his face and his hands behind his back. He had used to pace like that at Cubitt's when he was deep in thought. "Hawley is blackmailing you because he thinks you want Jessamine and the money. Have you explained to him why you don't?"

"I have not, and I'm not going to."

"Why not?"

"Because Hawley stains everything he touches," Zeb said. "That conversation with Jerome was important. It meant something to me, and I am not going to repeat it to someone who would tell me I'm a fool for thinking it matters. I refuse to do that."

"No," Gideon said, his voice low. "No, you would not. I... God damn it, Zeb. I think I have been extremely unfair to you."

It was a cold day. The Dartmoor wind had been

cutting through Zeb's coat for a while. His shoes were soaked through, his stockings wet, the bottoms of his trousers were slapping damply against his ankles, and now his entire body was suffused with a warm glow that went some way to counteracting the misery. "Well, yes, maybe. A bit."

"I had entirely the wrong idea. And that's because Wynn was mistaken, or deluded, in what he told me, but also..." He hesitated. "I think it was because of us. Because it was easier if I could think the worst of you. I'm sorry."

"It's all right."

"It's truly not. Thank you for talking to me, Zeb. I don't know if I'd have bothered in your shoes."

"Of course you would. In my shoes, I mean, not that you'd actually want to be in my shoes, they're drenched. Thank you for listening. Might we do a bit better, then? Because the prospect of a fortnight here with you hating me is pretty awful, honestly."

"I don't hate you."

"It feels like you hated me."

"I—" Gideon began, and then stopped. There was a long, painful silence.

"I mean, you can," Zeb said, when he could no longer stop himself filling it. "Hate me, that is. I quite see why you would. I just wish you didn't."

"I don't," Gideon said again. "I—God damn it. I have spent the last month hearing about your willingness to marry a stranger for a fortune, and yes, by the end of that I think I was coming to hate you, but that's hardly your fault if it wasn't true. Still, it raised a lot of other issues—memories, whatever you want to call it, and... Zeb, I need time to think about this. Could we leave it for now? Please?"

Zeb raised his hands and clamped his lips, biting them fiercely shut on the inside against the near-compulsion to speak, and the dozen things he wanted to say. He dug the sharp edges of the crucifix into his thumb as a distraction. They walked on.

After a few moments, Gideon let out a long breath. "Look. I truly don't hate you. But I also don't want to spend a fortnight with you, any more than I expect you want that with me. Not to mention you're being blackmailed over an inheritance and marriage you don't even want. It would be a great deal easier all round if you left."

"I can't."

"Why not? What is there to gain by staying?"

Zeb wished he knew the answer to that. Or rather, he did know; he just wished it wasn't a wispy impossibility. "Wynn asked me to stay."

"What does that matter? Why should you indulge his absurd plans at our expense?"

"At—?"

"Zeb, it hurts," Gideon said, low. "I was happy a year ago, with you. Having you here makes me very aware I am not happy now. I don't blame you for that—I'm well aware what happened was my fault too—but here we are, and it's making us both miserable. I would go if I could, but I can't. So I wish you would."

"But I promised." Zeb's lips and tongue felt oddly stiff, unwieldy. "I promised Wynn I'd stay and I don't want to break a promise. Not if I can help it."

"You won't break a promise to him," Gideon said. "Fine. You wouldn't even *make* one to me, but you won't— Whatever you choose. It's up to you. Fine."

Zeb wanted to cry out, *I have to! Wynn is dying!*, but he'd given his word to keep that to himself, and he couldn't think of any way to explain without it. He stared at Gideon, silenced. Gideon looked as though he was going to say something else, then he simply turned and walked away.

eight

ZEB RETURNED TO LACKADAY House alone, with sodden feet.

He wasn't sure if he was glad they'd talked. No, he was: more than anything, he didn't want Gideon to hate him. All the same, he felt even worse than he had before at the realisation his stupidity was still causing so much pain a year later. Although maybe that shouldn't have come as a surprise. Gideon's absence had hurt Zeb on a daily basis for months.

But they *had* talked, and resolved a misunderstanding. Maybe, if he stayed, they could talk about what had gone wrong. Maybe Zeb could explain—

Explain what? *Remember when you asked me for forever, and I said 'I dare say I could give you the evening'? And then the next day I pulled you into a stockroom at work, and we were caught and sacked for gross misconduct and damned lucky not to be gaoled? Well, about that...*

He was a damned fool to think Gideon wanted explanations a year too late, and a damneder one, if that was a word, to imagine that anything he could say would change matters. What did he think: that Gideon would say, *Oh, well, now I understand, it was all perfectly reasonable*? That he might give Zeb another chance?

The most likely outcome of all this wasn't reunion, or even forgiveness: it was him ruining Gideon's life by accident for a second time. He did not want to do that. Therefore he had to get a grip on the situation.

The walk had taken up much of the morning. (*Two and a half days down*, he found himself thinking, *eleven and a half to go*.) He took himself up to his room, changed his stockings and trousers, and wondered where best he could put his sodden shoes to dry, ending up propping them by the unlit fireplace. He had no other shoes except his dress shoes, but he'd brought slippers with him, being a man who lived in slippers, given the chance. They were a long-loved pair, tartan and extremely down-at-heel, and Bram would doubtless have plenty to say if he turned up for lunch in them, but there wasn't much choice.

He should have some laundry done while he was here, or he'd be down to slippers and a nightgown. He glanced ruefully at his muddy trousers, which he'd slung over the back of a chair, and saw a stain on the grey fabric that he was sure hadn't been there before. They'd been clean on three days ago, and he'd worn them yesterday, and... oh yes, he'd put his hand into a pool of something on the altar of the stone circle, wiped it on his trousers, and had been walking around with a stain on his arse ever since. For heaven's sake.

He squinted at the stain. It was dark red, oddly hard to the touch where it had dried, and he remembered the liquid's cold, viscous feel with a shudder. What the blazes had he put his hand into?

He donned his only pair of clean trousers with a vow to be more careful and went down to luncheon. There he found Dash, Jessamine, and Bram making stilted conversation, and Gideon sitting in silence over a spread of cold chicken, cheese, and bread that looked identical to yesterday's cold chicken, cheese, and bread.

"What on earth have you on your feet?" Bram demanded.

"Slippers," Zeb said. "Good day to you too."

"Why are you—"

"Because my shoes are wet. Because I went for a walk," he added, anticipating the next question.

"You have only one pair of shoes with you?" Bram demanded. "Really, your irresponsibility—"

"Where did you walk, Cousin Zeb?" Jessamine asked over him. Possibly she'd had her fill of Bram too.

"Round the grounds. I'm not sure how one walks anywhere else. Could we go into the moorland? I'd love to see a bit of Dartmoor. Who else would like a long walk?"

"Energetic fellow, aren't you?" Dash said. "Hopping around the place like a squirrel. Perhaps tomorrow. I should like to put my feet up this afternoon."

Apparently neither Bram nor Jessamine felt the urge to get out from under the encompassing walls either. Zeb helped himself to chicken, cheese, and bread, feet twitching under the table. Jessamine offered to have his shoes brought down and properly dried. Dash said that in his view, the weather was liable to close in, and Dartmoor weather was not to be sneezed at. Gideon said nothing at all. Bram launched into an analysis of the paintings in the dining room, none of which seemed to Zeb to have any artistic merit, and his monologue was still going strong when the door banged open.

Hawley marched in, red-faced. "What the devil is happening in this house?"

"Just luncheon, Cousin Hawley," Jessamine said, startled. "Would you care—"

"There is graffiti outside my room!"

"There's what?" Zeb said.

"*Graffiti,*" Bram said in a very foreign-sounding sort

of way. "A term from the Italian, referring to the common Roman practice of writing on walls—"

"The wall outside my room, you pompous arse!" Hawley spluttered. "Letters a foot high, and a damned offensive bit of spite with it. I want to know who did it, and I want it removed!"

"Writing on the *walls*?" Jessamine said. "Inside the house?"

"In the corridor!"

"That seems extremely unlikely," Bram remarked. "Have you been drinking?"

"It's there!" Hawley snarled. "And I won't have it! Who did this?"

Everyone exchanged glances. "I'll go and look," Jessamine said.

"No!" Hawley snapped. "That is, it is not fit for your eyes, Jessamine. You are above such spite and vulgarity."

"Then *I* shall look," Colonel Dash said, with a touch of annoyance. "Lead the way."

"I'll come with you," Zeb offered, since it was a fast exit from the table and Bram and Gideon.

Hawley was lodged on the opposite side of the house to Zeb. With so few staff in evidence, he really would have thought they would put all the guests together. He followed his cousins upstairs and along several corridors until Hawley stopped dead.

They were in a corridor very like Zeb's but without any paintings. That, unfortunately, meant they had an uninterrupted view of the extremely ugly wallpaper with its aggressively repeated pattern. Zeb had read a surprising number of stories featuring haunted patterns (well, two, but that seemed a lot) and was of the opinion that Lackaday House's walls could inspire another.

There was nothing else at all to see.

"Hawley?" Dash asked.

"But—it was here. What the—" Hawley took a few intemperate strides forward and ran his hands over the wallpaper. "There was writing here! Damn great letters, painted on the wall!"

"There's nothing there now," Zeb observed.

"I can see that, you bloody fool!"

Zeb put his own hand to the wallpaper. It was dry and a little dusty. "What did this writing say?"

"Offensive nonsense. A slanderous allegation."

"Personal?" Dash asked.

"Of course personal. It could hardly be slanderous otherwise."

"So, you had a vision—"

"It was not a vision!"

"You 'saw' abusive words written on the wall," Dash said, the quotation marks around the verb very clear. "But there is nothing there. Do you often see things that aren't there?"

Hawley indicated his opinion of that question in an explosive manner, added a few reflections on the intelligence of his companions, and stamped off into what was presumably his bedroom, letting a reek of stale-scented smoke and a distinct whiff of spirits into the corridor. Zeb and Dash turned as one and headed back to the main hall.

Once they were at a safe distance, Dash remarked, "Well, they do say that absinthe stuff gives a chap visions."

"But it makes the heart grow fonder."

Dash gave a moustache-ruffling snort. "What do you make of all that? Is he off his rocker?"

"He's playing the fool in some way. No idea what."

Dash frowned slightly. "You sound sure of that."

"Last night someone dressed up as the family ghost in an attempt to scare me," Zeb said. "You were playing billiards with Bram and Mr. Grey at the time, and I'd heard Wynn and the women talking downstairs. That leaves Hawley."

"Well," Dash said. "Is that so? Well, well. Someone dressed as a monk, was that?"

"In my corridor. You don't sound surprised."

"Saw it too."

Zeb turned to face him. Dash gave a mildly embarrassed shrug. "Late last night, going to bed. Ghostly grey hooded form, you know. Assumed it was my imagination or a servant or some such. Rotten low light here: I must say, I thought acetylene would be better. Hawley, you think?"

"Everyone else was accounted for when I saw my ghost."

"Hmph. Let's you and I keep an eye on Mr. Hawley Wyckham, shall we?"

"Let's do that," Zeb said.

Zeb headed down to the library with his satchel that afternoon, in the hope of getting some use out of the day, and found Jessamine. He would have retreated, but she looked up and smiled. "Good afternoon, Cousin Zeb."

"Well, good-ish. The weather's closing in a bit." It was decidedly grey outside now; he was glad he'd gone out that morning. "What are you up to?"

"I am going over the housekeeping accounts," Jessamine said composedly. "Learning how to manage Lackaday House, since I will be its mistress one day."

It was something to do, he supposed. He couldn't help noticing she seemed very confident about the success of the marriage plan. "I imagine there's a great deal to the running of a place this size, and such a remote one," he offered. "It must be difficult to keep it supplied?"

"The grocer sends a cart from town once a week. I

hope you don't find the food monotonous? I don't think Bram is very happy. He's a gourmet, isn't he? He must be finding our plain fare very tiresome."

"It'll do him good," Zeb said without sympathy.

"I hope so, but he often seems in a bad temper at meals. He was quite angry about the book, wasn't he? I am enjoying it a great deal."

"*The Monastery*? Are you really? Where have you got to?"

"The second volume."

"You, uh, didn't find the end of the first volume a bit much?"

"Oh, it was terrible."

"It is, isn't it?"

"In the sense of the poets. Awful and magnificent and sublime. Like the fall of Satan in *Paradise Lost*. That's what it makes me feel: pity and terror."

"Oh," Zeb said. "Gosh."

"And the cruelty of the monks, the evil of it. No wonder the ghost walks. No wonder it comes to punish wrongdoers and leaves its writing on the wall."

Zeb had forgotten that. "The ghost does that, doesn't it? In the book, I mean. It writes on the walls in blood."

"Yes, the ghost does that," Jessamine said. "Did you see what Hawley saw?"

"There wasn't anything there."

"Of course not. I knew there would not be."

"Sorry?"

"Don't you remember? The words can only be seen by the guilty one. A message just for him, or me, or you."

"That's in the book. In this case, there just wasn't anything there."

She frowned a little. "You think the ghost is a story, don't you?"

"Yes," Zeb said. "I don't believe in ghosts. Or disappearing writing, or disembodied footsteps, or any of it."

"But I have *seen* it. How can you dismiss the evidence of my eyes, and Cousin Wynn's, and Mr. Grey's, and so many others'?"

"I'm not saying you didn't see something. I'm saying, I don't believe what you saw was the spirit of a dead monk."

She pushed her chair back and stood. "I think you are calling me a fool, and if not, you are calling me a liar. Which is it?"

Zeb blinked. "Neither. I just don't believe in ghosts. If you do, that's your affair, but I don't think there's anything to be gained by discussing it."

Jessamine was staring at him with big, hurt, rejected eyes. "I thought you understood. Or, at least, that you would understand if you listened. I did think *you* would listen. Oh, I cannot bear it!" She left the room hastily; Zeb would almost say 'fled'. He thought he heard a sob.

"That went well," he remarked to himself.

He spent the rest of the afternoon in the library. The weather turned to gusts of rain that splattered against the windows and drove his fellow guests to look for comfortable places to sit. That, regrettably, meant Bram turned up.

He came in with a heavy tread and irritable movements, looked over, and snorted. "What are you doing?"

"Just my accounts. Robbing Peter to pay Paul, as usual." Zeb pulled his papers together as he spoke.

"As I would expect. Feckless and irresponsible."

Zeb had had all the unpleasant conversations he needed for the day. He tried to focus on getting everything into his satchel as Bram mooched around the shelves with the sort of dissatisfied air that demanded to be asked what was wrong.

"What the blazes is up with you?" Zeb snapped.

"Have you taken my cigars? I had them in the smoking room."

"Of course I have not. Why would I take your cigars?"

"You endlessly interfere with other people's things. I dare say you have half a dozen of Wynn's matchboxes on you now."

That was a gross libel: he'd only pocketed one. "I detest cigars," he pointed out. "And I haven't even been in the smoking room. It reeks of those rancid perfumed things of Wynn's."

"Well, my cigar case is gone. And I am quite sure I put a box in my luggage, but it is missing too."

"You probably meant to pack the box and forgot. I do that kind of thing all the time."

"*You* may. Some of us are rather more competent," Bram said.

"I'm not the one looking for his cigars," Zeb retorted, and stalked to the door.

As he reached it, Bram said, "Wait. This marriage business. What are your intentions?"

"Exactly what I told you. I'm not going to marry Jessamine."

"And do you stand by what you said? That this idea of Wynn's is misconceived?"

"I think it's terrible, but it's none of my business."

"I agree," Bram said. "Naturally Wynn is concerned for her future. But she is a pretty girl, if a foolish one. Elise believes she could very well find a more suitable situation—one more appropriate for her character and parentage—given the opportunity."

"I don't understand."

"Consider her background. Breeding will out. Let her but have a little time in London and the problem will take care of itself."

"Still don't understand."

Bram made an irritable noise. "With a reasonable sum

settled on her, she will doubtless make an appropriate marriage. Alternatively, and to speak plainly, I can well imagine her as a mistress, but not that of Lackaday House. Elise has proposed taking her to London and making introductions, and I imagine her future will resolve itself very quickly. We are putting that proposition—I mean a visit before any marriage is decided—to Wynn. I hope we can count on your support."

Zeb took that in. He could imagine Elise dangling charming young men at Jessamine until she fell in love with one, all the while quietly telling those men that she came from a long line of easily seduced young fools. *A housemaid's granddaughter, my dear, a bastard's bastard. Ripe for plucking.*

At best, Jessamine would end up discontented with her lot; at worst, used, disgraced, and discarded. Or maybe she would meet a good man and Wynn would give her a sensible sum and she'd live happily ever after, but Zeb wouldn't want to bet on it.

"Absolutely not," he said. "I'm all in favour of Wynn reconsidering this marriage plan, and if you come up with a way to change his mind that is fair to Jessamine, I'll support you. If your idea, or Elise's, is to engineer her ruin, you can go to hell."

"Don't be a sentimental fool. The girl is a cuckoo in the nest. She needs to be pushed out."

"Well, you'd know about that," Zeb said. "Wouldn't you?"

They stared at one another. Bram's jaw clenched in a very familiar way, one that heralded justifications. Zeb didn't have the strength. He shook his head and walked out.

nine

IT BEGAN RAINING PROPERLY after that. Zeb found a suitable small table in an empty bedroom and lugged it to his own room, intending to work there rather than encounter any more relatives. As it turned out, he was too frustrated and unsettled to get anything done, and felt uncomfortably conscious of the small room, the enclosing walls. Rain lashed the glass, the daylight dwindled, and as the shadows closed in around him, he was very aware of how far he was from human company. It was hard to remember that, in the circumstances, this was a good thing.

And then he heard footsteps again.

These ones were lighter than before, brisker. Zeb almost ran to the door, yanked it open, and jumped out of his skin to find himself face-to-face with a maid. They both shrieked.

"Sorry!" Zeb yelped. "I'm dreadfully sorry. Did I startle you? Of course I did; I scared myself half to death. I do beg your pardon. Sorry. Do come in." He stepped back, gesturing her in, and received a look of startling hostility.

That seemed unwarranted. He'd seen her around the house and noted her tense, unfriendly manner, which seemed common to all Wynn's staff. In her case, it might be linked to the fact that she was a very handsome woman but had her hair pulled back in an unflattering manner and wore a loose, shapeless dress. Zeb wondered whose attention she was trying to avoid—

And that would be the problem.

"Er," he said. "If you have duties in here, I can leave. I wouldn't want to be in your way. Give me a moment—"

"I just came to collect your shoes for drying, Mr. Zebedee."

"Oh! Oh, marvellous, thank you very much. I'm sorry to give you the trouble. Let me get them."

"I'll fetch them, sir," she said, her tone sufficing for the missing 'you idiot'.

Zeb retreated to the window to be well out of her way, shuddering at the cold it failed to keep out, and gazed at the dark rather than impose further on her notice.

Perhaps everyone else in the house hated him, but at least he could avoid upsetting the staff.

He went down to dinner in a mood of unpleasant anticipation. Drinks in the drawing room were negotiated without disaster thanks to Colonel Dash, who held forth at great length on the weather, with particular reference to the likelihood of a Dartmoor mist, then moved seamlessly into British foreign policy while everyone else nodded along. Hawley seemed less poised than usual and was unexpectedly silent; Zeb wondered if he had been drinking. Elise and Bram looked rather smug.

It started to go wrong as they ate yet another bowl of soup. This time it was parsnip.

"Are you feeling better, Hawley?" Elise asked brightly.

"I have not been unwell."

"Really? I understood you had an unfortunate episode. It isn't the first time, is it? Perhaps your constitution is strained. Your way of life does start to take a toll."

Hawley swung round rather than replying. "So, Jessamine. I have scarcely seen you today. I understand you were closeted with Elise this afternoon."

Jessamine dimpled. "Elise allowed me to try on some of her dresses, and arranged my hair." She did look different, Zeb belatedly noticed, with dangling ringlets. It made her look older, her neck longer. It suited her rather better than the more schoolgirlish styles.

"Really," Hawley said. "You certainly look very sophisticated and very beautiful. I myself think—but I must not be ungracious."

"No, do say," Jessamine said naively. "I wondered if it quite suited me, though it is wonderful. I look so grown-up. I tried a little lip-stain—"

Wynn made a noise. Jessamine said quickly, "Only to try! I wiped it off at once."

"I think all a young woman needs is the bloom of youth," Hawley said. "There is nothing so fresh, so perfect. Of course it doesn't last, and then the tricks come out in an effort to recapture the freshness that has passed. But it is, to me, a shame to see such falsities used on simplicity and innocence."

Elise's nostrils flared. "Really, Hawley? A *hairstyle* affects her innocence? How remarkably puritanical, from you."

"I don't think a hairstyle will affect her innocence. Corrupt company might do that."

"Yes," Elise said. "It would certainly be for the best if she avoids degenerate men."

"I would fear women more," Hawley retorted. "A man may have a past, but he can and will cast that behind him in favour of a new and better future. A woman's past is her present and her future too. And women are so *very* unkind to girls with youth and freshness they have themselves lost. *Women Beware Women,* isn't that the play? A virgin despoiled by her manipulative aunt?"

"Are you going to let him speak like this, Bram?" Elise demanded furiously. "Wynn? Is there not a gentleman at this table?"

Hawley smirked. "One might also question the number of ladies."

"Oh, for God's sake," Zeb said. "Stop it."

Hawley's eyes narrowed. "If I were you, I'd think before you speak."

Zeb truly loathed him in that moment. "All I want is to eat dinner in peace for once. Can we not do that?"

"I will not be silenced," Hawley said. "I think, since you force the issue, that Jessamine should not be expected to mix with a notorious woman at all, still less permitted to stay with one in London. I don't care to think what corruption she might be exposed to."

There was a moment of loud-voiced chaos. Elise and Bram demanded how Hawley dare. Hawley sneered. Dash made moustachioed noises of extreme disapproval. Jessamine looked between them, bewildered and distressed.

Zeb considered crawling under the table. "Stop it," he tried. "Stop!"

Nobody listened. The angry voices rose and clashed until the door creaked open, and the footman slouched in.

That, at least, shut everyone up. They sat in fraught, icy silence as the soup was cleared away and the main course brought in. It was beef stew, served with potatoes overboiled to obvious dryness. The cook was not helping matters.

The family waited in mutually bristling silence until the food was served and more wine poured. The footman maundered out, taking his time. Several people inhaled at once as the door shut, and Wynn said, "Wait."

He spoke with unusual sharpness. That might have got him listened to, or it might just have been the fact that he was the one with the money.

"That conversation was—I would normally say unedifying. In fact, it was most edifying. I had hoped for more from this gathering, this family."

Zeb couldn't imagine why. Wynn looked around them, face severe. "It seems I must make myself clear. Jessamine, you will not be accompanying Mrs. Wyckham to London, or anywhere. I do not find her a fit companion for you. Moreover, Bram, I regret to say that I will not be allowing Lackaday House to pass into your hands under any circumstances, at least in the current state of affairs. I would prefer to be sure the next inheritor will be a Wyckham, and your marriage does not give me faith in that."

Elise's head jerked back as if she'd been struck. "How *dare* you?"

"It was not my observation. Zebedee made an excellent point to that effect."

Bram's jaw dropped. Zeb said, "I did not!"

"There is no need to apologise. You drew my attention to the issue and I am grateful. We will have no Lady Ravendark here, foisting a bastard onto the family."

Hawley's mouth curved in a nasty manner. "Well, I must say, Zebby—"

"You must not," Wynn said coldly. "I have received information on your recent past that has shocked me to the core." He glanced at Elise as he said that. "You spoke about how a rake might reform: I should like to see evidence of that before I entrust my ward or house to your care."

"Yes, I have sowed my wild oats," Hawley said. "I admit it frankly, and I admit too that I regret it. I would have preferred to come to a pure woman with a clean slate of my own. But I hope I may be given a chance to wipe the slate clean, under her influence."

"You regret your wild oats?" Wynn said.

"I am deeply ashamed," Hawley said. "I look on my past with revulsion."

"I *am* a wild oat that someone sowed," Jessamine said loudly. "Am I shameful and revolting?"

Hawley's mouth shut like a rat-trap; Elise's smile flashed like a razor. "Zebedee," Wynn said, causing Zeb to jump. "You could put an end to this. You have expressed your scruples, and I respect them, but for Jessamine's sake, I must ask you to reconsider. You have impressed both of us favourably—"

"I wouldn't rush into this, Wynn," Hawley said. "Should he, Zeb? If we're talking about discreditable habits?"

"What does that mean?"

Zeb glared at Hawley. "I told you, I am not in this competition."

"It is not a competition, Cousin Zeb." Tears trembled in Jessamine's voice. "I am not a prize."

"Yes, you are," Zeb said. "You have been made one and you oughtn't be. Wynn, you must see that this marriage plan is a terrible idea. If you care for Jessamine's wellbeing, settle a sum on her—give her the lot, even—but let her marry as she pleases. And I have to say," he felt obliged to add, "the way you just spoke is not right. Elise is still a guest in your house."

"Hypocrite," Elise said with concentrated venom.

"Quite," Hawley put in. "The Little Lord Fauntleroy posture doesn't suit you."

"Shut up," Zeb told him. "All of you can shut up, actually: I'm fed to the back teeth with the lot of you. You can go to the devil, Hawley, and take Bram with you. And Wynn, I will not be proposing to Jessamine because, with the greatest possible respect, I don't want to marry her, any more than, if she met any other men at all, she would want to marry me. That's the end of the matter, and I will take my leave tomorrow."

Zeb was quite pleased with that speech, feeling he'd been frank, strong, and honest. He was therefore rather disappointed that the immediate effect of his words was to make Jessamine burst into tears.

"I told you," she sobbed to Wynn, big brown eyes overflowing. "I told you he does not care for me. Oh, why did you ask?"

She half rose from the table as she spoke. Wynn glared at him, indicating with a hand that he should go to her side. Zeb stayed firmly where he was.

"This is a shocking display," Dash announced, in tones so strong it got even Jessamine's tearful attention. "One man who cannot control his wife, one who does not deserve a wife, and one who, when offered the sweetest young lady as a wife, spurns her like a clod. I had not intended to speak—I am well aware my age is a disadvantage—but I cannot see Jessamine treated in this way. She should have a husband who will worship her as the treasure she is, not consider her a mere inconvenience in his path to a fortune." He extended his hand. "Jessamine, if you will let an old soldier express his heart, I would like a private moment's speech with you."

Jessamine looked around wildly. "Yes—no—I don't know—don't ask me! Oh, don't ask me!"

She was off on that, sprinting from the room at her usual breakneck pace. Dash moved to go after her, but Wynn said, "Wait. No, Dash, old friend, stop. Give her time to reflect. I think all of us need that. You can finish your meals without me; I shall go to my room. Assist me, Grey." He stood as he spoke.

"So shall I," Elise said coldly. "Since I find myself insulted by all and sundry, and my husband is incapable of offering me protection. And *you* are a pair of vipers," she told Zeb and Hawley. "The girl would be better dead than wed to either of you."

She got up on that and swept out, past Wynn, who was leaning on Gideon's arm.

"Well," Hawley said.

Bram had been staring at his plate. Now he looked up at Zeb with real hatred. "You cur. You backstabbing swine."

Zeb perhaps should have assured him that he had never intended the construction Wynn had put on a literary allusion. What he said was, "It takes one to know one, you stinking hypocrite."

Bram pushed back his chair and walked out. Dash said, "I also find the company uncongenial tonight. Wynn, old friend, let me take your other arm."

They departed, leaving Zeb with Hawley, who took a leisurely mouthful of wine. "Goodness, Zebby, you do have hidden depths. I dare say the Brams deserved that. But you would be ill-advised to try those tactics with me."

"Oh my God, just tell Wynn," Zeb said. "Get up, march into his room, give him the big speech that I'm sure you've composed in your head, and have done. I don't care any more."

He dolloped beef stew on his plate, grabbed it, and joined the exodus, leaving his cousin alone.

ten

ZEB ATE HIS PLATE of dry potatoes and chewy beef in his room because he might be seething with fury, including at himself, but he was also hungry. He'd bet money that Bram had ordered sandwiches. Assuming Wynn's dour serving staff even did sandwiches. They didn't serve afternoon tea or any such, and Zeb hadn't dared to make requests.

Bram had probably been eating angry sandwiches and fuming at Zeb's underhanded tactics all evening, and the worst thing, the stupidest thing, was that although he hadn't done it, and Bram would have deserved it if he *had* done it, he still felt awful.

He tensed as he heard feet coming along the corridor, not wanting another conversation that would make him feel worse. It came to something when you found yourself hoping that the footsteps you heard were ghosts.

There was a knock at the door. Zeb considered pretending he was asleep, but there was a second knock. He cursed internally, answered the door, and saw Gideon.

"Oh," he said. "Hello."

"May I come in?"

"Er, yes. If you like." Zeb stepped back. Gideon came in and closed the door behind him. "Is Wynn all right?"

"Perfectly. Are you?"

Zeb made a flappy-hands sort of gesture. "Well, you were there."

"I was." Gideon had a little frown between his eyes. "And I heard—as we all did—Wynn say you told him Mrs. Bram was liable to bring a cuckoo into the nest."

"I *didn't*. Or, at least, I didn't mean to. Wynn asked me what I thought of the blasted woman, and I made a throwaway remark comparing her to a Walter Wyckham character. I honestly didn't remember the character carrying another man's child in the book, and in any case, Elise hasn't had anyone's baby so far, Bram's or otherwise. I just said she reminded me of Lady Ravendark, and Wynn drew the inference that she'd produce a changeling. I'm not sure why he felt compelled to credit me for it, but now Bram is quite sure I was stabbing him in the back to get the money..." His voice faded as his brain caught up with his mouth. "And that's what you think too. Oh my God. It is, isn't it? That's what you came to say. If you think that, after everything I told you this morning—oh, go to the devil. Sod off. I don't need any more people in this house throwing accusations at me."

Gideon didn't go. He was watching Zeb's face with an expression that was hard to read.

"Don't just stand there," Zeb snapped, hot and miserable, his stomach churning at Gideon disapproving of him, again. "I told you why I don't want the money, and I find it damned offensive you think I'm trying to get it anyway."

"You did tell me why, and I believe you."

"Then why did you say that?"

"Because you have an excellent case for taking it."

"What case? It's not mine to take! It oughtn't be Wyckham money, and it certainly shouldn't be mine!"

"But if it came to you, you could give it back."

Zeb blinked at him. Gideon opened his hands. "Zeb, is that what you're doing? Seeking the money to make reparations? Because if you are, I could understand."

Zeb groped for a reply, simultaneously indignant and flattered. "I—no. I am not doing that. Perhaps I should be. Maybe that would be the best thing to do, even, but I literally, absolutely, do not want the money in my hands. Even temporarily, even to do good with it. No."

"Why not?"

"In case it didn't leave."

"I don't understand."

"Oh, *you* know." Gideon's face suggested he didn't. "I mean—well, can you not imagine? You'd say yes, of course I would return the money to its originators, and then you get it. A hundred and fifty thousand pounds: imagine what you could do with that. You would imagine, wouldn't you? And maybe you'd think, it would surely be all right if I gave most of it away. Two-thirds, say. Or maybe half would be reasonable. And of course there's taxes, *that* shouldn't come from my share. And it would take time to decide who to give it to, so naturally I should hold on to it until that was resolved. And perhaps giving it back wouldn't be straightforward. Perhaps it would only be wasted by people who never did anything to earn it themselves. And it was all a very long time ago, and plenty of British fortunes come from similar origins, and is there any such thing as morally pure money? And in the end... well, it's my money now." Zeb took a deep breath. "Do you see?"

Gideon was frowning. "I suppose so, but do you really think you would do that?"

"I don't know if I *would*—I hope not—but I can absolutely see I *could*. Love of money, root of all evil, that sort of thing, and I don't suppose I'm any less corruptible than other people." He shrugged. "I'd rather not put it to the test."

"I think you underestimate yourself considerably," Gideon said. "But if that is the case—"

That was when they heard the scream.

It came from some way away, but Zeb could still hear that it wasn't a shriek of surprise, any more than it was a fox in the night. It was a scream of pure human terror, a real throat-ripper, and it was followed by another, and another.

They both bolted out of the room. Zeb ran in the direction of the scream, down a corridor and right, which took him to a flight of stairs that split.

"It came from Mrs. Bram's room," Gideon said behind him. "That way."

"You stay here, then," Zeb said. Whatever god-awful chaos Bram and Elise had created would not go better in the presence of an unrelated witness: Bram got very heated about washing dirty linen in public.

He sprinted up the staircase Gideon had indicated and discovered a full-blown scene in progress on the next floor.

Bram, wearing a truly horrible smoking jacket over Indian silk pyjamas, was holding Elise, in a state of undress. She was clinging to him, sobbing. Zeb had never seen her cry before; judging by his expression, it wasn't habitual for Bram. Colonel Dash was also there, with his tie off and collar open. Given his usual neatness, he might as well have arrived in pyjamas.

"Is everything all right?" Zeb asked, in the pointless yet obligatory way of these things.

Bram gave a huff of annoyance to indicate that no, of course it wasn't. Dash said, "Lady seems to have had a shock."

Elise took the great shuddering breath of a woman pulling herself together, jerked herself upright, and stepped back from Bram's halfhearted embrace. "In my room," she said, voice distorted. "It was in my room!"

"*What* was?" Bram said.

Colonel Dash cleared his throat. "Something in your room? Would you care for me to check it? What, exactly—"

"The ghost. I saw the ghost."

"In your room?" Zeb said. "Can I see?"

"See?" Bram demanded. "What nonsense—?"

"By your leave, ma'am," Dash said briskly. She nodded, and he went through the door. Zeb followed him in.

Elise was clearly not sharing a bedroom with her husband. There were various feminine accoutrements around the place—pots of things, brushes, garments. The room had panelled walls, a bed, a dressing table, a wardrobe, another door. There was no ghost.

Dash began to look around as Zeb opened the other door. "Bathroom," he reported. "Nobody in here."

"Nobody in the wardrobe," Dash said.

Zeb squatted low. "Or under the bed."

Bram, from the doorway, said, "You expect to find a ghost under the bed?"

"Someone dressed as a ghost, possibly," Dash said. "What exactly did you see, Mrs. Bram?"

"A figure—a grey robe, like a monk. I couldn't see its face."

"And did the ghost come and go through the door?" Dash asked, his voice dampeningly practical.

"I don't know where it went or where it came from. It *appeared*. The room was empty, the door closed. I was putting things away in the bathroom when there was a rush of cold air and the gas flickered and went very low. I turned, and saw it, just there in the corner." She pointed.

"Close to the mirror of the dressing table," Bram observed. "A mirror, the curtain, an unexpected shadow: all that might create an effect in the mind—"

"I did not imagine it," Elise said, with teeth.

"So you were standing by the bathroom door, facing it," Zeb said. "What happened?"

"I screamed. It raised a hand and pointed at me and its hand was just bones. A skeleton," she said, sounding incredulous at her own words. "It crooked its finger at me, *beckoned* me, and it whispered."

"What did it say?"

"It said—It's none of your business what it said," she snapped, rather more like her usual self. "It reached for me with its vile whispering, and I ran for the door, as anyone would have. I got out just as Bram came out of his room."

"And did it follow you?"

"Of course not," Bram said. "I have not moved from the spot. Nothing—nobody—came out."

Zeb exchanged a glance with Colonel Dash. They both walked to the corner.

"What are you doing?" Bram demanded. "This is my wife's room, you know."

"Looking for a hidden door." Zeb wondered how one went about looking for hidden doors, and tried knocking on a panel, since people did that in books. It sounded very like every other time he'd knocked on wood. Colonel Dash ran his hands over the joints.

"Hidden *door*?" Bram said.

"Nobody came out, so either they're still in here, or there's another door," Dash said. "Stands to reason. You know this house. Any secret passageways?"

Bram's mouth open and shut a couple of times. "Good God, are you all mad? There are no secret passages!"

"So where's the person who was in here?" Zeb asked.

"There was nobody in here!"

"Do you mean she saw a ghost?" Dash enquired.

"There was no man and there is no ghost!" Bram shouted. "This is all nonsense and imagination!"

"I *saw* it!" Elise said, voice rising. "Do you think I am that deluded brat of a schoolgirl, wittering about her fancies? It was in here! It spoke to me!"

"Rubbish. Your feelings are overwrought and your mind ungoverned. What a fuss about nothing."

This went down as well as might be expected, and the marital discord escalated rapidly. Zeb sidled out, with Dash on his heels, and they retreated down the corridor, away from the raised voices. They were in the central tower, Zeb realised.

"Are you up here?" he asked Dash.

"Next floor down, east wing. Round the corner from Hawley." They headed for the stairs together. "What did you make of that?"

"I think she saw something," Zeb said. "And I think what she saw was someone dressed up in a monk's habit, just like I saw last night."

"And it was Hawley, you say." Dash's moustache rippled with outrage. "One thing to play a joke on one's fellows, but a lady—I think I shall pay a call on that gentleman. Do you care to accompany me?"

That sounded like a disaster waiting to happen, in the circumstances. "Honestly, no. I'm fed up of this nonsense and I'm going to bed."

Dash's expression suggested he was a spineless disappointment. It was water off a duck's back at this point, so Zeb merely added, "Good night," and hurried back to his room. He very much hoped Gideon might be there.

eleven

HE WAS, LINGERING IN the corridor, his tall frame distinctly more decorative than the wallpaper.

"I'm glad you're still here," Zeb said, ushering him in to the bedroom and shutting the door. He would have liked to flop onto the bed, since he was now feeling the backwash of far too many exhausting interactions. "Honestly, I'd run screaming into the night if I had the energy. Are there secret passageways here, do you know? There must be: my grandfather would never have built a Gothic mansion without them."

"Secret—Go back a bit. What was the noise about?"

"Elise saw a ghost in her room, which beckoned her with a skeletal hand," Zeb explained. "I dare say Hawley would know how to pull that sort of thing off—the theatrical effects, I mean—but I can't think how he did the disappearing act unless there are secret passages."

"You think the ghost is Hawley dressing up?"

"It must be him. He was the only one unaccounted for when I saw it, and he didn't come to see what the noise was about just now."

"But I saw it too, weeks ago. As have several of the other staff. All well before the family's arrival."

"You are *joking*," Zeb said.

"No. It's been something of an issue here. Several people have reported it—various staff members as well as Miss Jessamine, and there's no pattern of any one person being unaccounted for at its appearances. People are unnerved. The housemaid is genuinely afraid."

Zeb gaped at him. Gideon, apparently misinterpreting his reaction, added, "I'm not saying it's real. I'm saying it's cleverly done, persistent, and predates Hawley's arrival. I told Wynn about it, since frightening people strikes me as a rather unwholesome hobby. Unfortunately, he believes quite sincerely in the family ghost, and also fears that Miss Jessamine has become a little too interested in the topic."

"He's not wrong."

"So he ordered me in so many words not to speak of it. Not to deny it, because that would be untrue, but also not to discuss what I saw, or speculate on the subject. That has left me in a rather awkward position."

"Not just you," Zeb said. "I see that you didn't feel you could talk about it, but I thought it was Hawley, and told Dash it was Hawley, and he has just gone to confront bloody Hawley, which I expect he will do with the words *Zeb said it was you*."

"Oh," Gideon said. "Oh, hell's teeth."

"Hawley told me not to get in his way," Zeb said hollowly. "He's bound to think I'm stirring up trouble for him, and he'll talk to Wynn, and...oh my God."

"He can't do that tonight: Wynn has retired to bed. And Hawley is a late riser, so you can be gone before he gets up. I'll order the motor first thing. I realise you made a promise, but under the circumstances—"

"I made a promise on the clear understanding that I would not be marrying Jessamine, and then Wynn all but ordered me to propose to her, in front of her. I really don't know what the devil he was playing at tonight. I suppose his mind is becoming clouded."

"He seems sharp enough to me," Gideon said with a frown.

"But his behaviour is awfully erratic. And it's got me in a lot of trouble, which is about to get a great deal worse."

"Zeb—" Gideon stepped towards him, extending a reassuring hand, then pulled it back with a jolt. It was how he'd used to reach for Zeb in times of trouble, an instinctive movement, deep in the body. Zeb understood that, because the instinct to reach for Gideon now was engraved into his bones.

They stared at each other for a second. Gideon cleared his throat. "I'll have the chauffeur ready and waiting for eight o'clock. I dare say Hawley will spew his malice but you won't be here to hear it."

"Right. Good. Thank you." He was just a few feet away, so close. They were both still in evening dress and Gideon did look good in evening dress. He looked good in anything; he always had.

Zeb wanted him so much.

He'd never stopped wanting him, over the past year. He'd had better-looking lovers before and since, and more skilled ones, and certainly easier ones to get on with, and none of them had mattered a damn by comparison because none of them had been Gideon. And it probably wasn't sensible, or possible, or even fair, but they were here together, against all the odds, and he had to try.

"Look," he said. "Could we, perhaps—when you're back in London—could I see you again? I have missed you awfully, and it was good to talk, and I know I got things horribly wrong before so I quite understand you're still angry, but I'd very much like to make amends, if I could. If you want." He sounded pathetically hopeful in his own ears.

Gideon hesitated. "I'm not coming back to London

for the foreseeable future. I can't leave this job. I literally can't afford to."

"Then may I write to you here? Or was that a polite rejection? Not that you owe me a polite rejection. You could tell me to sod off and I'd have no grounds to argue. Only, you didn't, so *was* it a rejection?"

Gideon shut his eyes, possibly in despair. "God damn it, Zeb. What's the point of this? You have to go. I have to stay."

"Yes," Zeb said. "But we could have tonight."

Gideon opened his eyes at that. Zeb said, "Just tonight. No obligations. It doesn't have to mean anything if you don't want it to. But I missed you."

Gideon didn't speak at all for a moment. He looked almost blank, as if he didn't quite understand.

Then he grabbed Zeb by the lapels, shoved him back against the wall in a couple of stumbling steps, and kissed him.

Zeb grabbed him back, pulling him in. Gideon's mouth was urgent, as forceful as Zeb felt, and he was fisting Zeb's lapels, dragging him close, kissing him with frantic need. Zeb clutched his hair, his strong shoulder, then his arse, tugging their hips together, wanting all of Gideon's touch he'd deprived himself of over the past year, for which he'd never found an adequate substitute.

Gideon's mouth stilled, and he pulled back, leaving

Zeb's lips wet and bereft. Zeb stared up, praying he wasn't going to change his mind, and Gideon moved his hands gently up Zeb's lapels, took hold of the cloth on both sides, and shoved his jacket down over his shoulders.

Well, all right then.

Gideon had one knee up, trapping Zeb against the wall with his body. He used that position to jerk the sleeves down, without Zeb's aid, and tossed the jacket to one side. He didn't stop watching Zeb's face. He didn't speak.

He unbuttoned Zeb's waistcoat, eased that off, discarded it. He slid his hand down the front to Zeb's shirt, with its wretched fiddly studs.

"Just pull," Zeb said. "I won't be wearing it again."

Gideon paused, and then he did it. He pulled hard, with both hands, wrenching the sides of the shirt apart, sending fastenings flying. He shoved the shirt down over Zeb's shoulders, to his forearms, and stopped there. "Damn."

Zeb still had cuff links in, so the sleeves wouldn't go over his hands. The cloth of his shirt was tangled behind his back, restricting his arms. "Leave it," he said.

"Your hands are caught."

"Leave it."

Gideon inhaled, a little hiccupy noise. Zeb licked his lips. "Touch me."

Gideon spanned Zeb's chest with his hands, sliding

them up and down the bare skin, circling Zeb's nipples with his thumbs, running his fingers through the sparse hair. Zeb stood, bare-chested, fiercely erect, arms trapped, as Gideon explored. It was quite hard to breathe now.

When Gideon looked up at last, the hunger in his eyes was a physical shock.

"You are beautiful," he said, voice so low it vibrated. "Beautiful as ever, you scruffy, ridiculous stray cat of a man. God damn it, Zeb. What do you want?"

Zeb didn't know what he wanted, and if he did know, he wasn't sure he wanted to know. "Whatever you're doing, keep doing it."

Gideon's hands moved to Zeb's waistband, making short work of fastenings, working around his painful erection without touching, and pushing his drawers and trousers down round his ankles. Zeb kicked off his shoes, then the clothing, which left him in socks, suspenders, and shirtsleeves round his wrists. Somehow, he felt a lot more naked than if he'd been completely stripped.

Gideon, in impeccable evening dress down to the polished shoes, stepped back and looked him up and down.

"You look disgraceful," he said softly. "I missed you so much. And I missed—"

He closed the distance again and his fingers wrapped possessively around Zeb's prick. Zeb whimpered. He couldn't help it.

Gideon's fingers tightened, not stroking but squeezing Zeb's shaft, the touch pulsing through him. It was something he'd always liked doing, toe-curlingly good, and Zeb was liable to come in his hand if this went on.

Gideon gazed at him a moment longer. Then he tugged with his lower hand.

Zeb had frequently been led by his prick, but it had always been a metaphor before now. He followed Gideon because he had no choice, away from the wall, constricted and dreamlike. Gideon moved around behind him and wrapped his free hand round Zeb's waist, pulling him in, holding him tight. Zeb's arms were constrained by Gideon's and by the entangling shirt.

Pliant in Gideon's arms, held in his grip, just for tonight. It was very nearly unbearable. He wondered if Gideon's harsh breath was only arousal, or if he felt the same desperate longing for everything they'd lost.

Gideon kissed his neck. "Talk to me, Zeb."

"You talk. I talk too much."

"You do not," Gideon said. "I missed you talking. Although..." His free hand came up, stroking Zeb's neck, his jaw. He thumbed Zeb's lower lip, pushing it down, slid the thumb inside. "If you did want to use your mouth...?"

"Mph," Zeb said in urgent if incoherent agreement.

Gideon released his grip. He pulled Zeb round to face him, and leaned back against the bedpost.

Zeb went to his knees by reflex, only then remembering his hands were still tangled behind his back. That was fine, except that Gideon was still dressed. "Unbutton yourself for me?"

Gideon reached for the buttons at his waist, moving with dreamlike slowness, with Zeb mostly naked on his knees in front of him. He was so hard it hurt.

Gideon released his prick, which was standing proud. Zeb ran his tongue over his lips, very deliberately, and heard Gideon's sharp intake of breath. Zeb leaned in and licked the smooth head of Gideon's prick, relishing the feel of it, taut and full. He circled it with tongue and then lips, setting them round the shaft, just holding Gideon there.

"Your mouth, your fuckable mouth. Christ." Gideon ran his fingers through Zeb's hair. "You blasted beautiful alley cat."

Zeb purred round his mouthful, with a lot of vibration. Gideon gave a sobbing sort of gasp and his fingers tightened on Zeb's scalp. His thighs were flexing with tension. Zeb made a fruitless effort to move his hands, reminding them both he was pinioned by the shirt, and Gideon almost sobbed.

Who needed hands? Zeb leaned in, taking Gideon deep, using tongue and cheeks and the roof of his mouth, everything and anything for Gideon's pleasure. He could feel the fingers flexing and tensing in his hair, the motions of his hips, and then Gideon's hands clamped on his skull, and he was moving. Gideon fucking his mouth as much as Zeb sucking him, just the way they had always both liked it, and whispering as he moved. "Fuck, fuck, fuck. You wanted this. You're hard for this. You utter—Christ!"

His hips jerked hard. Zeb held on for the ride, letting him thrust deep into his throat, feeling him come. He stayed there as Gideon's breath sobbed out, and his chest heaved.

"Jesus," Gideon said after a moment. "Zeb."

Zeb pulled his mouth off and swallowed, then sat back on his heels, extremely aware of his own arousal. Gideon looked dizzily down at him. "Do you need me to untangle your arms?"

"No," Zeb said. "Don't."

Gideon contemplated him a second longer, then stepped around him, and Zeb heard and felt the movement as he came to his knees, once again wrapping his arms round Zeb's waist, a hand round his cock.

"Oh," Zeb said, leaning back.

There was a sudden wetness on his ear—tongue, the scrape of teeth. Zeb arched his neck, and Gideon kissed that. "God, you're hard. You always did love that." His voice shuddering through Zeb, resonating deep in his bones; his thumb at work, stroking, caressing; his arm tight round Zeb's waist, holding him close. "You're so damned good at it and you feel so good—so hard—and, God, Zeb, the way you looked." His hand tightened, his strokes speeding up, and Zeb could hear his breath, shallower, urgent. His own heart was thumping faster, his toes curling. "Can I make you come like this?"

"You can make me do anything you please," Zeb said, and heard Gideon's breath catch.

"I fucked your mouth and you loved it and I'm going to make you—oh God, I can feel you—Zeb!"

Zeb cried out, and arched his back into Gideon's grip, gasping his pleasure as it crested and spent.

He slumped back. Gideon bent forward, so they were wrapped around each other. Zeb felt warm, and cradled, and as if the aching hole in his heart was liable to rip the whole thing apart.

"God," Gideon said at last. He sounded much like Zeb felt: spent, sated, wretched.

"What are you thinking?"

"How much time we wasted. Where we went wrong. How I wish I had been less of a prig."

Gideon had been utterly, hopelessly inexperienced when they started. He'd never acted on his longings before, and those long, cold years of repression had marked him. It had been difficult for him to acknowledge his own wants, to touch freely, to voice his pleasures, or indeed to do anything at all without checking half a dozen times that he wasn't getting it wrong. Zeb had done his best, but a lifetime's denial and control couldn't be discarded in a few weeks or even months.

Gideon had talked more in this one encounter than Zeb thought he might have done in any five fucks when they were together. Maybe he'd found someone who'd taught him to voice his pleasures in a way Zeb hadn't managed, and if he had, that was excellent, and very much not something Zeb had a right to be wistful about.

"It was hard for you," he said. "And you weren't a prig."

"I was, and we both know it. I wish—never mind." Gideon shifted his head slightly. He might have been brushing a kiss over Zeb's hair, or he might have been scratching his nose. "And you? What are you thinking?"

"I was reflecting that I should have made you tie me up and fuck me a long time ago. And then you should have *kept* me bound and gagged, so I couldn't have said and done the things that ruined us."

"Don't." Gideon's sigh heaved both their bodies. "Please. It wasn't just your fault."

"Gideon—"

"There's no point talking about it. You're going home tomorrow; I'm staying here; that's all there is to it."

"I know. But may I write to you? You didn't say."

Gideon exhaled long and hard. "Do you recall the story of Pandora's box? She opened it and let out all the ills of the world, and the last thing to come out was hope?"

"Yes?"

"People always tell that story as though hope was a consolation, the one good thing, instead of the last evil in the box. I truly don't know why, because hope is unbearable. My life was perfectly acceptable before I met you—not exciting, perhaps not entirely satisfactory, but functional. And then you came along, and I started hoping for a lot of things I'd never imagined before, and which of course I couldn't have—"

"*Gideon—*"

"I don't want to hope any more," Gideon said. "I want to rebuild the wreckage of my career and my finances and my life, and not bet everything on a dream, or spend every waking hour wanting the unattainable. I've spent so much time in limbo over the past year, without you and because of you, and I can't do it any more. If that makes me a coward, I'm sorry. But I'm begging you, don't ask me for this. I *can't*."

"I see," Zeb said, his heart aching. "I'm sorry too. I wish you didn't feel like that, but—well, I understand, I suppose. Of course I do. I hope—I hope, if you can be happy, you will be. And...well, you know where I live. If you should want to find me, ever."

Gideon's chin came forward, resting on his shoulder. Zeb tipped his head sideways to meet Gideon's, and they sat in silence as the house cooled around them.

twelve

The next morning was, as predicted, thick with mist. Zeb, rousing himself at seven having lain awake, alone, and miserable until four, could see nothing from his window but vague shapes where trees once were. It was very cold. He dressed quickly and shoved his abused dinner clothes into his suitcase.

His shoes were outside his door, dried rather badly in front of a fire so they felt baked on his feet, and he went downstairs to breakfast with a sense of discomfort that wasn't improved when he saw Bram was there.

He gave Zeb a look of loathing. Fine. Zeb ignored him right back and went to pile his plate from the chafing dishes, trying to disregard the lump in his gut. His brother had unquestionably wronged him, whereas he hadn't actually wronged Bram, therefore he wasn't the one who should be feeling bad. Anyway, Zeb had to break a promise, get out of the house before Hawley woke, and leave Gideon again. He didn't have the energy for Bram.

He forced down his food in stubborn silence and went to find Wynn, who was sitting in the drawing room with a book.

"Good morning," Zeb said. "I hope you're well? You looked rather rough last night."

"Very well, thank you. Last night—well, the less said the better. I hope we can put all that unpleasantness behind us. What can I do for you, Zeb?" Wynn beamed like a Dickens character, all jolly benevolence. "I trust you have changed your mind as to your rash statement last night?"

"No, I haven't. I will be going home today."

Wynn's face was transformed by heavy disappointment. "I hesitate to remind you, but you made me a promise."

"I did promise to stay, yes. And *you* said you weren't going to push me to marry Jessamine, and then you all but ordered me to propose to her."

"You exaggerate a little, I think."

His cousin had an immensely reasonable manner that gave Zeb a constant nagging feeling he was overreacting. "You put me in a position where I had to tell her I didn't want to marry her," he insisted. "That wasn't fair to anyone. And—no, please let me finish—and I also don't think this is in any way the family reconciliation you described. I appreciate your intentions, but the effect has been to set us all at one another's throats."

"I fear you may be right," Wynn said heavily. "I am deeply concerned by both Bram's and Hawley's behaviour."

"I'm not sure how you expected them to react. Thank you for your hospitality. I'll ask Mr. Grey to order the motor."

Wynn sighed. "You must do as you see fit, though I am sadly disappointed. But not today."

"Yes, today. As soon as possible. I'm sorry to be disobliging."

"Dear boy, it is not a matter of choice. You *cannot* leave. Look at the weather."

Zeb glanced at the window. "It's misty."

"Dartmoor mist. It would be far too dangerous to take the motor out."

"Dangerous?"

"The mists render the moors a treacherous place. Every year, unwary travellers wander and are lost, never to be seen again. The road has sharp bends, sharp drops, mires, and bogs on each side. You cannot leave until the weather lifts. None of us can."

"Are you seriously telling me that a bit of fog confines you to the house?" Zeb demanded. "Are you joking? We have fog in London too, you know."

"Not like Dartmoor mist," Wynn said. "You must take my assurance that it would be quite wrong of me to call for the motor. You have the right to risk your own life; you may not risk my chauffeur's."

"But—!"

"No," Wynn said with finality. "I lost my father to the mist. He went out alone, believing that he knew his path too well to miss it, and drowned in the mire; his body was not found for days. I will not lose another life that way."

Zeb cringed: he should have recalled that. "Of course. I'm awfully sorry. I didn't think."

"You meant no harm," Wynn said kindly. "But let us have no more talk of leaving until the air clears. Good morning."

Zeb found himself in the hall, uncomfortably flustered. He knew that Dartmoor mists were bad—or at least, he'd read *The Hound of the Baskervilles*, which came to the same thing—and if it was genuinely dangerous to take a motor out, that would be something he'd have to live with, but if Hawley rose from his slumbers breathing vengeance, things were liable to get nasty. He stuck his head out of the front door, in case Gideon might have the machine waiting anyway.

There was no sign of life in any form. The mist was fairly thick, moving in slow drifts across the grounds. He wouldn't have said impassable: it looked no more oppressive and distinctly less filthy than a standard London pea-souper, but clearly Wynn had reason for his caution.

What in blazes was he to do if he couldn't leave? It was nearly nine; Hawley would be up by eleven.

This was absurd. Surely people on Dartmoor dealt with the weather all the time. He needed to talk to Gideon, who would doubtless have the authority to sort some form of transport out for him. He wandered the house for the next twenty minutes, looking for him in a state of rising alarm he couldn't suppress, and yelped, "Thank goodness!" when he finally saw him in the hall. "Could you order the motor, at all?"

"Unfortunately, I am unable to oblige," Gideon said, voice tight and formal. "Your cousin has given strict instructions that the gates should remain closed for the time being."

Zeb blinked at him. "But I need to leave. You know I need to leave."

"It simply isn't possible, Cousin Zeb," Jessamine said from behind him, making him jump. "The mist is treacherous. The paths betray."

"Then how am I supposed to get home?"

"You can't," Jessamine said. "We all have to wait for the mists to rise. *Pray* for the mists to rise."

Zeb gaped at her. Gideon said, "Perhaps the weather may lift in half an hour or so. Maybe read a good book while you wait." He put his hand on Zeb's back as he spoke, turning him in the direction of the library, and Zeb felt a finger draw an extremely firm circle on his back.

"Half an *hour*?" Jessamine said. "Goodness me, Mr. Grey, it will be days before it lifts. Three or four, I should think."

"Well, we may hope for half an hour"—Gideon's finger circled on Zeb's back a second time—"but you are doubtless right, Miss Jessamine."

He turned and left without a further word. Zeb stared after him, speechless.

What the devil. Days, trapped here? And why hadn't Gideon been more help, and what on earth had he meant with that peculiar touch? It hadn't been connection, or affection. It had felt more like...

...instruction.

He stood a moment longer in the hall, wondering if he was going mad or if that was everyone else, and then, for lack of better ideas, went to the library.

Bram was sitting in there, smoking one of the unpleasant perfumed cigarettes, with a half-full ashtray in front of him. He glared. "Perhaps you would have the goodness to leave me be."

"I didn't seek you out," Zeb assured him. "But since I'm here, I did not intentionally slander your wife to Wynn. He drew an inference I didn't intend from a throwaway remark, and I'm very sorry about that, but I did not set out to make him think ill of her or undermine you. If I wanted to do that, I would tell him exactly what you promised Father on his deathbed, and the thousand ways you have broken that promise since."

Bram gazed up at him. He looked twitchy, as if he hadn't slept well. "Why should I believe you?"

Zeb wanted to say, *I don't care if you believe me*, and was irritated it wasn't quite true. "I don't suppose you will, because your inflated self-esteem depends on telling yourself I deserve the shabby trick you played on me. But Wynn clearly doesn't like Elise and he didn't need my help to reach that conclusion."

"Is that his reason for changing his will? His sole reason?"

"I don't know. I don't care."

Bram shook his head, in dismay rather than denial. "I was promised this. I am the heir. To have it snatched from me because of *her*." The pronoun hissed out with venom. "That succubus has taken this from me as she has taken everything from me. She has drained me dry. Even you, even my own brother—"

"That was you," Zeb said. "You made a promise, and you broke it. Don't you dare blame Elise."

"She made me do it!" Bram shouted. "You don't understand how I loved her! It was an obsession, an enchantment."

"Oh, for—"

"I was under her influence! And look what I have gained by it. My inheritance exhausted, my brother estranged, my marriage a laughing stock. *She* did this to me. And I am irrevocably chained to her malice, her spending, her infidelity and spite."

Zeb shifted uncomfortably. He didn't know his sister-in-law well, or like what he knew, but nobody ought to be talking with such thick hatred about their spouse. "Then get a separation. A divorce, even."

"I can't. She would contest it, and the scandal would be intolerable."

"How could she possibly contest it?"

"Oh, she will make me out to be the villain in court. A roué, destroying his innocent wife. Ha."

"Innocent?" Zeb said incredulously, since Elise's adulteries were notorious, and realised too late that he'd been more accurate than polite. "I mean—"

Bram stubbed out his cigarette and reached for another. His hands were trembling a little. "It was before our marriage. I was in a fever before the wedding, consumed by anticipation of my wedding night."

"I don't want to know," Zeb said firmly.

"I needed a way to relieve my natural urges—"

"I *don't* want to know."

"—and to prove to myself that Elise did not entirely own me. To resist her spell. A man cannot be subservient to his wife, slave to her whims. I ensured my needs were met, that was all, and yes, perhaps I should have put an end to the business afterwards. I grant that freely. But it did no harm, and prevented me making excessive demands on a new wife. Is that so wrong? And yet, to hear Elise tell it, I ruined her life and despoiled the marriage bed. As though *she*—"

"Wait, wait, wait." Zeb had been translating that out of Brammish. "You're saying you took a mistress before your marriage and kept her on afterwards? While bleating about how much you adored Elise? For God's sake!"

"I have a man's natural urges!"

"You have a man's thick head, is what you have. She found out?"

"The wretched girl came to our house," Bram said. "I had been married less than two months when she forced her way in and told Elise everything. And Elise has punished me for a decade. Ten years of anger and resentment over a trivial affair! They ruined my marriage between them."

"Jesus wept, Bram. Elise was, what, nineteen, just

married? And your mistress turned up at the family home?"

"The girl meant nothing! I proved it at the time, but Elise has used her as an excuse for ten years of frigidity to me and harlotry with others, in which she has spent everything I have. I cannot rid myself of her because she will recount my every misstep in court—"

"More than just the one mistress, then?"

"And now this!" Bram said, ignoring him. "It is a bitter irony. She only stayed for the money, because I was to be Wynn's heir, and thanks to her I am to be disinherited."

"Look on the bright side," Zeb suggested. "If you don't inherit, she has no reason to stay married to you, and you can divorce one another like civilized people. What a rotten mess you have made of your life."

"That's rich, coming from you," Bram snarled, and the pure childishness of it landed a punch that no amount of bluster could have achieved because it sounded like the big brother Zeb had loved when he was six.

"Ah, God," he said. "Can we not do better than this? Can we just—"

He didn't even know what to suggest. He wanted to say *I forgive you*, but it wasn't true and he didn't know how to make it true. Maybe if Bram admitted he'd done wrong?

Pigs might fly.

"I'm sorry that what I said caused trouble for you," he said. "It wasn't my intent. But honestly, Bram, if you are unhappy with our estrangement or your marriage, you need to take a hard look at who is truly responsible and act accordingly."

Bram considered him unblinkingly for a moment. "Well. Thank you, Zebedee. And..." He drew himself up. "I accept your apology."

Zeb gave a moment's consideration to beating his brother's head in with a candlestick. On the whole, it didn't seem worth the effort.

"Fine," he said, and left.

He went back into the hall, wondering what to do now. Gideon and Jessamine had gone—

Gideon! Damn, damn, damn: he'd entirely forgotten, and he had no idea how much time had passed. He hurried to get his coat and slipped out of the house, heading for the stone circle.

Wynn's refusal to take the motor out seemed a little more reasonable as he stepped outside. The mist was clammy and bitterly cold. It drifted over the grounds, making them ghostly. He didn't feel entirely convinced it was a good idea to walk anywhere in this: the grounds were a circle two miles in diameter, which made for an area of—he attempted to remember what you did with pi—something over three square miles, probably. You could get dangerously lost in that if you couldn't see your way, given the cold. And his reason for leaving the house was...well, *tenuous* didn't come close. He'd probably invented the whole thing, or was horrendously late, and would stand out here like a fool getting wet and freezing half to death. His shoes already felt damp again.

But he set off down the path all the same, through the trees. It was hard to judge time or distance in the mist, but he trudged on, mist tickling his cheeks and drenching his shoes, and after what felt like a very long time, he saw the stone circle come looming out of the dimness in a way which would gladden the heart of any Gothic novelist.

He marched up, more relieved than he'd have cared to admit to have found it, and called, "Hello?" His voice sounded oddly flat and muffled, as though the mist cut off sound as well as sight. "You had better be here or I'm going to feel stupid."

A shadow detached itself from one of the stones. "I am."

Zeb felt a pulse of relief. "I did think you must mean the stone circle, but then I felt like some sort of secret agent. What the blazes are we doing out here in this stinking weather when Hawley is going to wake up at any moment?"

"Not being overheard," Gideon said. "Did you speak to Wynn?"

"He said the mist is too thick to drive in, which I dare say, but surely we can't all be trapped in the house. Can the chauffeur not go slowly? Or does he not have horses? I'm sure horses don't wander off paths and fall into grimpen mires."

"I couldn't say, but it's moot because Wynn's instructed the grooms not to have the horses taken out. And I've been to the garage and the chauffeur isn't budging either. Wynn has ordered that nobody goes onto the moor till the mist has lifted, and that's all there is to it."

Zeb stared at him. "But he can't keep me here! Hawley will be up and about in an hour at most. Shit, shit, shit!"

Gideon's arms closed round him. He was cold and damp, but so was Zeb, and the touch was at least an emotional comfort. He leaned in, pathetically grateful for this.

"Let's not panic," Gideon said into his hair. "How bad is this?"

Zeb attempted to think clearly. "Hawley will doubtless spill all the beans he can. I have no idea how Wynn will react. Bram will be awful." He set his shoulders. "But, you know, it will only be awfulness. Unpleasant remarks and such. I suppose I can put up with that."

Gideon's grip tightened. "You shouldn't have to."

"But Hawley is a prick, so I will. The main thing is, it shouldn't affect you. If Hawley knew you and I got sacked from Cubitt's together, he would have mentioned it before now, so—"

"He may not know that," Gideon said, voice hollow. "But Wynn does."

"What? How? *What?*"

"It was how I got this job. He sought me out after he heard from Paul Ellison at Cubitt's that I'd been caught up in a mess of your making. He said, specifically, that he was not going to ask what had happened, and that Ellison believed I deserved a second chance, so he wanted to offer me a fresh start."

"Good Lord. Well, that was good of Ellison—a lot better than I'd have expected, actually—but why? Not why you deserve it, but why would Wynn clean up my messes?"

"I didn't ask," Gideon said. "I latched on to the offer with no questions and both hands. I'd been out of work for months, and with my brother-in-law—"

"Oh Lord, I didn't ask. How is he? How are they both?"

Gideon's sister had suffered years of poor health after giving birth to twin girls, costing a fortune in doctors, and then her husband had been seriously injured in an accident that had left him unable to work for more than a year. It was the kind of bad luck that plunged people from comfort into poverty at frightening speed. Gideon had been spending most of his salary on keeping the family afloat; it was one of the reasons Zeb getting them both sacked was unforgivable.

"Eleanor is very well, and James has made a full recovery." The glow in Gideon's voice was audible. "He's back at work."

"Really? Oh, thank God."

"It's a huge relief. But of course they have debts still, and I'd long since run through my savings and borrowed all I could, and I didn't want to be a drain on their household when I finally had a chance at work. So I leapt at it."

"You spent everything you had on keeping them afloat," Zeb said indignantly. "They couldn't help you in return?"

"They did. I lived with them for eight months, for goodness' sake." Gideon spoke as if that went without saying; as if family could naturally be relied on and wouldn't let you down. "But they deserved their own lives back, and I didn't want to be dependent. I wanted a job, and when Wynn offered me this one out of the blue it felt heaven-sent. Board, lodging, good salary. A year of this and I'll have paid off my debts, *and* have a reference I can use."

"That is marvellous," Zeb said, resolving to think better of Wynn. "I'm awfully pleased."

"Well, yes. Except, I have this job because you and I

got sacked from Cubitt's together. So if Hawley spills the beans and Wynn draws the obvious conclusion—"

"Oh God. If you lose this because of me—shit, shit, *shit*. I'll do anything I have to. I could try grovelling to Hawley—"

"Wouldn't that just make him worse?"

"I'm not sure things can get worse. I cannot lose you another job."

Gideon's fingers bit into his arms. "If I lose this, it won't be your fault."

"Yes, it will. I shouldn't have come here at all, and I should have left when you told me, and I should never have done that stupid thing at Cubitt's, and I'm so sorry—"

Gideon jerked him closer, jammed his cold face against Zeb's, and kissed him.

It was not an elegant kiss, with numb faces and at least one party entirely unprepared for it. It was urgent and panicky and almost angry, and Zeb grabbed on for dear life, pulling Gideon against him, fists in his coat. Kissing in the mists, reckless, damp, frantic, together.

It didn't last nearly long enough. Gideon let him go, breathing heavily. "It is not your fault," he said again. "It's my fault for getting caught up in Wyckhams again, and Wynn's for not asking obvious questions, and Hawley's for being a prick."

Zeb released his lapels with regret. "Certainly the last

one. All right, look. If Wynn says anything, there was an unfortunate incident at Cubitt's, but it was entirely my fault for putting you in a compromising situation against your will. You were unjustly blamed, you haven't seen me since. Yes?"

"No," Gideon said flatly. "That's not fair."

"I will not lose you another job," Zeb said equally flatly. "I will not, and you can't ask me to. So you are going to blame me for everything, got it? I owe you this. You don't have to take the consequences of my actions again."

Gideon's lips parted. Zeb went on before he found an objection, not that there could be any. "And think about it. If we play this right, Wynn will insist I leave immediately, mist or not, and nobody in my family will ever speak to me again. I'd pay good money for that."

"Zeb," Gideon said again, and grabbed his hand.

Zeb squeezed it, hard. "You blame me, for everything. And that way you'll keep your job, and it will all be fine. Come on. We should get back."

thirteen

EB RETURNED TO THE house cold, sodden-footed, and dreading the near future. For all that, he felt better. He'd seen the expression in Gideon's light eyes, the hope, the warmth. It was nice to have put something good there again.

Beslippered—he might as well be comfortable if he was going to have unpleasant confrontations—he went downstairs and walked right into Hawley.

"Oh," he said.

"Morning." Hawley looked heavy-eyed. Zeb had no idea who he was staying up drinking with; possibly just himself. "Still here? I thought you were going."

"Wynn won't let me take the motor. There's a bad mist

and we're confined here till it lifts. I would go otherwise, I absolutely will, but it's not in my power—"

"All right, all right. I don't care." Hawley sloped away in the direction of the breakfast room.

Zeb followed. "Yes, but I am trying to leave—"

"Good God, Zeb, shut up. I don't know how anyone chatters so much."

He sounded hungover but not particularly malevolent. Could Dash have gone about things tactfully? "Look, did you talk to Dash last night?" Zeb blurted.

"Dash? Christ, no. Why would I do that?"

"He was looking for you," Zeb said numbly.

"Well, don't tell him where to find me. I can't be expected to tolerate that bore before coffee."

He lurched off. Zeb stared after him.

They hadn't talked. Dash hadn't accused him of being the ghost. He wasn't going to reveal Zeb's personal life, so Gideon's job was safe. Reprieve bloomed through Zeb like the sun as he realised that all the fretting and fear had been pointless.

Well, not entirely pointless. It had led to that kiss. And if he hadn't been able to make amends in action, at least he'd shown he wanted to, and perhaps, with that in mind, Gideon might be more open to just a *little* bit of hope...

He cut that dream off as self-indulgence and tried to think through the revised situation. His urgent need was to find Dash and ensure he knew that Zeb's suspicions had been wrong. And then he could keep his head down and last out the next couple of days, and everything would be absolutely fine.

Dash didn't seem to be around. Zeb skittered around the house, checking the various shared rooms, but had had no luck tracking the man down by luncheon. There was no Elise, as usual, and no Dash either. Bram forked food into his mouth in grim silence. Hawley ate in a perfunctory sort of way and made flattering remarks to Jessamine. Gideon was stony-faced, braced for trouble.

Zeb smiled sunnily at him and asked Wynn, "Is Dash about? I wanted a word with him."

"Ah, no, the poor fellow," Wynn said composedly. "Unfortunately, he is suffering an attack of malaria. He contracted it in Africa and it returns periodically."

"Really," Hawley said without interest. "He looked revoltingly healthy last night."

"I believe it comes on very quickly."

"Ought he not have a doctor?" Zeb asked.

"How would we obtain one? I am not on the telephone, and I cannot send a man across the moor in the mist. He has a supply of quinine with him, and I understand that he will simply endure the period of fever, which will last several days. Yes, indeed, he will need to endure. He must be left strictly alone except for the man who will attend him. No visits—not even a mission of mercy from you, my dear." He smiled at Jessamine.

That would be why Dash hadn't spoken to Hawley, and blasted lucky timing it was too. Not that Zeb wanted him to suffer an attack of malaria, but if he had to, it might as well be useful. He flicked a reassuring glance at Gideon and thought his face had relaxed a fraction.

The meal went well enough, considering last night's catastrophe. It was too much to hope that everyone was embarrassed about their behaviour; more likely, they were all gathering their strength for another round. Still, it was an oasis of comparative peace for Zeb's nerves, and he took it as such.

He worked in his room that afternoon, sitting by the mist-shrouded windows beyond which the air writhed like spectres. He would have liked to seek Gideon out, but knew he should not. The physical pull between them was as strong as ever, and they'd slid back into intimacy with an ease for which Zeb was heart-shakingly grateful, but Gideon had made himself clear: he did not want to be mooning over a man hundreds of miles away when he was stuck here for a year.

Well, nor did Zeb. Where they differed was that Gideon seemed to think it was avoidable. Zeb would be mooning, like it or not.

And it wouldn't be for a year either, because Wynn's

doctor had given him no more than a handful of months to live, a fact Zeb had temporarily forgotten and of which Gideon seemed to be unaware.

Hell's teeth. Gideon was depending on this job, and he didn't know his employer was dying.

Wynn had told Zeb about his health in confidence. Zeb had no right to break that, but presumably his cousin had taken Gideon on to put his affairs in order, so he would doubtless reveal the truth soon. And then, if Wynn's doctor was right, Gideon would return to London in summer. They would be geographically close once more and perhaps, maybe, then…

Then, but not now. Now Zeb was going to respect Gideon's wishes and avoid doing anything that would destroy anyone's life or livelihood, and if that meant sitting in his room with his mouth firmly shut until the mist lifted, that was what he'd do.

In that spirit, he got quite a lot of work done. He was feeling rather pleased with his newfound maturity until it was time to dress for dinner, and he realised his dinner clothes were crumpled in the suitcase, he hadn't retrieved his shirt studs from wherever they'd flown, and his shirt was stained with spunk.

Dinner passed as well as could be expected. Bram rolled his eyes at Zeb's daytime clothes, Wynn graciously accepted his apology for the informality, and Jessamine assured him she would have his laundry done. Elise was furiously silent. She'd probably wanted to leave too, and was demonstrating her displeasure by ignoring everything everyone said. Hawley held forth about the bohemian art world, telling stories that Zeb suspected were intended to be provocative. Bram stayed grimly silent, though his jaw twitched a few times as though he was clamping it shut.

By the time they'd reached the second course—a chicken casserole that seemed to be flavoured with marmalade—Zeb felt impelled to open his mouth, if only so Hawley would shut his. "Is there any sign of the weather lifting?" he asked. "I tried going outside this morning but it was awfully wet."

"I fear not," Wynn said. "We may expect another few days of this. Lackaday House has always been lonely, but it is when the mist descends that we truly feel our isolation. The outside world is a thousand miles or a thousand years away, and those in this house are transported. Out of time. Yes: you are all quite out of time."

He sounded almost dreamlike. Zeb said, "Uh, right, yes. Er, how is Dash?"

"I fear the dear fellow is suffering greatly."

"Poor Colonel Dash," Jessamine said. "But that is the

nature of the affliction, isn't it? One carries one's past, always, and at any time, it can return to strike you down."

They finished the meal in silence.

Wynn retired to the drawing room, inviting them all to join him. Zeb didn't think he could bear another evening in there. He had the fidgety feeling he got when he couldn't get out of places, which meant he'd be twitching his feet and fiddling with things all evening, which meant Bram would shout at him, and he didn't want to be the person who set off the next familial explosion.

"Join me for a smoke, dear boy," Hawley suggested.

At least it meant being outside and upright. They went on to the front steps, where Zeb shuddered against the cold. "I don't know what's worse, the mist or those gaspers."

Hawley puffed reeking smoke, reducing the quality of the air around them even further. "The gaspers aren't preventing you or Elise from going home. I am annoyed. I really did hope to see the back of the lot of you: you, your dullard brother, and that witch."

"It's entirely mutual, believe me. I'd love to show the lot of you a clean pair of heels."

"You've never had clean shoes in your life," Hawley pointed out. "I trust you intend to depart when you can, and will restrain your natural charm around Jessamine until that happy day. Tell me, Zebby, what happened with Elise last night?"

"In what sense?"

"You know very well. What she said she saw."

"She said she saw a ghost," Zeb said. "And before you say anything sarcastic, you claimed you saw writing on the wall."

"I did see it."

"Then I expect she saw a ghost."

Hawley exhaled a long stream of smoke in lieu of reply. Zeb was weighing up the relative merits of freezing to death out here or sitting inside with everyone else when his cousin spoke again. "Do you believe in the Wyckham curse?"

"If you ask me, the Wyckhams *are* the curse."

"I'm serious," Hawley said. "There are some odd things happening in this house. That writing. That damned ghost of Wynn's."

"It's not his ghost. It's from *The Monastery*."

"Wynn has evidence that Walter based *The Monastery* on what he saw here. He showed me letters from two of Walter's wives, letters from his father. People have seen it—the ghost—for years. And this cursed place—" Hawley turned abruptly. "For God's sake, can you not feel it? Can you not feel something wrong?"

"Oh, don't you start." If there was one thing, *one single thing* Zeb had thought he could rely on in Hawley, it was boundless cynicism, but apparently the man couldn't even be trusted for that. "Everyone's on edge, that's all, and hardly surprising."

Hawley shook his head. "The writing was there, Zeb. I didn't imagine it. It said things nobody here could have known, and I *saw* it. It was written on the wall, and then it was gone as if it had never been. And—Christ, have you not noticed the shadows?"

"What shadows?"

"In this house. The lights flicker, and they darken, and I can see things moving in the corner of my eye. The whole house is full of them, moving when you aren't looking. If you look directly, they're just shadows but when you turn away... For God's sake, Zeb, I see them now. Don't you? Can't you?"

Zeb couldn't help an instinctive look around. "There's nothing there, and you need to lay off the sauce."

"I can see them now. It's why I asked you to come out with me." Hawley's mouth twisted in what ought to have been a sneer but looked dreadfully like a man about to weep. "I didn't want to be alone. Ludicrous. Me, clinging on to you of all people because I'm frightened of the monsters under the bed. But I don't know how anyone can bear to be alone." He grabbed Zeb's sleeve. "God damn it, are you that much an oblivious fool? Do you really not feel it hanging over you?"

"Feel what?" Zeb said, resisting the urge to glance

around again. The back of his neck felt very cold and bare.

"Retribution. They say our sins will find us out. I never believed that. Humbug and prudery. But everything has a price, and we all have to pay in the end. That's what Walter believed. I see it now." Hawley threw away his cigarette end and fished out another with a shaking hand. "There's always a price to be paid. Don't you feel your sins waiting for you?"

"If you're having a religious awakening, I'm going inside."

Hawley didn't seem to hear. He was lost in his own world, and Zeb was glad not to be there with him. "Jessamine said it comes after the guilty. I'm not surprised it has come for Elise before me. It *should* take her first: she took everything from me."

"I didn't know you had anything to take," Zeb said. "You owe me five quid as it is."

"She took my enthusiasm! My artistic essence! Women are the fuel for my creative fire, but *she* never gave, just took and took and when she left me I had nothing. The spark, all gone. Just like our grandfather, sucking the life from his wives and children."

"Who is? Her, or you?"

Hawley didn't seem to realise that was a jibe. "Both. *That's* the Wyckham curse: we devour and devour, until we are devoured in our turn." He was staring into the shadows, the cigarette smouldering between his fingers. "So whose turn has come now? The shadows are closing in, but for whom?"

"Stop it," Zeb said. "Stop this nonsense about shadows. Stop drinking if you can't hold it, stop whining about Elise as if that was ever going to end well, and if you feel doom coming upon you, book yourself into a sanatorium."

Hawley didn't react to that; he didn't seem to have heard at all. He was staring off into the middle distance. It was too cold out here for Zeb's comfort, and Hawley's fug of perfumed cigarette stink was making him feel a little woozy. "Oh, forget it. I'm going in."

He would have liked to go straight upstairs, but Jessamine hailed him as he walked through the hall, and he found himself coopted into a card game with her, Wynn, and Gideon. Elise and Bram sat on opposite sides of the room, not speaking to each other or the players. Their presence meant the atmosphere was constrained, which was to say as thick as mud. It didn't improve when Hawley slouched in a few moments later, cold mist and perfumed smoke rolling off him, and went straight to the decanter.

Zeb played three rounds at Wynn's insistence, foot tapping under the table, aware of his brother's resentful gaze, and was relieved when the party broke up. He would have liked to head out of the room but Wynn said, "Sit with me a moment?"

Zeb reluctantly remained as the others left. Wynn said, "I wanted to speak to you privately. I have been considering your scruples and I believe I was wrong to press you."

"Oh. Well, thank you."

"It was not fair. I allowed my desire to see Jessamine established to overcome everything else. I hope you will allow me to offer a little explanation of my behaviour."

He launched again into the story of Jessamine's origins, in rather more detail, starting with his sister-aunt Laura and his father's resentment of her. "He considered her a cuckoo in the nest. She was Walter's legitimate daughter, but my father could not forget the fool Walter had made of himself and the disgrace to our family when he married the housemaid."

"Rather harsh to blame Laura for that. What happened to her mother?" Zeb said. "You said she wasn't competent."

"A very foolish woman, always crying and making a fuss. Naturally, she could not leave Lackaday House: she was not fit to look after a child. My father found it all most trying. And then, you know, Laura was sent away and she could not come back until he died. Which he did in the mire, of course, crying out for rescue, but there was nobody there to help him, and so he was gone at last, and she came back to me." He paused there, contemplating the portrait. Zeb twisted round to look at it, at the little smile on Laura's face.

"But the Wyckham curse took her," Wynn went on. "A handful of years and she was gone. At least I had my Georgina as comfort, until she was abused in my care and I lost her too. I cannot have history repeat itself with Jessamine. I need her to be secure."

"Of course you do. But surely the way to do that is to help her make good choices, rather than rushing her into a bad marriage."

"And what if she makes the error her mother and grandmother did? What if she trusts some villain with her affections?"

"Most of us fall in love with the wrong person at some point," Zeb said. "Or the right person at the wrong time. Or the right person at the right time and then we make a mess of it. It's her life, Wynn. You can't rule it, and if you try, things are bound to go wrong."

"But we see all around us the result of unruled, unruly lives. Look at Elise, at Hawley and Bram. At you."

Zeb blinked. "What about me?"

"You have plenty of ability but no self-discipline. And so you are jobless, aimless, failing to—"

"My career and my life are my affair," Zeb said over him. "You may not think much of either, but I don't need you to think of them at all. And as it happens, my father was very much of the opinion that he and Bram should dictate my every action, so if you want to use me as an awful warning, which I must say I find offensive, it should be a warning against trying to mould people to your specifications, rather than helping them to do their best. It did me no good at all, and I doubt it will work for Jessamine either."

Wynn was regarding him unblinkingly. Zeb said, "Well, that's what I think. I'm going to bed now. Good night."

He felt decidedly ruffled by that exchange as he headed upstairs. So ruffled, indeed, that he didn't realise at first how dark it was.

The gaslight seemed to be turned down extremely low and it flickered as he walked. The shadows were dark around him in this blasted shadowy house, and the jumping light made them move in the corners of his eyes; he cursed Hawley and his unexpected, contagious fears.

There was nobody around. Well, that was only to be expected. The place was understaffed; the family were scattered around the house; everyone else had gone to bed. There was no reason for him to meet anyone on his way up, and yet the house felt very dark and very lonely somehow, and the hairs were prickling on the back of his neck.

Stop it, he told himself. *Imagination*. He whistled a couple of notes and stopped because it sounded too thin, too frail.

He was being absurd. All he was doing was walking through the dark, empty corridors of a house built by a monster on the proceeds of obscene cruelty, and which its inhabitants believed to be haunted. There was no reason to be nervous at all. "Idiot," he said aloud, forcing a grin.

He was at the turning for his corridor, and the lights were very low indeed. Gideon had been waiting somewhere round here when he'd arrived. He'd give money to have Gideon waiting here now. Whereas, if he turned the corner and saw a cowled grey shape…

His heart was beating faster than it should be. Ridiculous to be afraid of the dark, and of some fool dressing up. His father had had plenty to say about childish fears; Zeb had never been allowed a night-light in case it encouraged him. His father would be furious with all the superstitious nonsense sloshing about.

His father had been wrong about a lot of things.

He was talking himself into a state of panic. He *didn't* believe in ghosts or moving shadows or mysterious dooms: he was just letting his imagination run away with him, as it so often did. All the same, he had to force himself to turn the corner.

And he did, and the corridor was empty. Of course it

was. Zeb let out a long breath, gave himself a shake, and headed briskly for his room, where he would be perfectly safe. And would lock the door, and sleep with a light on if he wanted, even though he wasn't superstitious, because he was a grown man who could do as he pleased.

He threw the door open. It was pitch dark inside. He groped for the matches and lit the gas.

The light bloomed. The shadows leapt, and moved, and kept moving. Zeb stared into the room, his heart seizing.

There were spiders everywhere. Spiders on the walls. On the ceiling. On the bed, making their way over the pillow and quilt with their dreadful mindless angular motion. Huge black spiders, their legs jointed and pointed, creeping and crawling in his darkening vision, hundreds, thousands, *spiders*.

He couldn't breathe, couldn't scream, couldn't move, could only stand, shaking and sweating, for the longest seconds of his life, and then a thing of legs dropped abruptly from the ceiling and Zeb broke.

He didn't even realise he was running, still less where he was running to, just away, *away*, frantically down the corridor, whimpering in fear, and when he turned a corner and collided with someone, he screamed.

"*Zeb?*"

"Oh Jesus," Zeb said, and clung on to Gideon as though he was salvation.

"Zeb? What the blazes? Are you all right?"

He was not all right. He wanted to crawl up Gideon and balance on his shoulders so no part of his body was touching any part of Lackaday House. "Spiders," he managed. "My room. *Spiders*."

He felt Gideon's breath hiss out in a 'for God's sake' way, but he didn't let go. "All right, don't panic. I can deal with a spider for you."

"There's hundreds of them!"

Gideon's hug tightened. He'd always been ridiculously kind about Zeb's childish fear. "I very much doubt that. Come on, deep breath. I will deal with it, all right? Let's have a look."

He led the way back to Zeb's room. Zeb trailed behind, feeling more and more infantile and absurd. If there were three spiders and he'd imagined the rest in a fit of panic, he was going to look like the world's most hysterical fool.

Gideon opened the door. "All, right, let's—Jesus!"

Zeb was not going to look. He stood at the other side of the corridor at a safe distance from crawling horror. "There are a lot of them?"

"Jesus *Christ*. Oh, I am not having this. Oh, no. Enough. What do you need me to get from in here?"

Zeb was strongly inclined to suggest throwing a lit match and some kindling in there, rather than taking anything out. "Clothes? Toothbrush? Oh God, my satchel! What if they got in it?"

"I will examine every inch of everything," Gideon said. "Stay there, wait for me, and for goodness' sake, *don't look*."

He went into the spider room as if it was just a room. Zeb sagged against the wall, trying to make his heart beat normally.

Gideon emerged with the leather satchel over his shoulder and a pile of clothes. "Come on," he said shortly, almost angrily, and Zeb followed.

fourteen

GIDEON'S ROOM WAS SOME distance from Zeb's, up a flight of stairs and towards the back of the house. Zeb collapsed onto the single chair while Gideon made a performance, greatly appreciated, of shaking out everything he'd brought, including emptying Zeb's satchel, riffling through the paper it contained, and checking the pockets. He found two spiders and disposed of them out of the window with a tumbler and a book. He could pick them up in his fingers if he wanted, being possessed of impossible courage, but he never had after Zeb had expressed his feelings at being touched by spidery hands.

"Clear," Gideon said at last. "All gone. I absolutely promise you."

"Thank you." Zeb felt suddenly tearful, and aware of how cold and sweaty he'd got. "I know it's contemptible."

"Zeb." Gideon dropped to a knee in front of the chair and gripped his hand. "The room was seething with spiders: there must have been a hundred of the things. Of course you were terrified. That was one of the cruellest things I have ever seen."

"What?"

"Cruel," Gideon said. "Unbelievably so. Someone emptied a box of spiders into your bedroom, for what, entertainment? What in the devil's name is going on here?"

Zeb blinked. "Someone put them there?"

"Well, they didn't just appear. Did you see the writing?"

"What writing?"

"The writing in large capitals scrawled across the wall?"

"Was there?" Zeb wouldn't have noticed a giraffe in the circumstances. "I wasn't looking. What did it say?"

"'Sodomite'," Gideon said crisply.

"Oh."

"It was written on a piece of wallpaper carefully attached over the existing paper, presumably for easy removal. I imagine you were meant to see the writing on the wall but be discouraged from investigating further. You'd flee the room and find it had disappeared on your return, much like Hawley did."

"I don't understand. Are you saying it was a joke?"

"No." Gideon sat back on the floor, long legs angling in a way that Zeb wasn't going to compare to anything else with angular legs. "This is well beyond a joke. This is malice taken to a frightening level. This is someone who is going to hurt people."

Zeb put his hands together in front of his face. "You aren't being awfully comforting." His voice still had a tremor in it; he couldn't seem to get it under control.

"No. Oh, blast it. Here." He rose, grabbed Zeb's hand, and tugged him to the bed. It was a plain bedstead, no frills for the staff, but a good size. He kicked off his shoes, sat on it, and pulled Zeb over. "Come on. Lie down with me until you're breathing properly."

Zeb lay down as instructed. It was cold. They were both fully dressed, but Gideon pulled a quilt over them anyway and put his arm firmly over Zeb. "Here. All safe. Take your time."

"Thank you," Zeb managed. He wanted to burrow into Gideon's arms and never leave. "How were you there?"

"I was coming to find you. I wanted to talk about—well, a few things."

"What things?"

Gideon exhaled, his breath warm on Zeb's neck. "Don't worry about it. We'll come back to that when you're in a better frame of mind."

"Tell me now. I'd like to talk about anything that involves not thinking about that room. Distract me, that would be welcome."

Gideon was silent a moment. Then he said, "I wanted to ask about how we ended. If that changes your mind, I'll quite understand."

Zeb actually laughed. It was a strangled sort of noise, but it was a laugh, and Gideon's arms tightened responsively. "Scylla and Charybdis," he said. "I would like to talk about it. I owe you an apology and an explanation, if you want to hear it."

"I would like the explanation, but you're upset. It can wait."

"Well, it can't," Zeb said. "Because I'm getting out of this damned house tomorrow if I have to walk the whole way to Exeter, so let's do it. Where do you want to start?"

Gideon's breath hissed out. "The part where I told you I loved you, and you looked like a trapped fox. And I said again that I loved you, and I wanted the rest of my life with you, and you said, 'I dare say I can give you the evening.'" His chest heaved violently. "That part."

They had met at Cubitt's. Zeb had worked in the clerks' office; Gideon had recently been brought in as the new supervisor. The work was tedious and repetitive, exactly the sort of thing Zeb hated, and things hadn't been going well. He had stayed late, hoping to finish a batch of work that he simply hadn't been able to make himself do all day; Gideon had stayed too, and helped him through it; Zeb had offered to buy him a drink as thanks. It had gone from there.

They'd had nine months. Not the smoothest nine months, not the honeymoon part where you fell in love and everything was rosy, because there had been so much to deal with. Gideon had spent thirty years choking down his desires and stifling his feelings; Zeb was emotional and uninhibited, and liked affection shown in words and touch. Gideon was tidy and organised and logical and good at his job; Zeb was none of those things. They'd both needed a lot of patience, a lot of reassurance.

They might have found it too, if they hadn't worked together. If Gideon hadn't been obliged to cover for Zeb's failings during the day—or, even worse, rebuke him for them, as his supervisor—he wouldn't have found them so grating in the evenings, and then perhaps he'd have found it easier to let go in the nights. If Zeb hadn't been so drained and belittled and miserable after work, he would have had more strength to support Gideon through his uncertainties. Come to that, if Zeb hadn't been so often reminded of his own unbearably exasperating nature through the years, he might have found it easier to believe Gideon could love him.

"I'm sorry," Zeb said. "I really am. It was a horrible

thing to say, but I was panicking. Things were going so badly between us. There was work and we'd had that row and I felt I couldn't do anything right. I was wondering if we could really be together at all, actually, and then you asked me for more—"

"That was stupid," Gideon said. "I know it was. I was panicking too, and I tried to—well, it was more or less the equivalent of asking you to marry me as a remedy when we weren't even getting on. I realise it was absurd."

"It wasn't absurd. But I didn't know it was coming, and I was so tired. And also, you don't have the words right."

"I remember exactly what you said."

"What you said. You didn't just say you wanted the rest of our lives. You asked me for a promise."

"Is that different?" Gideon demanded, and then Zeb could all but hear something click in his mind. "Zeb?" he asked, more gently. "You said you don't break promises. Is that why you wouldn't make me one?"

"I hate promises." Zeb was facing away from Gideon, staring at the wall. "I hate everything about them. If someone makes one to me I feel sick waiting for it to be broken, and if I make one it's worse because then I'm the one who'll mess everything up. A promise is just wrapping hope around lies, and I don't want to do that or have it done to me, and we'd only been lovers for what, nine months—"

"I spoke far too soon. I *know*. I was getting it all wrong

and it terrified me. I'd had to reprimand you at work that day, and it seemed that everything that came out of my mouth was a criticism, and I wanted to... I don't know. To make it clear I loved you."

"But I was terrified too. I couldn't seem to get anything right as it was, and then you wanted me to make this great promise and how could I? How could I promise you everything and not ruin it, not have to explain why I got it wrong? How could I spend the rest of my life with that hanging over me every day?"

"God," Gideon said. "That really wasn't the spirit in which I asked."

"I *know* that. But I also knew I wasn't capable of being what you wanted, so a promise would have been a lie, and I couldn't bear to wait for you to find out I'd lied to you. I'd be sitting under the Sword of Damocles until whatever I did to make it fall."

"You thought you couldn't be what I wanted?"

"I knew I couldn't."

"Oh God," Gideon said. "If you thought that—Zeb, you were *who* I wanted. I wanted you, and you are superlatively and marvellously you, and if you didn't understand that, it's because I failed to tell you. Because I didn't know how to be with you, and I got annoyed about the *what*, the lost keys and shirts on the floor, as if those were the things that mattered."

"But they do matter and you were annoyed," Zeb said. "There was work, and your family situation, and you were under so much stress, and I couldn't even do the little things to make it easier. I kept failing. And when you asked me for more, although I couldn't even seem to handle what we already had—it felt like a rebuke, I suppose, like you were pointing out another way I hadn't been good enough. And it hurt, and I hit back and pretty much said the nastiest thing I could."

He'd been ashamed of that for a year. Gideon had been very conscious of his inexperience compared to Zeb's extensive history. To have thrown *I can give you the evening* at him, with its implication that Gideon was merely a casual diversion, had been the sort of shitty thing Hawley would say to end an affair.

"It was horrible of me," he said. "I've no excuse. And we argued, and you went off and I thought, *but I could give you the evening.*"

"I don't understand."

"I mean—I could have been with you day by day. Not making big promises, or saying I'd always get it right, just waking up and deciding every day we were still us. I'd have done that. I'd have loved that."

"Oh Christ." Gideon's voice was raw. "So would I. I didn't think you meant that."

"I didn't when I said it, but I should have. It was what

I *wanted* to have meant, because it was what I wanted to have. I lay awake all night working out how to explain that to you. I thought, if I could just explain it, we could make things right." He smiled mirthlessly at the wall. "And then there we were at Cubitt's the next day, with you pretending not to look at me, and I had no idea how to broach matters, and the not speaking was unbearable. I had to say *something*. And, you know, I really did just pull you into that stock cupboard to talk, only the way you looked at me—I just wanted to kiss you, and I thought I'd latched the door, or maybe I forgot about it, but either way, I *didn't* latch it, and there we were. First I panicked and grossly insulted you, and then I decided that I was going to make things work, and managed to go about eight hours before I ruined your life. Sorry."

Gideon's free arm shifted. Zeb rather thought he was putting his hand over his face. "Oh, Zeb. Dear God."

"I'm sorry," Zeb said again. "I'm an idiot."

"No. I let you drag me into that stockroom. I let you kiss me, when I was well aware how stupid that was. And I shouldn't have pushed you as I did that evening. I knew at the time that I was going about it wrong, but I wanted to make a grand gesture instead of, I don't know, helping you find whatever you'd misplaced without complaining about it, which I expect you would have preferred."

"Well. Yes."

"I'm sorry," Gideon said softly. "I did know I was being a prick. I was so worried for my sister and her family, and Ellison was pushing for your dismissal and giving me a hard time for not supporting him—"

"You didn't tell me that!"

"No. I probably should have, but you were already so unhappy and nervous at work, I felt like it would only have made things worse. The fact is, I should have stopped being your supervisor as soon as we started. But if I'd passed you to anyone else—"

"They'd have sacked me."

"Probably. Yes. I was constantly on edge because of it, and I didn't know what I was doing with you. I couldn't seem to get it right. So I got it catastrophically wrong, and then you responded badly, so *I* got upset, so *you* did that at Cubitt's, and—God almighty, we're not fit to be let out."

Zeb snorted. "It does sound that way."

"And if that's anyone's fault, it's mine," Gideon said. "I spent a long time trying to blame you for everything that happened, but the truth is, I precipitated the whole mess."

"You were trying your best."

"You were trying when you dragged me into that storeroom," Gideon pointed out. "One can have good intentions and still make a pig's ear of things."

"Can't one just," Zeb said with feeling. "But I really

wouldn't have objected to a grand gesture of a different kind. It's just, I don't like promises. And the bigger the promise, the worse it feels, and it felt like you were asking me for so much."

"I was. I wanted so much. And...ugh. When you said what you did, I assumed you meant—well, that you were seeing other men. I know you are a great deal more, uh, free with your, uh, physical—"

"Slutty."

"I didn't say that."

"No, I did. I wasn't, though. Seeing anyone else."

"I know that," Gideon said. "You'd have told me. But I couldn't see it at the time. I put you on the spot, knowing you don't do well on the spot, and then I thought the worst because I was jealous, and therefore I didn't ask some simple questions that could have saved us both a lot of pain."

Zeb had never really been able to unpick the horrible mess of last year through the morass of guilt, self-blame, and regret. He let out a long breath now, with the sensation of a fog finally blown away. "You're right. It *was* both our faults, and we're *not* fit to be let out."

"Some sort of nursemaid is clearly required. Could you explain something?" Gideon said. "I heard what you said about promises, but I don't really understand. All I know is that you have a random but deep-seated fear of them that gets worse when they're larger. Are you confusing them with spiders?"

Zeb really did laugh then. He lay, shoulders shaking, under Gideon's arm, because with Gideon holding him, even the worst things seemed possible to be laughed at.

"Swine," he said. "It's not—not random, though."

"No?"

Gideon didn't ask more. He just waited. Zeb nuzzled back into him, blinking. He didn't much want to tell this, but the alternative was Gideon not understanding, and that was infinitely worse.

"I was brought up to take promises seriously. My word as my bond, the eternal disappointment caused by breaking either. It was one of my father's bugbears. *Promise you'll do better at school. Promise you won't lose this one. Promise you'll remember to go, that you'll get there on time, that you will be more like your brother. Why aren't you more like your brother?* And I'd make the promise because he made me, and be punished for not keeping it—*untrustworthy, irresponsible, feckless*. And then—do you recall asking why I was a clerk and Bram a wealthy man of letters?"

"You said your father left him all the money."

"I was eighteen when Father took ill, and Bram twenty-eight. Father announced he was leaving everything to Bram because I wasn't fit to manage my own life. Impulsive, incapable of applying myself, all that. But the thing is, in the same breath, he charged Bram to set me up in life and give me a kindly steadying hand. He specifically *wasn't* cutting me out: he was passing on his paternal responsibility. Bram swore to stand in the place of a father to me at Father's deathbed, and Father joined our hands as a sign of that pledge. It was utterly nauseating. But he *promised*."

Gideon's body had stilled. "So what happened?"

"Father died. The will was executed. And in the space of a few weeks, Bram went from 'I will pay your university bills and give you a generous allowance' to 'You cannot expect me to fund all your entertainments' to 'You should be grateful for anything' to 'You are wasting your education and must be made to grow up'. And that was it. He cut me off in the middle of the university term. I had about thirty pounds to my name. I had to leave off my studies and find work, with not the faintest idea what I might do. So, of course, I went around family friends, in the hope of at least finding a nice office job, and discovered that Bram had got there first. He'd told them all he'd been forced to take this step because of my gross unreliability and whatnot."

"*Why?* Why would he do that?"

"Why tell them? So people wouldn't think ill of him when I complained about his behaviour. Why do it in the first place?" Zeb made a face. "If you ask me, he made the promise because he wanted to be the family patriarch, and he broke it because he liked having twenty-five thousand pounds in the bank, and he lied so he could reconcile the two in his head."

"Which is why you don't want the Wyckham inheritance," Gideon said. "In case you do the same."

"Anyone can renounce money they don't have. I sometimes wonder, if Bram *had* shared, if I was living prosperously on Wyckham money when Jerome called on me, would I have listened? Or would I have told him to clear off? I should probably be grateful Bram saved me the moral test."

"Christ. Why didn't you tell me before?"

"I didn't tell anyone for years. I was too ashamed."

"You aren't the one who should feel shame about this."

"But I do. It's humiliating that my father had so much contempt for me, and it's hideously embarrassing that Bram could be so petty and greedy and *small*. I'm ashamed for him. The prick."

Gideon nodded slowly. "If I may say so, your family are some of the most awful people I've ever met in my life."

"Aren't they just."

"And I don't believe for a moment that you would behave like your brother," Gideon added. "You should think more of yourself. A lot more. You were the best thing in my life, and I was a damned fool to let you go."

"That's funny," Zeb said. "Because so were you, and so was I."

"Oh God. Zeb, could we—please—"

He sounded wretched and yearning and hopeful all at once. Zeb twisted urgently round in his arms, and then they were kissing frantically, a mess of flailing limbs and tangling clothes and trapping quilt, hands and lips and longing, and the bitterness of a wasted year.

Gideon ended up on top of him after a few overwhelming minutes, his long body sprawled over Zeb's, his light eyes looking down with the same confused mix of pain and joy and wanting that Zeb felt.

"God damn it," he said softly. "I missed you so much. I persuaded myself you were playing with me all along. That I would never have been enough."

"How could you not be?"

"How could I be? You're all charm and heart and exuberance, and I count pennies and tidy things up. You've so much joy, and I felt so joyless for so long that when you did share your joy with me, I couldn't embrace it even though I wanted to." He cupped Zeb's cheek. "It was a great deal easier to decide that you had brought my orderly life chaos and I didn't want it any more, rather than to realise you'd offered my trammelled existence freedom and I'd been afraid of it."

Zeb's heart was thudding oddly now, arrhythmically,

as if it wasn't quite in his own control. "I...didn't know you thought that. And I did bring chaos."

"You are excessively chaotic," Gideon said. "I'm excessively orderly. On average, we could work."

"Could we?" Zeb asked on a breath. "I know what you said about being stuck here, with me in London—"

"I don't think I will be staying at Lackaday House much longer, and we need to talk about why at some point very soon. But right now—"

"Sod Lackaday House and all who sail in her. I want you. And that's not *just for tonight* or *It doesn't mean anything* or any such rubbish. I want you back, which we can discuss later, and I want you now."

"Yes," Gideon said. "Yes. Oh, Zeb. License my hands—what is it?"

Zeb knew exactly what he meant, and what he was asking. He'd quoted Donne's poem to Gideon a very long time ago, a request and a seduction in one: *"License my roving hands and let them go, Before, behind, between, above, below."*

"I really must memorise that. Before," Gideon murmured, fingers skimming down Zeb's chest.

"Behind." Zeb slipped his own hand round to Gideon's arse, tense, a little thinner than it had been.

Gideon spent a pleasant moment on *before*, palming Zeb's prick, flattening his hand, touching, stroking, feeling. Connecting them, skin to skin, closing his hand possessively, finally sliding it down between Zeb's thighs. "Between?"

Zeb curled up and forward, getting his mouth to Gideon's neck, his ear, kissing, licking. "Above," he mumbled against the warm skin.

Gideon cupped his balls. "Below. I will definitely remember that. If we practice enough."

"Let's," Zeb said, and got his mouth to Gideon's, and then it was nothing but breath and touch, hands and lips, and the joy of Gideon's touch, Gideon's response, and its echo in his own shuddering pleasure.

fifteen

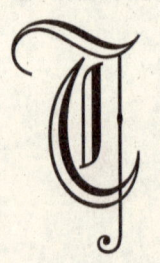HEY LAY ENTWINED AFTERWARDS, Zeb wrapped in the sprawl of Gideon's long familiar limbs, eyelids heavy, suffused with contentment.

"Hey," Gideon said. "Don't go to sleep."

"Mph. No. I should—"

Go back to my room was what he'd meant to say, and that brought his last sight of his room to mind. He jolted sharply. "I can't!"

"You're staying here tonight. Don't think about leaving. But we have to talk about why."

"Oh God, can we not?"

"You are in here because you were driven out of your room by frightening malice," Gideon said. "And we really do need to discuss that, which means we cannot allow ourselves to be sidetracked any longer by how ridiculously lovely you are, or anything of that nature."

"We can if we want."

"No," Gideon said firmly. "Sit up, and wake up. *Up*, Zeb, this is serious."

Zeb sat up reluctantly. They both propped themselves against the bedstead.

"Right," Gideon said. "Let's start with your room. Who knows you're afraid of spiders?"

"Bram. But I really cannot imagine him collecting spiders to put in my room; I'm quite sure he'd consider that beneath him. Hawley doesn't know my feelings on spiders or he'd constantly be mentioning it."

"Might Bram have told Wynn about your fear?"

"Possibly. But there was that writing on the wall, you said, and Wynn doesn't know I'm queer, so—"

"Doesn't he?"

That sounded meaningful. "No? That is—does he?"

Gideon took a deep breath. "You recall what I said about him hiring me. In retrospect, does that sound even remotely plausible? That Wynn went out of his way to find and help a total stranger because I got in trouble alongside a cousin he'd barely met in his life? That he'd give me access to his affairs without asking about the gross misconduct I was sacked for? It's nonsensical. I knew it was nonsensical when he hired me, but I was desperate enough to persuade myself it was charity."

"What are you saying?"

Gideon took his hand. "I think he knows I was your lover and we'd parted badly. I think he brought me here because of you."

Zeb blinked. "You can't mean to get us back together?"

"Jesus wept, Zeb. No. I think my purpose here was to unsettle you. To provoke you to misbehave."

"Um." Zeb gestured at their bare bodies.

"Very much not like that. Look, suppose you were less honest, less generous—in a word, more like your family. Suppose you wanted the incredible fortune on offer as much as the rest of them, but here I was, able to ruin your chances if I opened my mouth. What might you have done—what might Hawley do in your shoes—to silence me?"

Zeb thought about that. "Oh."

"And equally, I was terrified you might lose me this job. I thought you would try to get rid of me, and I was quite prepared to make this a battle. If you hadn't made us talk, what might we have done to one another?"

"But why would Wynn want me to fight you? He *invited* me here."

"He invited two estranged brothers, one with an illicit ex-lover, one with an adulterous wife, plus *her* ex-lover, and then threw a tiger among all those pigeons with this legacy business," Gideon said. "If he wanted to create the conditions for you all murdering one another, he's gone the right way about it. And I will tell you what else: on his account, you knew about the inheritance, you came here for it, and you've been actively scheming for it all along. He's told me all about his letters and conversations with you, which bear very little resemblance to what you've told me. Come to that, he made everyone think you'd slandered Mrs. Bram. He's doing a damn good job of making you look as bad as the rest of them."

"Oh God," Zeb said. "Is this his illness?"

"What illness?"

"He's sick. Dying. That's how he made me promise to stay. He says his doctor told him he had six months; he won't live till summer. He begged me for time while he has it." Wynn had also asked Zeb not to tell, but at this point, he was putting himself and Gideon first. "Maybe what's wrong with him is affecting his brain?"

Gideon's brows had gone up. "Well, possibly, but I've been here since September, and in that time he hasn't gone to see a doctor, or been visited by one, or had any letter that looks remotely medical or official, or had a visit from a solicitor, or spent any time in bed, or had me put his affairs in order. If he's dying, he's doing so in a remarkably self-effacing manner."

"He looked pretty bad in the dining room the other evening," Zeb suggested. "He needed your arm to leave."

"That was the first time he's done so. Are you absolutely sure about this? When did he tell you?"

"It was when I said I was going to leave, and...wouldn't be persuaded to remain by any other argument... Oh, no," Zeb said hollowly. "Really. He said he was *dying*. He can't have been joking about that."

"None of this is a joke. There was nothing funny about what was done to your room."

"But that couldn't have been Wynn. We were talking downstairs, right before I came up—Oh."

"What?"

Zeb grimaced. "He called me in to play cards when I was going to go up and then said he wanted to talk to me afterwards, but he didn't have anything to say. He just chattered on about Laura and Jessamine."

"In order to delay you while someone filled your room with spiders," Gideon said. "It's Wynn, Zeb. Whatever is going on, he's behind it."

"But why would he set out to make us all miserable? Anyone might dislike Bram or Hawley—it's hard not to—but why bring me into it? He'd met me twice in my life before this, both times as a child! What did I do to deserve this?"

"I have no idea, and I don't care. This is escalating towards dangerous cruelty, and I want you well out of it."

"What about you?"

"I'm quite sure I was brought here to get at you. He's barely given me a thing to do, and once you leave, he'll have no further use for me. The important thing is to get you out."

"Right," Zeb said. "How?"

Gideon's lips parted. He was probably thinking about high walls, locked gates, obdurate chauffeurs, and miles of empty, wintry, misty moor. Zeb certainly was.

"I don't know," he said at last. "Maybe the mist will lift tomorrow. We'll find a way."

We. Zeb and Gideon were *we* again. With *we* in his pocket, Zeb could face down Wynn or anyone else. And Gideon would come back to London soon rather than an indefinite time later, and everything really was going to be all right as soon as they both left this blasted, cursed, haunted house.

Haunted. "What about the ghost business? Do we think he's behind that too?"

Gideon stretched in that way he had that seemed to elongate his already long body by about eight inches. "Surely. It's intended to put you all on edge, I suppose."

"But it's been going since you got here, well before we arrived."

"This has obviously been long planned. Where do you think the spiders came from?"

"Hell, like all their kind."

Gideon gave a pointed sigh. "You can't just nip outside and collect an entire crateful of spiders in an afternoon. Can one breed spiders? Either way, it must have taken time and work. This is a long-term, elaborate scheme that involves quite a few people."

"It must, but who? Everyone was downstairs at the point I saw the ghost."

"No, they weren't."

"They were. You were with Dash and Bram and I heard Wynn and the women—"

"There are plenty of other people in the house."

Zeb had a sudden, terrifying image of Walter's last wife, now a withered old spectre huddled in an attic, creeping the corridors in silent shadows, picking spiders off the walls. "What do you mean, other people? Where?"

"The staff, Zeb. It's very clearly the staff."

It took a second for Zeb to digest that. "Why on earth would Wynn's servants dress up as ghosts or collect spiders?"

"Because he ordered them to?"

"Come on. Would you do that for an employer?"

Gideon made a face. "It might depend how desperate I was for a wage. And—have you noticed that this house is grossly understaffed? Wynn let go three maids and a footman just before the family arrived, for no offence I could discern. All the staff we have left are notably unfriendly, relatively new to the house, and not very good at their jobs."

"Especially the cook."

"Indeed. So I have to wonder what they were hired for. I suspect it's this."

"Can you hire people to be awful to your guests?" Zeb asked.

"I expect you can hire people to do anything if you pay enough. Which—I don't suppose you have a large sum in cash on you, for bribery?"

"Only about three quid. Who do you want to bribe?"

"The chauffeur, to get you out of here. I doubt three pounds will do it, but let me see."

"Or I could talk to Wynn. Say I know what he's up to, and demand to leave."

"You could," Gideon said slowly. "I'm not sure you ought to, without an exit available. Perhaps I'm being overly cautious."

"You're a cautious man."

Gideon shifted onto his side so they faced each other, eyes locking. "I am, yes. Except when it comes to you, and then I don't have any self-preservation at all."

Zeb lunged. Gideon's mouth met his, and for a blissful

moment, he didn't need to think about his cousin, or his situation, or anything.

They were both up in a timely fashion the next morning. Gideon went off to extract Zeb's remaining belongings and then try to bribe the chauffeur or, failing that, groom. Zeb went downstairs and made an early breakfast in blissful solitude, wondering what might be useful to do.

He ought to warn his family about all this. Unfortunately, he couldn't believe any of them would listen. Bram and Hawley were both convinced that Zeb was manoeuvring against them; Elise had never liked him. Dash might have listened, but he was ill, which was rotten timing. A military man of action who didn't believe in ghosts would be a very useful person to have around: it was a bit of bad luck he was locked away from the rest of them now.

Zeb paused on that thought, kipper congealing on his plate as the waters of panic lapped his metaphorical ankles.

It would not do to overreact, he told himself. Wynn was clearly on the far side of eccentric, his practical jokes malicious and frightening, but there was no reason to suppose he would actually harm anyone, especially his old friend and cousin.

All the same, Zeb would drop in on Dash, just to put his mind at rest.

That turned out to be easier said than done. Dash had mentioned he was lodged in the corridor round the corner from Hawley's. Zeb wandered up and down, listening for the sounds of a man suffering from malarial fever, or sleeping, or talking to a nursemaid, or anything at all. There seemed to be absolutely nobody about, and it felt not just quiet but uninhabited. Was he in the wrong place?

Damn and blast. He made his way up the corridor again, this time trying door handles. The first three rooms he opened were empty, with dusty floors, furniture shrouded in holland covers, and a lot of cobwebs; he shut the doors with speed.

The fourth door opened on an obviously occupied room, with things on the dresser and chair. The bed had the covers pulled back but didn't look as though it had been slept in.

"Hello?" Zeb said. His voice echoed flatly.

He edged in, feeling like the trespasser he was. The room was cold, the solid cold that came when nobody had lit the fire in a while. He noted water in the jug, shaving things on the dresser, a nightshirt over the back of a chair, a book on the bedside table. It looked like a very dull military memoir. He opened it and saw *Wyckham Dash* written on the flyleaf.

So this was Dash's room, but not his sickroom. They must have moved him to a different, more convenient location. And since a man in the grip of a malarial attack wouldn't need a book, or consider shaving, they had left his bits and pieces behind, and it hadn't been considered urgent to make up his room.

He glanced at the dresser again. It bore the usual sort of clutter out of pockets, and some less usual items such as a pocket compass and a penknife. Dash was clearly a practical sort. There was also a toothbrush and a pot of tooth powder. He might have thought Dash would want those, at least. He looked again at the nightshirt on the back of the chair.

Zeb was not a particularly logical thinker, at least in the commonly accepted sense. His train of thought didn't generally chug from station to station in an orderly manner, taking him from A to B to C on the rails that other people would use. What he could do, now and then, was leap halfway down the alphabet, reaching conclusions in a single intuitive bound he often couldn't explain, and as he stood in Dash's empty room, that was exactly what he did.

"Shit," he said quietly.

He had to look. Feeling both intrusive and alarmed, he opened the wardrobe, and at that moment, a floorboard creaked outside the room.

Zeb froze dead. If Dash was about to walk in, this would be unbelievably embarrassing. He stood, heart thumping. There was another creak, and then the sound of footsteps.

Zeb instantly forgot that he was trespassing, took two long strides to the door, and stuck his head out. The footsteps were clearly audible as they passed, but there was nobody in the corridor. Nobody at all.

To blazes with this pestilential house and its phantom feet. He was going to finish what he was about, and quickly, before he got caught. So he searched the wardrobe, the suitcase, every drawer, looking through it all, with the panic that had been lapping his ankles steadily rising as he failed to find what he sought. His heart was thumping in a way he didn't like, and he couldn't shake the feeling that, while he was delving into Dash's wardrobe, someone might silently open the door and creep in, and he would turn and they'd be there...

He left the room at last, shutting the door behind him with peculiar care, although there was nobody around to hear, and headed downstairs. He needed to talk to Gideon.

As ever, finding anyone in this blasted house was

impossible. He might be in Wynn's study, but Zeb did not want to go there if he could avoid it. He tried the library instead and came across Jessamine. She was staring out of the window, into the grey drifts of mist.

"Good morning," Zeb said. "Have you seen Mr. Grey, at all?"

Jessamine turned, startled. "Oh! Zeb. No, I have not."

"Bother. Thanks. Actually, have you seen Dash?"

"He's ill. A malarial attack."

"Yes, but he's not in his room. Was he moved somewhere else, for nursing?"

"Why, no. I shouldn't think a sick man ought to be moved."

"Nor would I, but he isn't there," Zeb said. "Who would know where he is? Who's in charge of caring for him?"

"I don't know. I have not seen him since he was taken ill." Her brows came together. "Is something wrong?"

"He's not in his room, that's all. What is it?"

Jessamine's hand had gone to her mouth. She stared at Zeb with stricken eyes. "Do you think—do you think something has happened to him?"

In another house, that would have seemed something of an overreaction. As it was, Zeb was deeply grateful that someone else seemed to be noticing. "Why? Do *you* think something's wrong?"

Jessamine bit her lip. "Do you know how old he is?"

"Late forties? Oh Lord, you're not going to talk about the Wyckham curse, are you? I just want to know where he is."

"But it might matter," Jessamine said. "Will you come with me?"

"Where?"

"Just come. I can't explain. Please?"

"Is this important?" Zeb said. "Because I have things to do, and if it's about curses and ghosts—"

"Cousin Zeb." Jessamine dropped her voice low. "There is nobody else I can speak to. Wynn doesn't want to know. If you don't think it's anything once you've seen, you may decide never to listen to me again. But come now, *please*."

"All right," Zeb said reluctantly. "But can we make it quick?"

It was not quick. It was a trudge outside, through the clinging mists. Cold, damp tendrils brushed Zeb's face and he batted them away.

"It's sticky, isn't it? I always think the mist is like cobwebs," Jessamine said. "As if a great spider was crouched over the house, spinning and spinning."

Zeb had not needed that mental image. He slapped at a finger of mist that twined in his hair. "Could you tell me what we're doing?"

"I will tell you, but you have to promise me to listen to me without interrupting and saying it's nonsense. Do you promise?"

"No," Zeb said. "I'll do my best to hear you out, though."

"Then listen. You know the Wyckham curse: that Walter sold the lives of his wives and children, exchanging their futures for his—"

"I'm interrupting, and this is nonsense. I don't want to hear it." He needed to find Gideon and go home, not be wandering in the fog, listening to doom-laden gibbering. And they weren't even wandering, he realised. Jessamine was leading them purposefully through the mist; Zeb recognised the path.

"Very well," Jessamine said. "Then you may just hear what I saw."

Zeb sighed. "What was that?"

"You know my room is on the west side of the house. I heard a sound last night, very faint. It was awfully eerie, and I thought it might be the wind or someone singing in the house. It was all on one note, and then it went up and down." She sang a few notes, just *la la*, that resembled plainsong. She had an excellent voice. "And I looked out of the window and I saw light. Flames. As if a line of people were carrying torches."

"Good heavens. What did you do?"

"I shut the curtains at once, went to bed, and pulled the covers over my head," Jessamine said, which struck Zeb as the most sensible thing he'd heard from her in some time. "But I got up early this morning and came out, and...well." She gestured ahead, to where the stone circle loomed out of the mist, every bit as ominous as Walter could have hoped. "Look," she said, heading up to the altar stone. "Come."

Zeb approached cautiously. The stones loomed out of the drifts of mist, grey and ancient and forbidding. The altar stone—

"What the devil?" he yelped. *"What?"*

"It's been like this before," Jessamine said, with terrible simplicity. "I have seen it several times. But I've never seen so much."

There was blood, pints of it, pooling on the top of the altar stone, in the dip where Zeb had put his hand what felt like months ago. It was dripping over the top, spilling down the sides, droplets splashing darkly on the grass. He stared, speechless.

"I thought—I don't know what I thought," she said, voice sounding rather fuzzy through the ringing in his ears. "I have seen blood on the stone before, but I told myself it was foxes, or a hawk killing a pigeon, or some such thing. It was never so much. But now, this—and the chanting—and you say Colonel Dash is missing."

"You cannot think—" The words stuck in Zeb's throat. He stared at the bloody sacrificial stone, the steady dripping. Eight pints in a human body, he vaguely thought. That was a bit more than a jeroboam.

Jessamine's mouth turned down at the corners, like a child about to cry. "I don't know. Zeb, I'm frightened."

"We need to get inside. Right now. *Now*, Jessamine." Not that inside felt a great deal safer, but he did not want to be out here, in the mist, unable to see more than a few feet, with God knew who lurking, listening, following them. "Come on. Quick."

"You believe me," Jessamine said on a breath. "You do, don't you?"

"I believe there's a man whose whereabouts are currently unaccounted for," Zeb said grimly. "He may be perfectly well—apart from the malaria, of course—but I should like to assure myself by seeing him. And, beyond that..."

Beyond that, someone had set out to terrify Jessamine, and that meant, when he got out of here, he needed to take her with him. He couldn't just flee and leave her to whatever hellish imagination had conceived this tableau.

Actually, now he thought of it—

"Beyond what?" Jessamine asked. "What were you going to say?"

"Uh—" Train of thought entirely derailed, Zeb tried to remember what he'd been talking about. "Just that this all seems to me like a very unpleasant prank."

"*Prank?* Can you not see—"

"This isn't ghosts, Jessamine, it's people," Zeb said over her. "Someone is playing the fool here. Trying to frighten you, trying to make you believe nonsense. It's cruel and very peculiar, and it needs a stop putting to it."

He strode back to the house, Jessamine hurrying at his side. They came into the hall, and as they were divesting themselves of damp coats, Zeb heard Wynn.

"Zebedee!"

Zeb turned and saw him, with Gideon looking decidedly tense at his side. "Wynn. I wanted to speak to you."

"And I to you. I made myself very clear yesterday, Zebedee. Nobody is to venture onto the moors while the mist remains. I will not risk my people, do you understand? Your wishes are nothing to their safety—their lives, even. I told you that in so many words and gave you my refusal, yet now I find you have been playing upon my secretary to have your way. What makes you think you can overrule me in my house? What right have you to countermand my orders?"

Zeb felt the colour rush to his face. Wynn's tone of angry rebuke was all too familiar, and it gave him the sick, crushed feeling in his stomach of finding himself in the wrong, again, as always. *Idle, irresponsible boy, why don't you ever learn? When will you grow up?*

He opened his mouth in automatic response to stammer some sort of apology, and Gideon cleared his throat. One single sharp cough, that was all, but it was enough.

Gideon was not impulsive or irresponsible or credulous. Gideon was sure there was something wrong in this house. Gideon was standing right there, and Zeb was absolutely not going to fold in front of him.

Also, some bastard had put spiders in his room, so if anyone had a right to be outraged, it was Zeb.

"Where's Dash?" he said.

Wynn's head went back. "What has that to do with anything?"

"Colonel Dash. Where is he?"

"He is suffering a malarial attack."

"I said *where*."

Wynn scowled. "He is unwell, and this is hardly the point."

"It's my point. I want to see him."

"I am speaking of your behaviour. What makes you think you can have your way with my secretary at your pleasure?"

Oh, that's nice, Zeb thought. He was probably supposed to panic at that, and wonder what Wynn knew. In the corner of his eye, Gideon looked superlatively blank.

"If you don't like how I conduct myself, Wynn, I suggest you order the motor and I'll go," he retorted. "But before that, I want to see Dash and assure myself he is well."

"He is *not* well. He is far too ill for visitors."

"Then he needs a doctor," Zeb said. "So why don't Jessamine and I take the motor to town and get one."

"Because it is too dangerous!"

"The man can drive slowly. I'll walk by the motor to ensure it doesn't lose the road."

A muscle jumped in Wynn's jaw. "It's too far for that."

"Then two of us can walk. Mr. Grey can come and we'll take turns. Elise can accompany Jessamine as chaperone so there can be no objection."

"I have every objection. You cannot order my staff or demand to see my guests. This is my house, and you may not behave as though you are already my inheritor!"

His voice got louder on that last. Zeb had heard a footstep on the stair, behind him. He would put money it was Bram or Hawley.

"So order the motor," he said. "Frankly, Wynn, your hospitality is starting to resemble a stay at His Majesty's pleasure. I would like to leave, and it sounds as if you would like me to leave, so I really cannot see any reason why you should be trying to prevent me."

They stared at each other. Wynn had gone brick-red; Zeb was probably much the same.

"I suggest you consider your position and your manner," Wynn said thickly. "This is no way to speak. I will talk to you later before I say something I regret."

He walked off. Zeb said, "Don't just go like that!" but Wynn didn't turn round.

"Well, well," Hawley said behind him. "Good Lord. Has little Zebby found a spine? I must say, I've always taken you for one of nature's invertebrates. Or do I mean inverts?"

"Sod off, Hawley," Zeb said. "Go on, scamper after Wynn, slander the rest of us, and beg for his money. It's what he's brought you here to do, and you're living up to expectations."

"Ah, yes, your ostentatious lack of interest in filthy lucre," Hawley flashed back. "I warned you about scheming for the inheritance."

"For the last time—"

"Cousin Zeb!" Jessamine said. "Are you not going to speak to Wynn? About our walk?"

"Oh, you two went for a walk?" Hawley asked, barely masking the snarl. "How very interesting. I wouldn't have thought it was the right weather. I would not have advised the company."

Jessamine turned her shoulder to him, a little snub that made his nostrils flare with anger. "Will you, Zeb?"

"Why bother?" Zeb said. "I should think he knows all about it already."

Jessamine's jaw dropped. "But how could he?"

"You seem to be stirring up trouble between our cousin and her guardian," Hawley struck in. "I consider that very questionable behaviour."

"Miss Jessamine is capable of making her own judgements," Gideon said. "Mr. Zeb, if I could have a moment's private speech with you?"

"Is that what we're calling it now?" Hawley curled his lip. Zeb gave him two fingers and turned away.

sixteen

HEY RETURNED TO GIDEON'S room, in which Zeb discovered his suitcases, neatly packed with the rest of his things. Gideon shut the door behind them, locked it, put his back against it as if holding off a siege, and said, "This is bad."

"What's happened?"

"I tried offering the chauffeur money to drive you to the station. He—I'd say laughed in my face except he doesn't laugh. He frog-marched me out of there and dragged me straight to Wynn, who gave me a very nasty ten minutes, with a great deal of hinting about the difficulties I'll find in obtaining another post and how I should consider where my loyalty lies. He absolutely knows about us."

"Oh God. I'm sorry."

Zeb reached for him; Gideon's fingers wrapped around his. "Not your fault. I shall worry about my employment when I'm well out of this bedlam."

"About that," Zeb said. "It *is* my fault, as we both know, even if you're being awfully good about it. And it's going to be rotten for you finding another job if Wynn gives you a bad reference, so—could I help?"

Gideon pulled him over and kissed his forehead. Zeb wrapped his arms round him, thrilling in the touch. He liked touch. Gideon was not an effusive man, and he had schooled himself to be more physically affectionate for Zeb's happiness. He hadn't forgotten, and he was doing it again, and Zeb melted into him with the pleasure of it.

"I really would like to help," he said into Gideon's chest. "Let me?"

"Sweetheart, that is very much appreciated, but it really can wait. What's the issue with Colonel Dash?"

"He's gone."

"Gone where?"

"I don't know. I last saw him the other night, when Elise saw the ghost. He was wearing evening dress, with the tie off as if he'd been starting to get ready for bed, and seemed perfectly well. We spoke, and he went off to confront Hawley."

"I recall."

"But he never reached Hawley, and Wynn said the

next morning he'd been taken ill. I went in his room, and he's not there. I found his toothbrush and things, including two nightgowns, one laid out over a chair. Would you bring more than two nightgowns for a fortnight's stay? But what I *didn't* find was his evening clothes. His other clothes are hanging up, or at least what looks like a reasonable wardrobe for two weeks, but I looked everywhere and his dinner things aren't there. Do you see?"

Gideon did not look like he saw at first. His lips and fingers moved slightly as he tracked through Zeb's argument. "You mean, this malarial attack came on so suddenly that he was taken to a sickroom still wearing his dinner jacket?"

"And yet, since then, nobody has brought him his nightclothes or hairbrush or toothbrush. And Jessamine doesn't know where he is, and Wynn won't tell me, and last night she heard monks chanting, and now there's blood on the altar stone."

Gideon stilled, then leaned back to examine his face. "Go over that part again."

Zeb explained Jessamine's night-time experience. "The altar stone is covered in blood, pints of it. Jessamine says there's been blood on it before—in fact, I put my hand in some when we were speaking, a few days back—but nothing like these quantities."

"Monks and blood," Gideon said blankly. "But—are you suggesting—"

"I'm not suggesting anything. I'm just telling you the facts as I know them."

"Or have been presented with them. Do you believe in the monks?"

"I'm quite prepared to believe someone dressed people up in robes and sent them marching around the house," Zeb said. "Wouldn't surprise me in the slightest. As to the blood, I dare say having a guest vanish mysteriously, followed by dark hints of human sacrifice, would be a lovely effect if you were trying to scare people out of their wits."

"Quite."

"Only, the problem is, Dash hasn't gone missing in a frightening sort of way. Wynn gave a good explanation for his absence, and I don't suppose anyone else has given him a thought since. If you were using his disappearance to alarm people, would you really just hope someone might start asking questions eventually? Especially people as self-centred as the Wyckhams? Would you count on me searching his room and wondering where his dinner clothes are? Even Jessamine didn't put his absence together with the blood on the stone until I asked her about him. What I mean is, the altar stone is intended to be very frightening and noticeable, but Dash has been quietly removed, and those things don't *fit*."

"No," Gideon said slowly. "No. That is true. And... So far, Wynn can deny having anything to do with the strange goings-on. He's made sure he's downstairs when the ghost appears upstairs, that sort of thing. But he told everyone Dash had malaria, and that would be a very easy lie to catch him in. As you say, it doesn't fit." He scowled. "But why would Wynn want to remove Dash if *not* to frighten people? What's the point?"

"He's the only man of action in the house. I was going to talk to him about all this. Now I can't, and nor can anyone else."

Gideon's lips parted. "Right. I could wish you hadn't said that."

"Sorry. And I could be completely wrong. Maybe he does have malaria, and it does come on in the course of a three-minute walk. On the face of it, that's still more plausible than Wynn's staff helping him kidnap someone."

Gideon frowned. "Would he need help? There are a lot of unused corridors, and rooms one could lock someone in, and Wynn could do that without assistance. *Come with me a moment, old friend; there's something I want you to look at in the attic*, and then shove him in and turn the key."

"If he was locked in a room, we'd surely have heard him shouting and banging. I'd break a window and yell out of it."

"And he hasn't. So either he's not locked in a room at all, or he is not in a position to protest about it, which rather brings us back to where we started. Mother of God."

He sat down on the bed with a thump. Zeb sat next to him. Gideon put an arm over him and pulled him close, and they sat like that for a moment because silent proximity was a lot better than anything they had to talk about.

"I don't like to say this," Gideon said after a while. "But Wynn is currently refusing to let you leave, with the mist as an excuse. What happens when it lifts?"

"Well, he'll have to let me go. Won't he?"

"I'm not sure what's going to make him. He can order the gate to stay locked, and forbid the motor to be taken out—"

"He can't do that forever!"

"I don't suppose he wants to," Gideon said. "The question is how long he *does* need to keep you here, and what he's trying to achieve by it."

Zeb grabbed a couple of handfuls of hair, tugging at it as if that would relieve his feelings. "Suppose I confront him? Push him into a corner where he has to stop pretending to be a genial host?"

"Do we want him to stop pretending that?"

"Then what are we going to do?" Zeb demanded. "Because I've got to do something. Get Jessamine out of here, for a start, and warn the others, and what about the staff? We can't just leave everyone to fester in this madhouse, and especially not if Dash is locked in a room."

"We don't know he's anything of the kind," Gideon said. "He may be assisting Wynn's little game and have his feet up in perfect safety. That's very much the problem: we don't know who, if anyone, we can trust. Honestly, I think our urgent problem is to get you out of this mess, and we should not be worrying about anyone else."

"Dash is missing. Jessamine is a *child*."

"I very much doubt Wynn will harm Jessamine. Zeb, now is not the time for your absurdly generous nature. Please promise—" He stopped himself sharply.

"Gideon—"

"Let me rephrase that," Gideon said, voice steady. "I don't give a damn for anyone else in this house. I realise you do, and that you are a better man than me for it, but I nevertheless beg you will look after yourself first. Because there is something dreadfully wrong here and I'm afraid for you."

"Noted," Zeb said. His mouth felt oddly dry. "I do want to go, don't think otherwise. It's just—I'm tired of walking away from messes. I walked away from you—"

"I sent you away."

"I let you do it. If I had fought for you a year ago, if I

had faced the difficult things instead of scurrying away, we would neither of us be in this ghastly house right now."

"You didn't make this mess, though, and I doubt you can mend it."

"But I'm neck deep in it. So I am going to—" What *was* he going to do? "Talk to Elise," he decided. "That would be a start."

"Do you think she'll listen?"

"She's got nobody else on her side. And she's got plenty of character, and is exhibiting more sense than Bram or Hawley right now. If we had her on our side, that might do something."

"All right. And I'll see if I can come up with anything useful among the staff." He stood, pulled Zeb up by the hand, and kissed him, swift and firm. "Just, please, take care."

Zeb headed directly to Elise's room, on the grounds that she had yet to leave it before two in the afternoon. He hoped she'd got a good book.

He knocked. She answered the door herself with the expression of a woman who was not used to answering doors, or pleased about it, and Zeb blurted, "Did Wynn not let you bring a maid?"

"He claimed there would be staff to assist me, by which he seems to have meant one sulky, incompetent woman. What do you want?"

"May I come in?"

She gave him the thinnest possible smile. "That would hardly be proper."

Zeb glanced up and down the corridor: there was nobody in sight. "I'll stand out here if you'd rather. I wanted to talk about what's going on in this house."

"Meaning?"

"Someone dressed up as a ghost to frighten you," Zeb said. "Not just you, either, there's a lot of it about. People dressing up as monks to scare Jessamine, a lot of spiders put in my room, slander written on walls—" He saw her mouth tighten. "Was there writing on your wall too? Did it disappear inexplicably?"

"Are you part of this bizarre practical joke?" she snapped. "Is Hawley behind this?"

"I had some on my wall too. It was on a piece of wallpaper, stuck over the actual paper, if you see what I mean: that's how they took it away again. I don't think it's Hawley, myself, because I don't see where he'd find a spare roll of wallpaper, and also, he's clearly going off his chump. And Colonel Dash has disappeared. He's not in his room and Wynn won't say where he is."

"He's unwell."

"I don't think he is," Zeb said. "I think Wynn's lying about that, as he's lying about a lot of things. I know he's been misinterpreting what I've said, including about you. He's trying to set us all fighting over the inheritance, not to mention scaring everyone half to death with ghosts and footsteps and strange writing, and let's be honest, it's worked."

She was looking at him properly now, intent and unblinking. Zeb ploughed on. "I don't like this at all and I want to leave. I think you should too, because the things he's been saying about both of us are awful. He's been refusing to have me driven to the station because of the mist, but if you added your voice to mine and showed we won't put up with this, we might be able to put enough pressure on him."

Elise's face hadn't changed. "You think I should leave. Why, exactly?"

"You were literally crying with fear the other night because of this business. And given the way Wynn has spoken to and about you—"

Her upper lip lifted into a touch of sneer. "Do you disagree?"

"Your personal affairs are none of my business."

"Have you spoken to Bram?"

Zeb had no desire to repeat any of their recent conversations. "I can't get much sense out of him. He feels unjustly done out of his inheritance."

"And is blaming me, of course. My faults as a wife are legion. There is no need to consider Bram's infidelities, his endless pawing of the maids."

"Uh." Zeb had no idea how to respond to that. "I'm sorry to hear it."

She smiled like ice. "Rather them than me."

"Well," Zeb said uneasily. "The point is, I don't trust Wynn's behaviour or intentions, there's a worrying amount of money at stake, and Bram and Hawley are being awfully odd. I'm fed up of it all, and I thought you might have had your fill too."

She gave him a long, considering look. "You don't trust Wynn's intentions."

"No. Not at all. I think, for whatever reason, he's tried to stir up trouble between us all."

"That's not hard," she pointed out.

"No, true, but why invite us in the first place? If he wants to leave Jessamine the house, why not just do that? He could ask her future husband to change his name to Wyckham, if that matters to him."

Elise gave a little tinkling semi-laugh. It was the sort of noise elegant women made rather than snorting. "You believe in Jessamine?"

"Sorry?" Zeb said. "Of course I do, I've seen her—what do you mean?"

She rolled her eyes. "If that girl is seventeen, so am

I. She's unquestionably over twenty-one, and you may detect a resemblance to the Wyckhams in her face, but I don't."

Zeb's jaw dropped. "You don't think she's really Jessamine Wyckham?"

"*Is* there a Jessamine Wyckham?" Elise asked. "Bram attended the funeral of precious Laura's bastard to ingratiate himself with Wynn—"

"Her name was Georgina."

"He saw no baby at the graveside and heard nothing of Wynn raising a child from that day until this visit. Are we really to accept Wynn never divulged the existence of his own granddaughter from birth to now? I don't believe a word of it."

"Jessamine's not his granddaughter," Zeb pointed out. "She's, uh—well, she's Laura's granddaughter, and Laura was Wynn's aunt—"

"And Laura's child was Wynn's," Elise said. "Do pay attention."

Zeb blinked at her. "You think Wynn and Laura—But she was his aunt. She was brought up as his *sister*."

"And she got in the family way at sixteen, while living here with sixteen-year-old Wynn, and Wynn still seethes with hatred of the father who sent her away, and as soon as the old man was dead, Wynn brought her back and filled the house with very expensive portraits of her."

"Well, if you put it like that," Zeb said. "Right. Gosh. That's sordid."

Elise slanted a brow. "So why would Wynn not bring up his granddaughter, the last remnant of beloved Laura, here? Adopt her, even, and make her his heir?"

"He would, wouldn't he? Oh God, you're right."

"Of course I'm right. The little witch is a patent fraud."

"So who is she if she's not Jessamine? And why is Wynn pretending she is?"

Elise shrugged. "I expect she's an actress or some such. Probably sleeping with Wynn by now; she's clearly enterprising. As to why, are you aware Wynn's dying?"

"He says he is."

She paused for a second. "Have you reason to doubt it?"

"He's lied about everything else. And it's been a very useful way for him to get everyone worked up to fever pitch about the imminent inheritance."

An expression of slight annoyance crossed her lovely face. "Well. In any case, my view is that Wynn doesn't want to give his money away."

"If he's not dying, he doesn't have to."

"Even when he's dead," Elise said. "I think he's worked himself into a frenzy about any of you getting your hands on it, because I think he is exactly like Bram, and like his own father come to that, and the very idea of being obliged to part with his fortune puts him through the agonies of the damned."

"A bit harsh?" Zeb suggested. "I know Bram doesn't like to share—"

"Wynn's father falsely imprisoned a woman rather than give her her lawful inheritance."

Zeb stared at her. "What do you mean?"

"Laura's mother. Walter's last wife. Did you not know?"

"I thought she was unwell."

Elise gave a mirthless smile. "Walter left her a very generous legacy, which Wynn's father was disinclined to hand over. He didn't want her spending his money, you see, any more than Bram wanted you spending his. So he kept her confined to the house after the child was born, and brought in a series of complaisant doctors to agree she was ill, then unfit, then mad. I believe she lived some seven years in those conditions before she put an end to herself."

Zeb's stomach lurched. "But—how do you know? I didn't know anything about this!"

"Bram had it from your father. Oh yes, your father knew all about it, but he greatly disliked the idea of a housemaid running around calling herself Wyckham. It would have been so embarrassing, and your father did loathe embarrassment, didn't he?"

"That's not a reason to lock someone away!"

Elise didn't answer. In particular, she didn't say, *Wouldn't he have locked you away if he could?* Maybe she didn't even think it, but Zeb felt the words anyway, felt them heating his face, squirming in his stomach.

"If Wynn's father did that to save money, he was a monster," he said. "And if my father knew and could have stopped it and didn't, then I am ashamed to be his son. But you said Wynn's doing the same thing, and we're talking about the disposition of money after his *death*."

"Maybe he wants to take it with him," Elise said. "There is an Egyptian pyramid in the grounds, after all. Or perhaps he has something else in mind. I am merely speculating, and it scarcely matters anyway."

"It doesn't?"

"You came here to tell me Wynn isn't to be trusted, and I quite agree. I resent being made a part of this as much as you do. And? What's your conclusion?"

Zeb opened his mouth and found he wasn't sure what to say. "Um—well, it's all awful?" he tried. "I want to go home, only Wynn's refusing to let me have the motor or any sort of ride to town and one can't leave terribly easily without that. And I'm afraid Bram is determined to stay—"

"He won't leave while he thinks there's money on the table."

"No. But if you and I both insisted on going, we

might force Wynn's hand, and I could escort you back to London."

Elise considered that. "You are offering to travel across the country with me, and without my husband?"

"I'm your brother-in-law. Nobody could think that inappropriate."

"I feel quite sure a number of people would consider it highly inappropriate. In fact, if there is anything that would help your brother get his precious divorce—"

"That is absolutely not my intention."

She folded her arms. "I dare say not. Whose intention was it?"

"Nobody's!"

Elise looked him up and down. "Do you know, I almost believe you? Hawley did say that your naivety was astonishing."

"I'm not naive," Zeb said. "I simply don't choose to think the worst of people all the time."

"In this house?" Elise said with light astonishment. "Good heavens. But notwithstanding your optimism, I can see the likely outcomes very well. So I will decline your kind offer to run away with you and thereby free Bram and remove an obstacle from Hawley's path. I don't see any advantage for myself in that."

"You could stop caring what either of them think."

That startled her, Zeb could see. He pressed on.

"Hawley isn't worth a snap of your fingers. Bram is clearly not much of a husband. They are greedy, tawdry men and you could stop having them in your life. You could be *happy*."

"I don't think Wyckhams are terribly good at happiness," she said with a twist to her mouth. "That has certainly not been my experience."

"Well, I am," Zeb said. "Or, I have been, and I'm going to be again. And the reason is, I walked away from all this rather than sitting around thinking about how much people wronged me and trying to hurt them back."

Her lips parted, then snapped tight. "Perhaps you are more forgiving than me. And rather more easily walked over."

"Maybe. But I'm happier."

They looked at one another. This was by far the longest conversation he'd ever had with Elise; in fact, it was probably their only exchange that could really be called a conversation. She must be desperately lonely to have talked to him.

"Please," he said impulsively. "I don't like this house, I don't like Wynn, I don't like any of it. Come away from it with me. Leave all this behind. I promise I'm not trying to seduce you."

She gave him the look of a woman who didn't need to be told that, and then she smiled. It was a real smile, one that looked almost rueful, almost affectionate, and it took his breath away. Zeb had always found her glacial beauty mildly intimidating, but he could imagine falling hopelessly in love with that smile.

Bram had probably fallen in love with it too, before he wiped it off her face.

"Well," Elise said as he gazed speechlessly. "I will think about it. Thank you, Zeb. You intend to leave tomorrow?"

"I want to."

She gave a decisive nod. "Talk to me in the morning."

She shut the door. Zeb stood in the corridor, lost for words.

seventeen

Wynn did not appear at lunch. Hawley and Bram were both there, looking frankly shocking, as if neither had slept much. Bram was pouchy and exhausted; Hawley appeared to be grossly hungover. Zeb wondered about making conversation, ran through his options—*By the way I asked your wife to come to London with me* or possibly *Why are you the most selfish, greedy man alive?*—and decided not to bother.

He and Gideon had moved his things to another room, for discretion, and let Jessamine know there was a small problem with insects. Zeb retired there now and was sitting on the bed, running the rosary through his fingers, when he heard a knock. He sprang to the door, hoping for Gideon, and saw the dowdy maid, bearing his evening clothes, cleaned and pressed.

"Thank you so much," he said, stepping well back as she came in to put them in the wardrobe. "I'm very sorry for giving you the trouble, and changing rooms like this."

"Sir."

He wondered if he should go and stand by the window again, but he saw the lines between her eyebrows, the little hints of tension, and the words sprang to his lips. "Is everything all right?"

"How do you mean?"

"Is anyone bothering you?"

She stilled. "Why do you say that? What do you want, sir?"

"I'm not trying to intrude," Zeb said hastily. "You can tell me to mind my own business and I will do just that. But if, for example, someone ought to tell any of the family to keep his hands to himself, I would be happy to step in. If that would help."

"Why?" she asked, a rap of a question. "Why would you?"

"Because you look awfully unhappy. I've actually just been sacked myself, from a rotten job with a dreadful bully who shouted at me all the time, and I have quite strong feelings about making people miserable at work." She was looking at him oddly. He was probably babbling. "I don't want to put you in a difficult position, so ignore me if you prefer. I just thought I should ask if you were all right."

She looked at him a moment longer. Then her face crumpled, and she put her hands over it.

"Oh Lord," Zeb said. "Uh, would you like to sit down?" He grabbed the chair and put it under her, then retreated to the other side of the room, away from the door, so she had a clear path out.

The maid sobbed silently, shoulders heaving. Zeb put his hands behind his back and leaned on them, rather than give in to the urge to offer a consoling touch. "I'm sorry for upsetting you. Is there anything I can do? If you just want to cry in here for a little while, feel free. I can go away." He cursed himself internally. Elise's remark about Bram pawing the maids had been sitting uncomfortably in his mind, and he'd blurted the thought out, and now look what he'd done. "Or I really will do my best to help if I can."

"Can I trust you?" she said into her hands. "In confidence?"

"Yes."

"Do you promise?"

Zeb couldn't help his jaw tightening. He said, "I will keep any confidence unless there is a true and urgent need to reveal it. I won't take it lightly, I swear."

She was silent for what felt like a very long time, then

she spoke deliberately. "It was Mr. Bram, sir. He made… advances on me. He insisted. I couldn't—he would not let me refuse. I did refuse. He didn't stop."

Zeb couldn't reply for a second. He would have liked to deny it, to say his brother couldn't possibly have done such a thing, but he knew very well that men did. His stomach was clenched hard.

"I'm very, very sorry to hear you say so," he managed. "Are you hurt?"

"No. No, I—" She gave a sudden, ugly, heaving sob.

Zeb fished out his handkerchief but a quick glance showed it was unacceptable. "Would you like a handkerchief? Er, I will have to walk by you to get a clean one."

She hesitated, then nodded without looking up. Zeb skirted her as widely as he could, grabbed his last clean handkerchief, and offered it with the longest possible arm. She took it and applied it to her face. "I beg your pardon, sir," she said, muffled. "You're very kind."

"Take your time."

She sniffled a bit, then looked up, face red and eyes wet. "Thank you, sir," she said softly.

"I'm so sorry. Can I do anything? If you want me to speak to anyone—"

"No! Don't say anything, to him or anyone. I don't want to lose my post, or my good name. I don't want Mr. Bram to know I told."

Zeb wished he could say, *Of course you will not be blamed or dismissed*, and knew perfectly well he couldn't; even in a normal household, that would not be a given. He wanted to do something and had no idea what it should be. The helplessness was enraging. "I won't do anything to risk your post without your permission. But at least you ought not have to go anywhere near him."

"I have seen to that." She dabbed at her eyes, recovering her composure. "I beg your pardon, sir, but there is nothing to be done, or at least, nothing for you to do. I told you so you know what kind of man your brother is. That's all I wanted. Thank you for the handkerchief." She rose.

"Wait," Zeb said. "I'm sorry, Miss—what's your name?"

"Rachel, sir."

"Miss Rachel. Is there a woman here? I mean, do you have someone you can talk to?"

She hesitated. "Do you think I should tell Mrs. Bram? Would she help me?"

Rather them than me rang in his ears. "I...don't know," he said. "I'm not sure I'd risk it."

Her shoulders sagged. Zeb cursed his family, again, and his own uselessness. "Look, I won't do or say anything unless you want me to. But if you think there's any way at all I can help, please tell me, and I'll do what I can. And, for what it's worth, I am truly, deeply sorry."

She met his eyes, examining his face in a long, silent look. "Yes," she said at last. "I think you are."

Zeb could do nothing after that but pace restively around the room. There was no sign of Gideon, and he kept thinking about Rachel's wretched tears, Elise's cold facade breaking with that smile, Jessamine-who-might-not-be-Jessamine. And of course, Colonel Dash, even now trapped in a dusty room, banging on the door, thirsty, panicking, unheard. The feeling that gave him—claustrophobic, confined, constrained—made him want to kick off his own skin.

He tried to tell himself that they had no idea what had really happened to Dash. It did no good. Once the thought had come, it wouldn't leave him, and he ended up prowling the house again, ears straining for cries for help.

He heard nothing. He saw nobody. His footsteps echoed flatly, the mist lay thick around the house, and it felt like the end of the world.

It was past four, the mist-thickened day starting to dim into night, and the twilight cast shadows that gathered in the corners and shifted around him. It would be very easy to imagine them moving as he walked, as Hawley's living darkness or just a mass of thick-legged spiders.

"Oh, stop it," he muttered under his breath. He had no need to do Wynn's work by scaring himself half to death.

He made his way around the west wing as best he could, trying every door he came across, and then went up into the central tower. He didn't really think Dash was being kept here—there were only four rooms on Elise and Bram's floor; they would surely have heard shouts or thumping—but he was trying to be thorough and methodical, and that meant every door. One led to a stair, and curiosity took him upward, into what was clearly the cupola.

This floor looked unused, with a few old pieces of furniture haphazardly stowed by the walls and a lot of dust on the floor. There were two doors. Zeb opened the first and saw a dark lumber room, cluttered and cobwebbed. He shut the door hastily and turned to the second.

It was locked, but the key was in the keyhole. He turned it.

This room was also dark, but Zeb could just about make out what looked like a bed. There was no gas mantle, but a candlestick stood on a little table near the door. He patted his pockets for matches, found a box, and lit the candle. It flared, bringing the room to life, and Zeb sucked in a breath so hard it hurt.

"What the—"

The room had a single bed frame, a small table, a

metal chamber pot, a single window covered by crossed iron bars. That was all. There was no place to put things, and no things to be put.

And there was writing all over the walls. It went from the floor to a few inches higher than Zeb's head—perhaps the full reach of a short person on tiptoe—leaving only a strip at the top where the writer apparently couldn't reach, and every single accessible inch was written and rewritten on, in layer after layer of scrawled pencil or chalk or even carving, viciously dug into the plasterwork with a nail or scratched with a pin. It was the work of years, Zeb thought as he turned and stared. Someone had been in this room for years, with nothing else to do but write on the walls.

He moved towards the walls, not wanting to see, compelled to look. It was hard to make out anything in the overlapping jagged scribbles at first, but he held the candle close, and saw the words emerge, horribly and urgently repetitive, like the patterns on the wallpaper downstairs.

LET ME OUT

LET ME OUT

LET ME OUT

There were other words too. *Walter*, gouged into the walls, and *Wilfred. Pig. Die.* That was Wynn's father. And again and again, *Laura. Laura. Laura.*

Laura's mother, Walter's widow, the nameless

housemaid. Wynn's father had called her mad and kept her confined to the house. She had been locked up here for seven years to keep her legacy, Wyckham money, in the family.

Cabin'd, cribb'd, confin'd. Zeb could feel the sensations building up in his own muscles, the angry jittery cramping misery of being trapped. If it had been him in this room, this long, he'd have gone mad. He'd have smashed the window in sheer, unbearable desperation to get out, no matter if the only way was down—

There were bars on the window. She couldn't jump. They hadn't even let her do that.

The walls closed in on him like the squeeze of a giant fist. He stood in the room, hands shaking, the wobbling candle making light and shadows jump on the walls that shrieked rage and pain and despair, and he didn't notice the tears in his eyes till they started to fall.

Zeb did not want to go down to dinner. He didn't want to see anyone in his family ever again.

He'd more or less run down from the terrible tower room and headed straight through the hall and out the front door. He'd wanted to walk for hours, or days. Unfortunately, it was sodding cold, very dark, and unpleasantly thick with cobwebby mist, and after about a minute outside, the horror of confinement started to be replaced with thoughts of getting lost in the grounds and death by exposure.

He returned, chilled and damp, paced the halls a bit more, and finally went and sat in his room for what must have been an hour, running his beads through his fingers, staring at the blank walls, imagining words. He'd heard nothing from Gideon and he wanted, *needed* to get out of here with an urgency that clawed at him. He could not spend another day in this accursed house with its pestilential inhabitants, or he would rip off one of Wynn's limbs and use it to beat his brother to a pulp. Or, at least, would stand in strong danger of losing his temper.

Elise had listened. She'd help him leave, hopefully with Gideon, and the first place he was going to go after that would be a lawyer, or a private enquiry agent, or the police. He would tell people and someone would surely do something about some of this, even if Zeb wasn't quite sure of what he could prove to be a crime. It was all too wrong and he couldn't bear much more.

He dressed, more out of excessive nervous energy than enthusiasm. That involved a lengthy search for the shirt studs he still hadn't picked up, but even so, he found himself first down. Apparently everyone else was even less enthused about the evening to come than he was.

Gideon appeared in the drawing room a few moments later with a rat-trap mouth suggesting he had also had a trying day. He glanced swiftly around, and strode to join Zeb at the drinks table.

"I have to get out of here," Zeb said without preamble. "Any luck? Hello."

"I've achieved nothing. Wynn kept me busy all day. Which, in the circumstances—" Gideon rolled his eyes.

"Has something happened?"

"Did you not hear the commotion? Good Lord, I thought people would hear it in Exeter." Gideon poured himself a very generous sherry. "This afternoon, Bram and Wynn had a long discussion about your and Hawley's failings. As a result, Wynn said he would make Bram his heir if he divorced Mrs. Bram and promised to marry Jessamine as soon as decency allows. He agreed."

"Of course he did. I hope he enjoys seeing his divorce proceedings in the papers," Zeb said. "But—"

"I haven't finished; I have barely started. Your brother agreed to seek a divorce and marry Jessamine. He went out. Ten minutes later, Hawley came in with Jessamine and said she had consented to be his wife."

"Oh my God."

"Wynn said he would need time to think before giving permission, and called Bram back to advise him of developments. That went down poorly. Wynn then told them he would need to consider which of the two was the more fit to wed his ward, and they both went out in some discord." He knocked back half his sherry in a gulp. "And twenty minutes later, Mrs. Bram descended and asked for a private conversation with Wynn."

"Oh my *God*."

"Wynn said he needed to rest before dinner, and will see her at nine tomorrow. I assume she knows where the bodies are buried and intends to destroy both of their characters to Wynn. Tonight should be special."

"If that is what she intends," Zeb said. "She might just have wanted the motor: I spoke to her today and I think she agreed to come with me. Or maybe it's both and she wants to fire a parting shot before we leave. Burn it all down and sow the ground with salt. I don't suppose I'd blame her."

"Perhaps not. But Bram and Hawley both really believed the prize was within their grasp this afternoon and they were both very seriously disappointed. If they think Mrs. Bram intends to scupper them tomorrow, they won't take it well."

"No. Ugh. Does Elise know what's going on? Because if she just wanted to talk about leaving—"

Gideon took a swift step away from him. "I hope the mist will have cleared tomorrow, yes. I understand it can linger for several days, but I expect the severity to decrease."

"We shall see," Wynn remarked from the doorway.

He had Jessamine on his arm, in a pretty cream frock, wearing her long hair down. She still looked very young to Zeb, but then, he had no sisters and had never mixed with young ladies, so what did he know. "I would expect at least another day of mist, perhaps two, and I shall not have the motor taken out before I am quite sure it is safe. I dare say I am a very cautious man, but I should not care to be responsible for something happening to my staff or my family." He beamed benevolently. Zeb thought of Rachel, and the silent agony of the walls upstairs, and took a deep, preparatory breath.

The scream was high and dreadful, a shriek of pure fear that cut off with a sickening crunch and thud. Zeb sprinted out to the hall, just behind Gideon, and saw a crumpled form at the bottom of the stone staircase. Her satin gown pooled ivory around her splayed legs. Blood pooled deep red around her head.

"Christ," Zeb said. "Elise!" He ran forward and dropped to a knee, reaching for her, but didn't touch: not with the angle of her neck and her wide, sightless eyes. "Oh God, I think she's dead. Gideon, she's *dead*!"

There was no reply. He looked up and saw that Gideon was gazing at the top of the stairs. Zeb glanced that way, saw nothing. "Gideon?"

"Oh, dear," Wynn said behind him. "Oh dear, oh dear me. Lady Ravendark herself."

Zeb had never hated anyone more than in that moment. "She's dead, you shit," he said thickly. "Someone fetch Bram. And send for a doctor, I suppose. The authorities."

"Police," Gideon said, the single word bitten out. "We need to summon the police."

"Elise!" It was a shriek. Jessamine pushed past Zeb and fell to her knees at Elise's head. "Oh, Elise, no, no!" She curved forward over the body.

"What the devil?" Bram was standing at the top of the stairs. As Zeb stared up, he saw Hawley arrive on the landing, behind Bram. They both looked down with expressions of almost comical horror, then Bram said, "Elise?" and began to descend.

Jessamine rose. Her expression was ghastly, her hands bloody, and blood stained her cream dress at the knees. It looked obscene. "Dead!" she said wildly. "She's dead! Oh, she's dead!"

Bram was at the bottom of the stairs now, standing over his wife's crumpled form, mouth slack. Zeb said, "Wynn, take Jessamine away."

Wynn didn't move. Zeb looked round and saw he had his hand clutched to his heart. Gideon took Jessamine by the arm and said, "Let us give Mr. Bram room."

"He hated her!" Jessamine shrieked. "She hated him! And now she's dead!"

Zeb shot a look at Gideon, who pulled Jessamine so

hard she stumbled sideways, still wailing. He looked like he was thinking about administering a slap, and Zeb wished he would. He said, "Bram?" and was ignored.

Hawley had come down now. He and Bram stood over the body of the woman they had both loved, at least in their ways, at some point, probably. They had wanted her and fought over her and hated her. She had perhaps loved them both once, certainly humiliated them both, and unquestionably stood in the way of either of them getting his hands on a hundred and fifty thousand pounds.

Bram looked stunned. Hawley's face was twisted in a way that suggested he might weep, or laugh.

"There's been an accident," Zeb said redundantly. Nobody replied.

And the proper thing now would be for Zeb to comfort his brother, so suddenly and violently made a widower, but he looked at dead Elise and thought of Rachel, and he couldn't choke out a word.

eighteen

ESSAMINE WAS REMOVED IN hysterics. Wynn indicated that he was in a state of shock and tottered away on Gideon's arm. Hawley stood by the body for several moments without speaking, then went out for a smoke. Bram announced, "See that she is decently disposed," and walked away.

That left Zeb to supervise the footman and chauffeur carrying Elise's body with its horribly lolling neck into an anteroom in the east wing. He saw her properly disposed and covered by a blanket, then he went to his room, washed his hands till they felt raw, although he had not touched her, and sat alone on the floor, knees to his chest, running the rosary through his fingers.

Eventually, there was a knock, and Gideon came in with a plate of sandwiches.

"Oh," Zeb said, suddenly realising he was very hungry. "Oh, that's a good idea."

"I made these; the kitchen is deserted. Are you all right?"

"Not really."

Gideon folded himself down onto the floor, next to him, and put an arm over his shoulders. Zeb leaned in to him. They both munched sandwiches, more through necessity than enthusiasm, and Zeb slumped back as soon as his immediate hunger was assuaged.

Gideon pushed the plate away once they were both done. "Have you converted?"

"Converted what?"

"Yourself. I mean, have you become a Catholic?"

"No?" Zeb said, bewildered. "I don't go to church." He wasn't an atheist as such, but divine service had been a torture instrument throughout his childhood: be ordered to sit still and silent for an hour, fail, be punished, regular as clockwork. A benevolent deity would surely have kinder worshippers.

"I didn't think so, but—" Gideon pointed at the floor.

Zeb looked down and saw the rosary where he'd dropped it. "Oh! Oh, yes, no. I lost my beads. That string I used to carry? So I thought I'd get a rosary instead.

People think it's odd if a man plays with a necklace, but if the beads are divided into groups of ten and there's a cross on it, that's perfectly reasonable. I say reasonable: I've had three people on omnibuses call me a Papist."

"May I?" Gideon waited for his nod and picked the string up. It was a nice rosary, with smooth, dark brown oval beads on a chain, and a thick, chunky metal cross. He ran it through his fingers, thumbed the edges of the cross, twisted the string into a cat's cradle in imitation of Zeb's frequent practice, then handed it back. "That's quite satisfying. I'm sorry you lost your other beads."

Zeb shrugged. It didn't do to get too attached to portable things. "I suspect my supervisor at my last job threw them away. I left them on my desk and they were gone when I got back. He hated it when I played with them."

Gideon's breath hissed out. "Did you explain to him why you have them?"

"No point. Once people have decided you're not listening to them, they don't listen to you. It's always *Stop fidgeting and pay attention,* as if that wasn't what fidgeting is for. Gideon, what's going to happen? With Elise?"

"I can tell you what should happen. The police should be summoned, urgently. Wynn insists that he can't send someone out to travel for hours on a cold misty night, and perhaps that's reasonable, but he certainly ought to do it in the morning."

"You said before that we need the police," Zeb said. "But she fell down the stairs. If she tripped and fell, it's an accident. I would like you to tell me she tripped and fell, please."

"I'm sorry." Gideon grimaced. "I saw movement at the top of the stairs. It was an impression only, not enough to identify or even guess at a person. But I saw someone moving away; I am absolutely certain of it."

Zeb hunched in on himself. "Hawley and Bram were both up there. Close by."

"I know. And those are steep stone stairs, and... If she was pushed, it's murder, Zeb. I don't know if anyone would be able to prove it, but morally at least, it's murder."

Murder. Zeb tried to make his mind fit around the word. Could he imagine his brother walking up behind Elise, for whose love he had betrayed Zeb, and putting out his hands and pushing? Could he picture Hawley doing that to a woman for whom he had once felt passion? All for the sake of a hundred and fifty thousand pounds?

Yes, of course he could.

"Shit," he said. "*Shit.* This might be my fault. If she only wanted to talk to Wynn about leaving, and they thought she was planning to spill the beans—"

"She probably was planning that. Do you really think she would let one or the other of them win?"

"Maybe not. But I think she wanted to come with me."

Zeb felt horribly small and sad and lonely. He'd barely known Elise. She hadn't been a very nice person. They'd shared a single proper conversation and one real smile, and now he felt nothing short of bereaved. "I wish—I wish—"

"I'm so sorry." Gideon tightened his arm. "God almighty, what that damned fellow has done. Can one be prosecuted for inspiring people to murder one another?"

"Wynn can't have meant this. Surely it's gone too far now. He must see it's gone too far. That is, if he suspects—"

"Of course he suspects. He asked me repeatedly how I thought it could have happened, and talked about the family difficulties and how she had wanted to speak to him tomorrow. He didn't say, 'Which of Hawley or Bram did it?' but he might as well have. Sorry," Gideon added swiftly. "He's your brother. I'm sorry."

"Did you tell him what you saw?"

"I did not, but it was obvious they were both near the top of the stairs. And I didn't get the impression he was panicking. If anything, he was enjoying himself."

"Christ." Zeb took that in. "You think he *wanted* this to happen?"

"Or doesn't care that it did. I don't know. I have no idea what's going on in his head, except that I very much doubt it's remorse, because he is still stirring the pot."

"This is insane. *He* is insane. We can't just sit here and let him do this!"

"I quite agree. The question is what we can do about it."

Zeb had no immediate answer to that. Gideon hugged his knees to his chest. "You've repeatedly confronted him to no effect. He's got the footmen and the chauffeur on his side, and they're all thugs. We've no allies in this house. So—"

"But Elise is dead! He can't just pretend it never happened, not with a houseful of people. What's he going to do, kill us all and hide the bodies? That was a rhetorical question," he added quickly.

"Was it?" Gideon said. "What *is* the damned man's intention here? Because he seemed determined to wind up all your nerves to snapping point, and now someone has snapped, and I don't know what the devil he'll do next!"

His voice had risen. Zeb said, "Are you all right?"

"No! We're trapped in here! The walls are twelve feet high, Wynn has suborned the staff, Mrs. Bram has been *murdered*, and we can't get out! What the devil are we going to do?"

Zeb somehow hadn't expected that. He'd come to know Gideon as the calm, rational supervisor who always seemed to see a solution or a sensible path. He'd looked on in awe in the nine months they'd had together, wishing he could be like that, knowing he couldn't. Gideon was self-controlled, remembered what needed remembering, made and kept plans, organised his life. Gideon didn't make mistakes and lose his head.

Except he did, and Zeb would do well to remember that. Gideon could be unable to cope, just like everyone else, and now he was on the verge of panic in a situation wildly outside his experience.

Well, Zeb had plenty of experience of panic, and uncontrolled situations, and Wyckhams. He might as well use it.

"Gideon." He squirmed round and grabbed his face. "Gideon. Lover. *Listen*. Tomorrow Wynn will surely have to summon a doctor, if only for the look of it. So when his messenger leaves, or returns, or the doctor leaves, we are leaving with them. Simple as that. We'll ask for a lift, but if we have to walk out with just the clothes on our backs, we will do that. We'll wait by the blasted gate all day if we have to. And if he doesn't call someone, we will find a ladder and scale the sodding wall, but either way we are *leaving*. All right?"

"Not really," Gideon said through his teeth. "That is, yes, absolutely, we will flee from here like thieves. Good idea. It merely entails abandoning my post and my possessions, which I can't afford to replace, just when I had thought I was clawing my way out—sorry. Sorry." He took a deep, shuddering breath and let it out slowly. "You're absolutely right, of course. We concentrate on getting out, and I'll worry about the future when we've dealt with the present."

"Well, don't worry about money, at least," Zeb said. "I can float you until you have a new job, and if you have to abandon your wardrobe, I'll replace it. So forget about that entirely, and concentrate on getting us both out of here."

Gideon looked at him for a moment. Then he said, "Zeb, I really cannot bear it if you're going mad too. You just got sacked, if you recall? So while that is a very kind offer—"

"I have money, or I will. What day is it?"

"The first of December."

"Then I have money. My publisher pays quarterly."

"Your what?"

This was really not how Zeb had wanted to tell him this. He'd thought of quietly dropping the news later, in London, over dinner, when he was sure of how it might be received. "I've written a couple of books. The advance for the first two wasn't very generous, but they've sold rather well. Very well. Actually, between the advance on the new contract and my royalties on the current books, I'm due about three thousand this quarter. So you see—"

Gideon was waving his hands. "Wait, wait, wait. You wrote a *book*? When did you do that?"

"I've been doing it for a while. Mostly at work. It's probably why people keep sacking me."

Zeb could see Gideon putting together memories. "You were writing a book. In the office. Well, that explains why I never had more than about forty percent of your attention."

"You always had my full attention," Zeb assured him. "The job didn't, I grant you."

"And—did you say three *thousand*? Three thousand pounds?"

"Guineas, actually."

He hadn't told anyone this before: as a habitually broke man with habitually broke friends, he didn't want either to brag or to be deluged with requests for ten pounds till next quarter day. He felt a certain embarrassment telling Gideon now. But he'd asked, and he needed to believe Zeb could cushion his financial catastrophe, plus it was a conversation about something other than this house, Elise, Wynn.

Gideon looked stunned. "But that's astonishing. That is absolutely wonderful. My God, Zeb, congratulations! Why did you not say? And why on earth have you not told your family this? They've been calling you a worthless sponger for days!"

"Because they think I'm a worthless sponger, I suppose," Zeb said. "Hawley and Bram would have a field day mocking what I write, and I would rather not be ridiculed for it."

"Well, I'm sorry. You *should* be able to share this with your family. You should be immensely proud of yourself because this is tremendous. Ah, what is it you write that's so unfit for the family?"

"It's fit for most families, just not mine. I write children's stories."

"Good Lord. Really?" Gideon cocked his head. "Actually, I can see that, now you say it. That's marvellous. My sister's twins are six now, and I'd love to find them a new favourite book because we've all read them their current obsession to the point of nausea. Might they like your work?"

"Possibly. The first one is called *The Fairies of Faraway Meadow*."

Gideon's mouth dropped open. "What," he said with force. "*What?* What the—*You* wrote that? *You* are Zinnia Waters?"

"You know it?"

"Know it? I can recite it!" Gideon yelped. "'Around the corner, down the lane, and just a little way out of sight lies the doorway to Faraway Meadow'—I have read that more times than I want to remember. I can't take the twins on a walk without them spotting a dozen corners, lanes, and doorways that might lead to your blasted fairyland! My brother-in-law says he forced himself back to work just so he wasn't at home being ordered to read *Faraway Meadow* twice a day!"

It was always nice to hear one's work had caused significant anguish. Zeb beamed. "He'll be horrified to know the third one comes out in February, then. And I've signed a contract for another three."

"My nieces will be overjoyed. They eat, sleep, play, and live *Faraway Meadow*. You can have no idea how they love it. Or do you? I suppose England is full of similarly possessed children."

"The publisher does receive quite a lot of letters."

"I imagine they do. Good God almighty, Zinnia Waters. I don't suppose you'd sign my nieces' books for them?"

"I've actually just got early copies of the new one. They could have it for Christmas? One each to avoid fighting?"

"My nieces will adore me," Gideon said. "Oh good Lord."

"What?"

"I was just imagining telling the girls that I know Zinnia Waters and how excited they would be. And then I thought about trying to explain *how* I know her."

"You will need a story," Zeb agreed.

"I don't want a story. I want to tell them at the very least that Zinnia Waters is my friend and I am immensely proud of that. Proud of her. I don't know if I have the right to say I'm proud of you, but I really am."

"Well." Zeb could feel himself going pink. "It's just books."

"It's not just books. You've obviously worked extremely hard, for a long time, and—" He stilled, then went on, slower. "And you didn't just hide that from your family. You hid it from me."

Zeb's stomach dropped. "It wasn't a secret. I just—well, I didn't know if it would come to anything. It might very well have failed, and I didn't want to have to tell you about another failure."

"God," Gideon said. "You should not have felt like that. I shouldn't have made you feel like that."

He had, though. There had always been that element of Gideon the sensible one, wearily dealing with Zeb's disorganisation, reminding him of things to be done, finding things he'd put down somewhere, coping with another job of work undone. Zeb hadn't minded, precisely, or if he had minded, that was his problem. Gideon was competent and organised; naturally it was tiresome for him to deal with habitual chaos. Zeb had grown up used to endless exasperation from his father and brother, and Gideon had been infinitely more tolerant than either of them. All the same, Zeb had undeniably wanted to show him a proven success, rather than a manuscript he hadn't finished, a dream that might founder.

"I wanted to see if it would go anywhere before I told you, that's all," he said. "I wanted to get something right."

"You got so much right." Gideon's voice was aching.

"So much. I'd never kissed a man before you, and you made me fit into my own life. You were endlessly patient with me. You made me laugh. You made me *happy*. And in return, I didn't make you feel you could trust me with your dreams, or your trouble with your brother, or—Jesus, did I do anything at all for you?"

"You bent over backwards for me at work. You sorted out a thousand problems. You took out spiders and never laughed at me for it. For God's sake, I still use the magic box!"

Gideon had instituted the magic box. If Zeb emptied his pockets into the box by the door when he came home then, as if by magic, things would be there when he looked for them. It was a ridiculously simple idea—perhaps one he might have or should have thought up for himself, but he was never terribly good at that sort of thing. In any case, it had worked like, well, magic. Gideon had bought him a lovely carved wooden box for the purpose, and then a second one that lived by his armchair, and repeated *Magic box!* every time he saw Zeb with unconsidered things in his hands until it had become habit. He still heard Gideon's voice in his ears every time he came home and had got really quite good at not losing his keys.

"That's still working?" Gideon said. "Oh, good. I did think—wait. Wait. The magic box. As in, the *queen's* magic box?"

"Oh. Um."

"The Queen of the Fairies' magic box, which contains whatever you need when you open it?"

That magic box had been stolen by goblins in the second Faraway Meadow book, thus putting the plot in motion. Zeb realised he was flushing. "Well, it gave me the idea."

"I thought of you every time I read that blasted book," Gideon said. "Every single time. I thought it was just—I don't know. Fate being unkind."

"No, it was me. Not me being unkind, I mean; I wrote it because it's such a good idea. Your idea. And what I said before about another failure—I didn't mean you made me feel incapable. I meant, you always said I just needed to find work that suited me, and I wanted to show you that I had. Ta-da, look at me, published author!" He grimaced. "This wasn't quite how I imagined telling you."

"But if I had paid less attention to your inability to put your clothes away and more to what you were actually doing and thinking—"

"Look, I'm a shambles," Zeb said. "I turn up late, fail to get my hair cut, and forget everything, and it drove you mad. I do know that."

"You are also profoundly kind, have behaved through the nightmare of the last few days with astonishing decency and steadfast courage, *and* you're a bestselling author. And something of a shambles, granted, but right now, I cannot remember why I let that matter."

"It does matter sometimes. I know it does. It's not precisely entertaining always losing my things and leaving jobs undone and having people be cross or disappointed. I know it bothered you." He took a deep breath, letting the truth bloom in his chest. "But you wanted me anyway."

Gideon's eyes snapped to his. "Yes," he said quietly. "I wanted you from the moment I saw you, and that was terrifying. You changed my practical, functional, joyless life when you offered to buy me that drink, and then you built me—us—a new life, one I'd never had the nerve to reach for myself, over every day that followed. Losing what we had was the stupidest thing I have ever done."

"We both made a pig's ear of it. Could we stop doing that?"

"I doubt you could stop being a shambles," Gideon said. "It seems to me an inherent part of your nature. I could approach that better."

Zeb had to swallow a hard lump in his throat. "But you did. You helped me make my life function, so it wasn't a sequence of small disasters, or big ones. If I'd listened to you, I wouldn't have messed everything up."

"If I had listened to you, neither of us would have."

Zeb took his hand, feeling the fingers interlace, the palms connect, a shiver running up his arm. "Suppose we start again. Suppose we get out of this house, and go home, and do better this time."

"Yes," Gideon said. "Please."

They stared at each other. It was cold, and the candles were guttering. Elise was dead, Wynn was deranged, and the house was a prison, but here they were, hands twined, together.

"I expect a sensible person would say, now we've got that out of the way, we should discuss all the terrible things," Zeb said. "But I think you should come to bed with me, because I want to hold you and be with you, and I can't think of anything that matters more than that."

Gideon's hand tightened. "Agreed."

nineteen

Zeb woke with Gideon's arm heavy over him and dread heavy in his stomach. He couldn't remember why either of those was the case for a moment, and then he did. He didn't realise he'd made a noise, but Gideon said, "Good morning."

"Morning."

Gideon kissed his ear, presumably because it was all he could reach. "We're us, today? Us again?"

Zeb didn't know what he meant for a moment, then he remembered. The promise he'd wanted to make that wouldn't feel like an impossible pledge. It sent a shudder of joy through him. "Still us."

Gideon's arm tightened. "Good."

They'd clung to each other for what had felt like hours

last night, relishing touch and skin and breath. Zeb hadn't wanted to fuck, with Elise's broken body downstairs, and Gideon hadn't suggested it either. They'd just held themselves together by holding one another, letting closeness salve the little wounds and silence make promises that neither of them dared voice.

They were going to start again. Gideon still cared. Everything was going to be all right—for them, if nobody else—as soon as they could leave this bloody house.

"I'll need my satchel," Zeb said aloud. "I brought the manuscript of book four and it's nearly done."

There was a tiny pause, then Gideon said, "Keep it with you so we can leave in a hurry. Good thought."

He didn't say *What are you talking about?* or *Could you try to make sense?* or complain about Zeb beginning a conversation halfway through. He'd just worked out where Zeb's thoughts must be. He'd always been good at that.

"I missed you so much," Zeb said into Gideon's shoulder.

"So did I. Daily."

"Will you come home with me? My landlady lets me have people sleep on the sofa for an extra ten shillings a week, not that I'd want you to sleep on the sofa. I know you have to find a new job and all that, of course, and I dare say we oughtn't rush into anything, and I really am trying to be sensible, but—"

"I will absolutely come home with you, if you want me to." He kissed Zeb's hair. "There's something I think I should tell you."

"Mmm?"

Gideon took a deep breath. "I went to a club. That one you showed me, but I didn't want to go in? Well, I did. I went."

Zeb had felt quite strongly that Gideon should meet more people of their sort. Gideon had resisted. He'd been terrified of a police raid, the risk of exposure, and, Zeb suspected, of the reality of it. One thing to have a lover in a room away from all eyes, quite another to go to a club and be seen.

"I'm glad you did. Was it good?"

Gideon grimaced. "It... I think it was good. I spoke to some people. Everyone was very friendly."

Zeb cast an affectionate glance at him, with his striking features and patrician nose. "I bet they were."

"And, uh. There was a man. Two men." It was still dark, but Zeb would put good money Gideon was blushing. He could imagine the heat sweep over his skin. "It was a performance, I suppose, or at least I hope it was, because...well. One of them announced the other had lost a bet. He told him to get on his knees in the middle of the room with his hands behind his back and suck him. He held his hair, and called him names, and it was—Christ."

"Did you like it?"

"I don't know. Yes. Yes, I did."

"Just watching, or…?"

"No," Gideon said. "No. I, uh, it was very—and a man—he sucked me off. I let him."

Zeb reached for his hand. That would be the second man Gideon had ever done anything with, and he hoped the fellow had made a decent job of it. "Was *that* good?"

"Yes. Sort of. Yes, it was good, but I didn't know him. I kept thinking, I wished I'd gone with you. If you'd done that there and then, it would have been—Lord."

"I'm at your disposal. Did you go again?"

"I was going to. But when I was approaching, there were police on the street, a couple of them loitering as they do, and I walked past without looking and went home. And before I got the nerve up to try again, I ran entirely out of money, so that was that. But I wanted you to know, I did try, and I'd like to go again. With you."

"Then we will," Zeb said. "Is there anything else on your mind, at all?"

Gideon took a deep breath. "The things that chap was saying to his partner—"

"You liked it?"

"He was quite offensive. But some of it—telling him he wanted it—"

"The other night," Zeb said. "I was on my knees with

my hands behind my back, and you were telling me how much I loved it."

"That," Gideon said hoarsely. "Exactly that."

"Well, I do, so if you tell me how much I love it, that's just true. And what I most want in the world right now is for you to tell me exactly what you want me to do, and then point out what an eager little bitch I am while I'm doing it."

"Oh Jesus, Zeb. Please," Gideon said helplessly. "Please. Can I?"

"I absolutely insist you do. I will tell you if I don't like anything," he added, knowing Gideon as he did. "I will say if it's too much, and not take offence. But that is *very* far from my problem right now."

Since his erection was jammed into Gideon's hip, this was inarguable. Gideon took a deep breath. Then he rolled over, pushing Zeb gently onto his back, swung a leg over his chest, and straddled him.

"Go on," Zeb said. "Just as you imagined."

"I thought about this so much," Gideon said softly. "Over you, watching your face. And—" He caught Zeb's hands, leaning forward to pull them above his head, interlaced their fingers, pressed down.

Zeb twisted under him, feeling his weight. "Yes. Like this."

"I thought sometimes about holding you and fucking

between your legs," Gideon whispered. "I thought about how you'd be so hard, and those noises you made—make—when you want to come, and the way you look. How I'd make you wait till you were moaning."

"Did you let me come?"

"You did anyway," Gideon said on a breath. "I'd pleasure myself between your legs and you'd love it so much, you begged for it, and came because you couldn't help it—"

Zeb whimpered. Gideon's breath hissed out harshly. "That. That noise you make. That's what I want."

He shifted, working his prick between Zeb's thighs and holding them shut tight with his own legs, hands entwined. Zeb's blood was thudding in his veins. His prick felt hot and tight, and incredibly sensitive to the lightest possible brush of Gideon's belly above him.

They were watching each other's face as the slowly brightening grey dawn lit the room. Fingers embracing, palms kissing, and Gideon thrusting gently. No lubrication, just warm flesh, the friction of a smooth prick against his thighs, Gideon's eyes on his, and the fact that he'd spent solitary nights wanking over this image. Zeb tilted his hips up, trying to press them together, the pressure in his own prick demanding touch, but Gideon was holding himself up just a little too high for anything but an occasional slide over the very head of Zeb's prick.

He gave a frustrated moan and felt Gideon's shudder of response.

"Please," he whispered. "I want to hear it."

Gideon paused. Zeb said, "Say it."

Gideon swallowed audibly. "You are so desperate," he whispered. "You want it so much. I can feel you shaking and hear you moaning. God, you love it."

Zeb could hear the naked desire in Gideon's voice, and it felt like an electric charge all over his skin. "Please. Please, Gideon, touch me."

Gideon's hands pressed harder. "Not yet."

Zeb was squirming now, entirely trapped by Gideon's hands and constricting legs. Gideon's cock was wet now, leaking against his skin, rubbing his balls, his motions becoming more urgent, less controlled. "Oh God, please," Zeb said. "You know I want it. Anything, if you let me come."

Gideon reared up. "Roll over."

Zeb rolled, with due care for his rigid erection. Gideon straddled him again, once again nudging his prick between Zeb's thighs, this time rubbing against his balls and buttocks, moving in short thrusts. His hand came between Zeb's shoulder blades, pushing him down.

"Please." Zeb was writhing in earnest, for the friction of cloth under him, and the joy of Gideon's weight, and very much for the provocative value. "Tell me."

"You know you love it. You love to fuck and you love me fucking you, and you're such an eager little tart—"

Oh, that's my good boy. "Hopeless," Zeb agreed. "Show me how I love it."

He felt a hand snake under him, wrap around his prick, and for a second he thought he might spill there and then. He let out a shuddering moan. Gideon whimpered himself. "Oh, God, Zeb, tell me—"

"I am an absolute shameless fucking *slut* for you," Zeb said, and then Gideon was driving between Zeb's legs, spasming, coming over him as he convulsively jerked Zeb's prick without rhythm or skill, just frantic need, and Zeb had to muffle his shout as he spent into the bedclothes.

Gideon slumped over his back. Zeb lay, flattened, with Gideon's hand still clutching him, both of them heaving with the need to get their breath back.

"God," Gideon said at last. "*God*. Christ. Uh, was that all right?"

"Is that a serious question?"

It wasn't the acts, or even the words themselves. It was the desire that had wracked Gideon's body, and the fact that he'd dug out the truth of that desire and trusted it to Zeb. That was what he'd wanted; that was a gift he'd hug to himself all his life. "It was very much all right," he said, because Gideon might need that. "Only, next time, I want you to fuck me all the way, and call me a trollop while you do it, please."

"You're going to give me a stroke. I will actually die in bed and then you'll have some explaining to do. Would you like that? Not the stroke. The other thing."

"I feel like a man who's saying he'll do anything should be taken at his word."

"When you put it that way," Gideon said, and buried his face in Zeb's neck.

It was the best possible start to the day. Zeb had a strong suspicion that things would start going rapidly downhill once they got up, so he made no effort to move, and they lay for a few more hazy, loving moments, until Gideon grunted. "I should get back to my room before people start rising."

"Eh. What's the worst that happens if we get caught? Wynn throws us out?"

"If I thought that was the worst that would happen, I'd ravish you in the main hall. Sadly, it wouldn't be, so we need a plan."

Zeb shrugged. "You do your best to find out about anyone coming or going; we lurk by the gate and ask for a seat in the motor as they leave. Or just hang around there and walk out as they arrive, come to that."

"I'm unsure about walking," Gideon said. "If Wynn sends at eight o'clock, there's very little chance of anyone arriving before noon at the earliest, and it'll be pitch dark by four-thirty. We might cover twelve miles in that time on a good road, and if we didn't get lost—"

"But the roads are shocking and we might well get lost. And there's a lot of Dartmoor and it's awfully cold at night."

"It would be much the best to get whoever comes to take us to town. So we'll need to seize the opportunity when it arises, which means being ready to go. Keep anything you can't leave in your satchel. Money, manuscript. Rosary."

"Yes, Mr. Grey."

Gideon kissed him, hard and deep. "All right, I must get ready to deal with your monster of a cousin. Oh God. We can do this. Face the day."

He'd used to say that on the weekday mornings they woke up together, when Zeb lay in bed whimpering about how much he didn't want to go to work. Zeb had always thought sourly how nice it must be to have such energy and dedication. He'd never wondered if Gideon had been exhorting himself too.

Gideon rolled out of bed, donned his evening trousers, and made a run for it with the rest of his clothing. Zeb lay back a moment, luxuriating in the warm bed and the mild stickiness.

That didn't last long, because of all the other thoughts

crowding his brain. Elise, and Rachel. Colonel Dash. Jessamine.

He hadn't told Gideon about Elise's suspicion of Jessamine; she had entirely slipped his mind what with one thing and another. They would need to discuss it at some point, because if Elise had been wrong and Jessamine was an innocent girl, Zeb could not possibly leave her in this hellish place where her grandmother had been confined, and trapped, and died.

He should dress, he realised. He therefore lay there for another twenty minutes or so before he finally forced himself up and went to look out of the window, since the grey light was finally making a lacklustre effort at daytime.

What he saw made him catch his breath, because it was trees. The mist had lifted.

Zeb felt a thump of excitement. Wynn couldn't possibly maintain the pretence of being cut off from the world any longer. They were going to get out of here.

He hurried to ready himself, then headed out for breakfast. When he reached the top of the stairs, he paused, looking down the steep, sharp-edged stone steps. It was hardly surprising Elise's fall had broken her neck.

Three corridors came on to the landing from different directions. Anyone staying in the house might easily have come from their room at the same time. Had they simply seen her and taken advantage of the opportunity, or had they waited quietly, with intent, until a chance presented itself?

He imagined her last moments—pausing, looking down, perhaps planning her grand entrance and considering how she intended to ruin Hawley or Bram or both. Maybe exchanging words with someone who had emerged onto the landing to join her? And then the hands on her back, the sharp push, the fall.

Zeb shuddered convulsively, put his shoulders to the wall, and made his way down the stairs crabwise. Call him paranoiac but he wasn't turning his back on anyone today.

The breakfast room was populated only by Gideon, which was welcome, and Wynn, which wasn't.

"Ah, Zebedee," Wynn said. "Good morning. If one can say as much, with poor Elise." He shook his head sadly. "I suppose you have seen the mist has lifted. I have sent the car to town—"

"You've sent it?" Zeb demanded. "It's already left?"

"At the first hint of dawn. It was the only possible course with a death—I suppose we must call it an unnatural death—in the house. I expect the motor back with Dr. Rudyard and perhaps the police by noon."

"Oh. Good." Zeb felt slightly off-balance at this unsought capitulation and the idea that Wynn was summoning the police himself. Perhaps there was no law against driving people to murder. Perhaps he was trying to put himself in the right. Perhaps Zeb had somehow been wrong about this whole bizarre sequence of events and Wynn had done nothing wrong at all.

He glanced at Gideon, who gave him the barest fraction of an eye-roll.

"That's excellent," he added, heading for the chafing dishes. "Making sure everything is dealt with properly, I mean."

"Oh, I will," Wynn said. "We must discover how she came to have that terrible accident. A woman of so much poise—it is hard to imagine how she could have slipped and fallen. I dare say the police will have many questions for the family."

Well, that hadn't taken long. Zeb glared at the sausages. Wynn went on, "I must ask you all to remain until that has been thoroughly resolved."

"Surely Mr. Zeb need not," Gideon said. "The three of us were together in the drawing room with Miss Jessamine when Mrs. Bram fell, so he can have nothing to offer in evidence."

Wynn's face hardened slightly. Zeb hastily put in, "I suppose when the doctor comes, he'll be seeing Colonel Dash."

"I could not say if Dash will want to see him," Wynn

said. "He has expressed the strongest disinclination to see anyone; he prefers to recover from his fit in peace. But I shall certainly ask. Poor Dash. Poor Elise. It seems that suffering is coming to us all. I wonder who it will strike next?"

Zeb had piled his plate with toast and bacon and added a boiled egg to fuel him for their escape. Somehow, he wasn't hungry any more.

twenty

IDEON WENT OFF SHORTLY after that, presumably to go about finding out what he could, as well as to pack. Zeb had packed his things, such as they were, before coming down to breakfast. Hopefully, the doctor would have the space to take the bags while giving them a lift to town. If not, Zeb would happily abandon his luggage as the price of departure.

They were assuming Gideon could just leave along with Zeb, of course. Would that look odd? Did Gideon have to resign? Did he have a notice period, and was that enforceable when your employer was an unconscionable swine morally responsible for a death? Zeb had always been sacked, so the question of notice had never arisen.

Gideon would know his own situation and make his

own plan. Zeb just had to make sure he was ready to go whenever the doctor got here. It couldn't possibly be before noon, but he intended to be poised and waiting by eleven at the latest, in case.

As he was finishing his third cup of tea, reiterating *Ready at eleven* in his head to fix it there, Jessamine walked into the breakfast room. She wore a long black dress with an extravagant black lace shawl around her shoulders, like a dowager of the previous century.

"Good morning, Cousin Zeb," she said in the hushed tones appropriate to a cathedral. "Oh, you have breakfasted. I don't know how anybody could."

"You're in mourning," Zeb said.

"Of course. Poor, poor Elise." Her mouth worked, and she pulled out a black-edged handkerchief. Clearly, they had all the funereal trappings conveniently to hand.

"It's very sad. I hear you're going to marry Hawley."

"He asked me to. And I said yes, if Wynn will give his permission—because I do need someone, one of you, but—but Zeb, oh, Cousin Zeb—" She gave him big liquid brown eyes in a pleading look. "I don't know how to say this, with poor Elise lying dead, but I must. I could not bear it if I lost my chance at happiness, even if it costs my modesty. Zeb, will you hear me out?"

Zeb was absolutely not going to sit through a girlish proposal, and particularly not since everything about her was cementing his conviction that Elise had been right. There was something studied in her manner, something knowing or even mocking behind her eyes, and he felt a violent prickle of hostility. "Sorry, I don't have time to talk now."

"Why not? What else have you to do?"

Zeb grabbed at the first excuse that presented itself. "I have to pack," he lied.

"Pack? You're leaving?" Something in her face changed just a little. "But you promised to stay."

"Well, I'm not going to," Zeb said, and left the room because there was a limit to how much he could tolerate before ten in the morning. He headed for the library instead. A room full of books felt safe.

He walked in, took a long breath of relief, coughed at the taste of it, and realised Bram was in the most comfortable chair.

He looked appalling, hollow-eyed and pallid, sucking on one of Wynn's vile cigarettes. There was a pall of smoke around him already; God knew how long he'd been here. He glanced round at Zeb as he came in, but said nothing.

"Bram," Zeb said, and realised he had no idea how to proceed. *I'm so sorry your wife's dead, unless of course you murdered her. I'd offer my condolences but you raped the housemaid. I don't know how to think about anything any more.*

"Bram," he said again. "Nice day. Er, I mean the mist. Lifted." Bram didn't respond to that hopeless display. Zeb could hardly blame him. "How are you?" he tried.

"She's dead," Bram said.

"Yes. Yes, she is."

"They're both dead."

"Both—who?"

"The women. The women are dead."

Zeb pulled over a chair and sat down. "Elise is dead, yes. What happened to her?"

Bram shook his head. He looked—Zeb was trying very hard not to think *haunted*—dismayed. "I did as she asked. I tried to please her, but nothing was ever enough. I could have been better, more generous to you, if *she*—"

"Elise didn't owe me anything," Zeb said over him. "You set us against one another from the start, as if she and I were fighting over your money, but you made that happen. You broke your promise to me: nobody else. And I don't know what you mean by 'more' generous," he added, unable to stop himself. "You couldn't have been less."

"She was my wife!"

"You had a mistress!"

Bram didn't respond with a jab of his own, for once. "I did," he said. "And I repented. I pledged my fidelity to Elise. I *proved* it. You have no idea what I did for her."

There was something in his voice as he said that. Zeb felt an unpleasant prickle down his spine. "What did you do?"

Bram sucked hard on the dog-end of his cigarette, stubbed it out, lit another in a puff of cloying smoke. Zeb said, "What, Bram?"

"It was the girl. Florence. She came to my house, made demands. I told Elise she didn't matter. I showed her in word and deed. I could hardly risk my marriage. What did she expect? How should I have known?"

"Known *what*? What happened?"

The fingers of Bram's free hand were tapping convulsively on the arm of his chair. "She claimed she was in a delicate situation. Her father had thrown her out of her home. She said it was mine, my child to provide for. That she needed my help."

"Your mistress came to your house in the family way? Mother of God!"

"She told Elise. Elise—Elise told me to prove that I cared only for her. And I did, I proved it. Not one penny, and so I told Florence. Coming to my home, forcing herself on my wife's notice—Elise would have left me, scarcely two months after the marriage! What would people have said? And Florence had no claim on me, in law. No proof at all."

Zeb took a deep breath. The smoke caught unpleasantly in his throat. He glared at his brother. "So she was expecting your child, her father threw her out, and then you threw her out. Congratulations, you upstanding pillar of the community. What happened?"

"She attempted an illegal act to rid herself of the consequences. That wasn't my fault. It wasn't my fault!"

"She attempted an abortion," Zeb translated. "And—?"

"Died."

Zeb stared at his brother. Bram's hand shook as he brought the cigarette to his lips. "Don't look at me like that. She came to my house, talked to my wife. She ruined my marriage, and she stopped me having children!"

"What?"

"Florence. When we told her to leave—Elise and I together—she prayed we would never have children. Called on God as her witness. She cursed us then, and she has come back to finish it now. Elise is dead, and she has come for me."

"What are you talking about?"

"On the wall of my room," Bram said hoarsely. "Last night, after—I returned to my room and there was writing on the wall. A message from Florence."

"And don't tell me, after you went out, it vanished?"

"No," Bram said. "It's still there."

"Oh. Well, that's hardly supernatural," Zeb said. "Anyone can write on a wall. Except a dead person, obviously."

"She signed her name. She wrote that she will have her vengeance, and she signed it *Florence*."

"For goodness' sake, man. Who else knew about this girl?"

"Elise. Elise and I killed her. Elise made me choose, and I chose her, so Florence died and now Elise is dead and Florence has come for me—"

"Bram!" Zeb yelped. "Stop it! Look, are you absolutely sure she's dead?"

"She fell down the stairs! You saw her!"

Zeb breathed deeply. "Not Elise, Florence. If Florence's still alive, she could have—"

"I saw her grave," Bram said. "I did not go to the funeral—I should hardly have wished to associate myself, in the circumstances. But I went to the grave."

Zeb briefly constructed a plot around a death elaborately faked a decade ago and then told himself not to be ridiculous. "Right. Well, clearly someone else knows. This house contains at least one peculiarly unkind practical joker, and you are the latest victim, that's all. You mustn't believe this stuff or you'll run mad."

"But she blames me," Bram said, with terrible simplicity. "She blames us for her death, and she has avenged herself on Elise, and now she will come for me."

Zeb's loathing of him in that moment was a physical force. "Everything's about you, isn't it? You and the women you pick up and throw down. What about Rachel?"

"Who?"

"The housemaid!"

"What?"

"The one you had your way with," Zeb said savagely. "Remember? In this house?"

Bram looked utterly blank. "What are you babbling about?"

"You forced yourself on one of the maids!" Zeb was spitting furious. It swamped his usual feelings towards Bram, the complicated, ugly mix of anger, sorrow, and weary resentment. "This visit or a previous one, I don't know which, but you screwed one of the housemaids and she did not want you to! Jesus Christ, you can hardly have forgotten! Or did you simply not notice you were committing a rape, you prick?"

"I did nothing of the sort." Bram didn't look defensive, or guilty, or even self-justifying, an expression with which Zeb was all too familiar. He just looked confused. "You must mean Hawley."

Zeb gaped at him. Bram returned an equally baffled look. "I should hardly trouble Wynn's staff in my position as his heir, Zebedee. That would be foolish in the extreme."

"Wait," Zeb said. "Have you bedded—pawed, touched,

had any form of congress with—any of the staff here? Ever?"

"No."

"The housemaid with dark hair? She wears it pulled back?"

Bram gave a tiny shrug, its sheer indifference more convincing than any oath. Zeb put his face in his hands.

He didn't believe that Rachel had lied; he knew too many people who had suffered intimate assaults, and how much shame was attached to victims, to dismiss any such claim, and in any case, it had *sounded* true. He was also depressingly aware that Bram had a talent for believing his own bluster.

And with all that, he couldn't help thinking the bloody man was telling the truth. Maybe he just wanted to believe that. Maybe he was a fool.

He looked up. Bram was staring at the wall, mouth moving.

"Stop it," Zeb said. "What are you going to do now? I suppose Elise's body will have to be transported to London?"

"A funeral. Yes. No. It must be here."

"She has family in London."

"I can't leave," Bram said. "Don't be a fool. Hawley will take full advantage if I do."

"Advantage of—?"

"Jessamine. He will secure her unless I act. He has already stolen a march on me, thanks to Elise."

Zeb needed a moment there. "Do you not think you should bury your wife before planning your next marriage?"

"Elise squandered my inheritance from my father," Bram said. "How much more must I lose because of her?"

The library door swung open. "There you are," Wynn said. He was dressed in funereal black like Jessamine, who stood behind him. Hawley was at his other shoulder, with the rather blurry expression Zeb was getting used to: he wondered how many bottles the man could possibly have brought with him.

"This looks like a delegation," Zeb said.

Wynn gave a sombre inclination of his head. "Rather, a ceremony. Dear Elise's passing should be marked, to pay respect to her spirit although her poor broken body cannot yet be interred. Such a lovely woman reduced to cold clay. How she will be missed, by so many of you."

Zeb gave sincere thought to punching Wynn in the face as hard as he possibly could. He couldn't look at Bram or Hawley.

"You will all please accompany me," Wynn went on. "We will take her to the crypt."

"Crypt?" Zeb said. "Wynn, the doctor is coming, and the police. They will want to see her."

"They can see her laid out with respect in the appropriate place."

"But I don't think we should be moving her around, should we? More than we already have, I mean."

"We must," Jessamine said in a thready voice. "To know she is here—no, she is gone, gone forever, but her body is here, lying cold, in the house. To know every time I walk through the hall that that dead thing is there, waiting, behind a door—I can't bear it. It's too horrible."

"My Jessamine is sensitive," Hawley said. "Do give her nerves some consideration."

"Jessamine's feelings are first in my thoughts," Bram said with an effort at charm that landed like a thrown brick. "It is quite appropriate to use the crypt. It will be Elise's final resting place."

"She did always hope to be mistress here," Hawley remarked. "At least she can be a permanent inhabitant."

Zeb stared at him speechlessly. Wynn ignored him. "Come. The men are ready."

"I have armbands," Jessamine said, holding out strips of black cloth. "Put them on over your coats."

⁓

The family crypt added a new terror to death, being a grotesque piece of Gothic that suggested Notre-Dame de

Paris was contagious. It had gargoyles like witches had warts.

They walked there in sombre procession: two footmen carrying a stretcher to serve as funeral bier with the swathed burden, and five live Wyckhams walking with Victorian solemnity. They were all Edwardians now, of course, but most of Zeb's life had been spent under the old queen's rule, and her culture of mourning was deeply instilled. The decencies had to be observed. Hawley wasn't even smoking.

They arrived at the crypt, which had two doors: the first an iron grille, the second an old oak door that looked as hard as iron. The combination seemed as secure as the Bank of England. Zeb found it had to believe that they needed such precautions against grave robbers out here.

Wynn drew out a large, ancient-looking key ring and unlocked the rusted grille door, which swung open with a resentful creak, and then the oak. He paused for a dramatic moment, then pulled the second door open.

It was pitch dark inside. Well, it would be: the dead didn't need windows. Zeb could just make out something that looked like a central slab, and a stairwell going down into the earth, where coffins would take their final place.

"She should be left to her rest by those closest to her," Wynn said. "Bram, and—" For a hideous second Zeb thought he was going to say Hawley. "Zebedee."

Bram, moving like an automaton, came to take the ends of the stretcher from one of the footmen. Zeb took the handles at the other end. He wasn't sure if Elise was unexpectedly heavy or unexpectedly light; he didn't know what he'd expected.

"Good," Wynn said. "Carry her in, both of you. Place her there, where she can lie in peace until the final rites can be completed."

Zeb looked into the cold, lightless space. Somewhere in there, Walter Wyckham's corpse lay shrivelling to a husk in the darkness. He looked at the two-inch-thick oak door and the iron grille that would close up the vault, and he thought of a mind that had filled his room with spiders and poured blood on a sacrificial stone.

He swung round to look back at Wynn, who was watching, his expression avid.

"Absolutely not," Zeb said. "The devil I will."

"Zebedee!" Bram barked.

Wynn's nostrils flared. "It is only right—"

"I will not be setting foot in there," Zeb said. "You, take this off me."

That was to the surly footman's address. He stepped back, holding his hands up with a mocking smile.

Zeb probably couldn't drop the end of the stretcher, what with his sister-in-law's corpse lying on it. "Someone take this end. Wynn, you do it. You can go in there."

"Are you afraid of the dark?" Hawley said, but it wasn't quite the sneer it should have been. It had something thready in it, and a little too much emphasis on *you*.

"No," Zeb said. "But I'm reluctant to accept Wynn's hospitality for whatever period he's got in mind, so I'm going to put this stretcher down unless someone takes it."

Wynn made a noise of outrage. "Show respect to the dead. How dare you!"

Nobody was coming to take the handles. Zeb said, "Putting it down, Bram."

He bent at the knees, lowering his end of the stretcher, which tilted dangerously. Bram gave a squawk as Elise's weight shifted and hastily bent to lower his end rather than have her slide off. "*Zebedee!*"

"I'm going," Zeb said, and walked away, ignoring the outraged cries behind him. His shoulder blades were itching with the consciousness of being watched, and if he heard feet behind him, he was going to run. He didn't care how foolish he'd look, or if they laughed; he was going to run like hell because he could imagine, as vividly as if he'd lived it, the feeling of being inside that cold, dank, dark stone building and the door thumping shut, the light gone forever, and Wynn laughing outside.

twenty-one

Zeb walked back to the house at a painfully fast pace, breath steaming and ears straining, and almost sobbed with relief when he reached the building. As he approached the front, the door swung open and Gideon stood silhouetted in the doorway, as he had that first night, an aeon ago.

"Oh thank God," Zeb said.

Gideon stalked out, grabbed his wrist, and dragged him down the steps, a little away from the house. "Where have you been?" he demanded, strangled.

"The crypt."

"*Why?*"

"What's wrong?"

"The motor is back," Gideon said, with tenuous

patience. "I was looking for you half an hour ago to suggest we wait by the gate, but I couldn't find you, and now the motor is back and it won't be going out again."

"Of course it will," Zeb said blankly. "The police and the doctor—"

"Haven't come. Won't."

"What?"

"The chauffeur returned alone. I asked where the authorities were. He said he was very sorry, but he encountered a bad patch of mist and felt unsafe driving through it, so he came back. He was laughing at me when he said it. So now the gate is locked again, and I have no doubt that Wynn will announce it's too dangerous to send the motor out until tomorrow. We're stuck, Zeb. We missed our chance."

"Because of me," Zeb said, with a cold feeling in his gut. "Shit. Wynn got me out of the way, didn't he? Shit!" And if he hadn't been sucked into that mock funeral procession, if he'd just refused to be involved with Wynn's nonsense, if he had paid attention, they might have been outside the wall now. His heart constricted with guilt. "Oh God. I'm so sorry. This is all my fault."

"Why the blazes did you go off with him?" Gideon almost shouted. "You have to stop playing his games!"

"It was a particularly good game," Zeb said numbly. "We just interred Elise—"

"*What?*"

"And I think Wynn intended to get me in the crypt with her body and slam the door."

Gideon stared at him, mouth open, for a moment, and said again, as more of an acknowledgement than a question, "What."

He was wearing his overcoat. "Come on," Zeb said, tugging him down the path. "We need to speak in private and that means not in the damned house."

They walked in silence, except for the percussive thud of self-reproach in Zeb's brain. He'd been so easily distracted. He'd taken Wynn's bait, and now Gideon was caught here with him, flies in a web. All Zeb's fault. Ruining his life. Again.

He led the way into Wayland's Smithy, the faux-prehistoric folly. Nobody would see them in there without actually sticking their head into the building, and nobody was likely to pass by. He had to duck his head low to enter; Gideon, several inches taller, bent double.

There was a sort of stone bench. Zeb sat on it, and Gideon joined him. It was extremely cold and felt damp.

"All right," Gideon said. "Why are we here?"

"Wait. Listen. I'm so sorry—"

"Don't. Really, Zeb. Wynn is very good at manipulating people, and I might have done the same in your shoes. We're where we are; we have to concentrate on what we're going to do. Rosary."

"What?"

"Rosary. Start fidgeting and pay attention."

Zeb blinked. Then he hauled the string of beads out of his pocket, flicking the smooth ovals through his fingers, letting a little of the pent-up tension in his body leak out through his hands.

"Can I go on? Right," Gideon said. "Firstly, this is Wynn's fault, every damned part of it. He won that round, so now we need to win the next. For that, I need you thinking, not mired in guilt or might-have-beens. So with that in mind, what did you want to say?"

Zeb took a deep breath. "I know what's going on. Not why, but what."

"In what sense?"

"It's the books. I think Wynn is recreating the Walter Wyckham books."

Gideon frowned. "You said the ghost was copied from that one, *The Monastery*."

"And the writing on the walls. Then there's Lady Ravendark. She's a character in *Coldstone Abbey*, the one I compared Elise to." When she was still alive. He shuddered. "Lady Ravendark is a very lovely woman but an unfaithful wife. She eventually gets pushed down the stairs of her stately home by—" He stopped.

"By?"

"Her cuckolded husband," Zeb said reluctantly. "But

the point is, she gets pushed down the stairs, just like Elise. And the same book also has a truly horrible scene where a character finds herself trapped in a room that's crawling with spiders."

"Right," Gideon said slowly. "That is a pattern, yes. Does it have sacrifices in a stone circle?"

"No. That's in *The Stone Circle*."

"Are you serious? There is a Walter Wyckham book with a sacrifice on the altar of the stone circle? By hooded monks?"

"Robed druids, but yes. It also has a scene where a character is locked in the family crypt with a recently murdered corpse. He's left there overnight and goes raving mad. And just now Wynn asked me and Bram to put Elise in the crypt, and he nodded at me to go in first, and I remembered—I thought…"

He shuddered again, violently, as though he was chilled to the bone. Gideon put his arm round him, and Zeb leaned against him, feeling safe in the embrace even though he really wasn't.

"I don't know if he meant to lock one or both of us in," he went on. "*Clara Lackaday* has two brothers fighting over a fortune who are locked in a room, so maybe that was in his mind. And I don't know, if he'd locked me in, if Bram would have objected or if he's too addled by now. The point is, it's all Walter. Even the basic premise is

Walter. *Clara Lackaday*'s entire plot is her being trapped in a great house with a wall round the estate. I literally thought about that when I arrived. We're in a cocktail of my grandfather's books, and if I had to be caught in an authorial world, I would not have picked his!"

"Makes one think longingly of *Faraway Meadow*," Gideon agreed thinly. "What about Colonel Dash? Are there mysterious disappearances?"

"Several, most ending badly. And secret passages. And there's also the sinister secretary."

"Do I want to know?"

"He's the villain of *Coldstone Abbey*, and father of Lady Ravendark's baby, but it's hinted he's also sleeping with Lord Ravendark, inasmuch as you could hint it at the time. In the end he gets put at the bottom of a well, standing with water up to his neck, and left there knowing he'll drown once he falls asleep. Which, of course, he does eventually, after lots of terrible hallucinations and slowly rotting away alive. It's horrible."

There was a nasty pause. Gideon said, "You don't think—"

"I don't know," Zeb said. "I don't know how much Wynn has planned or how mad he is. Not that 'mad' is the word, really. I think he's perfectly sane, just *wrong*. If you told me he was possessed by Walter Wyckham's ghost, I'd probably believe you." He thought of the portrait, his ancestor's sly smile on that cherubic face. "I just wanted to make sure you knew about the secretary and, uh, don't go near any wells?"

It was just a joke. A whistling-in-the-dark joke, but a joke nevertheless, so it was unfortunate that his voice cracked on the words.

"Zeb." Gideon's arms closed round him. "Zeb. Sweetheart. It's all right."

"It is not all right! It isn't nearly all right and I keep thinking of that cursed scene—"

"I'd rather not dwell on that. What else happens in the books? What about this Lord Ravendark?"

"The sinister secretary drops a chandelier on him."

"There's a chandelier in the hall."

"I'll look up," Zeb said, feeling rather sick. "Oh God."

"At least we know what's going on, and that will surely help." Gideon kissed his hair. "We're getting out of here. Both of us. I promise."

"You can't promise me that. It's not in your power."

Gideon paused. "No, perhaps I can't. But I can promise that I won't leave without you."

"Well, don't. What if you have to?"

"I will not leave without you," Gideon said steadily. "That is a promise. Now stop recriminating: we need to work out what to do."

"Not believe Wynn, for a start," Zeb said. "I really

thought he'd sent for the police, just like I've swallowed a great deal of lies since I got here."

"We all have. I believed his lies about you."

"But then you stopped. Whereas I—oh, hell. Gideon, I told Jessamine I was going to leave today. She was going to propose to me again and it was too awful and I said I was leaving, and the next thing, Wynn turned up with this plan for a funeral march for Elise and I felt obliged—"

"She's working with Wynn," Gideon said. "That's been fairly obvious."

"And she's also not Jessamine. I mean, there is no Jessamine. Elise says the woman here is at least twenty-one and probably an actress."

Gideon's jaw dropped. "Good God. Really?"

"Elise said so, and she was right about Laura's mother."

"About—"

"Laura's mother, the housemaid. She was locked up here. They kept her imprisoned for years rather than hand over her legacy. I found the room, her prison. It's one of the worst things I've ever seen."

"My God."

"Wynn's father did it, which might explain a lot about Wynn. Oh, and Elise also thinks—thought—Wynn and Laura had a Romeo and Juliet sort of affair and Wynn fathered her baby."

"I don't think the play would be the same if Juliet was

Romeo's aunt," Gideon said in the very calm sort of way of someone trying not to lose his grip. "Although I suppose that explains all the paintings. Ugh."

"Wynn clearly hated his father for getting rid of Laura. And, uh, he told me that his father drowned in the mire, alone. That it took hours for him to die, all the time crying for help that didn't come."

"If he died alone, how would Wynn know—"

"That's what I was wondering."

"Christ above," Gideon said. "Right, well, the relevant part of all this—aside from Wynn being a very dangerous and entirely unhinged man—is that Wynn and Jessamine are in cahoots. We can't doubt that. That business the other night, Wynn selecting Bram while she accepted Hawley, was a masterstroke. It all but forced Bram to push—"

He stopped abruptly. There was a frozen silence.

"Are you saying—did you see—"

"No. No, I didn't, Zeb. That was an assumption only. I've no evidence. But...it's what I think."

"He's my brother. You're saying he's a murderer and Rachel says he's a rapist—"

"Oh my God, *what?*" Gideon said, a man who couldn't handle any more revelations.

Zeb hurriedly told him about Rachel and Florence. "He admitted the whole thing about Florence. There's a threatening message on his wall now, signed with her name, and he insists nobody else knew about her. He's in rather a bad way. But the thing is, with all that on his mind, he still denied having anything to do with Rachel, and I... I wanted to believe him. I did believe him. But I believed her too."

"But she's one of Wynn's staff, so you probably shouldn't."

"Are you serious?"

"I think we have to treat everyone in this house as the enemy, at this point. We have to assume they're all playing Wynn's game."

"But what *is* his game?" Zeb demanded. "Elise thought he hated us because he didn't want us to inherit his money, but he could have left it all to a cats' home. Instead, he brought us here. Why? And why are the staff joining in with this? I thought the footman was going to shove me into the crypt by main force. How much can Wynn possibly be paying them to do this? Are they all escaped from Dartmoor Prison?"

"I truly don't know. All I know is that we have to get out, because I have no more desire to end up in a well than you do in a crypt. You mentioned scaling the wall: I think we might be reaching that point."

"Right," Zeb said. "Any idea how one does that?"

"I've walked the perimeter and there are no trees close

to it, so we'll need a ladder, and a rope to get down the other side, I suppose, unless we think we could jump safely? Twelve feet—I'm not sure. I suppose one can hang off the side and drop, but if one of us were to sprain an ankle, that would be bad."

"A bedsheet would do at a pinch, and be easily found," Zeb suggested. "And we need warm clothes—oh, and there was a compass in Dash's room. I should get that. And a map. So we can navigate if we're walking."

"Suppose I look for a ladder, then," Gideon said, in the very calm tones of a man dealing with a nightmare. "You see about the map and compass."

"I'll do that. Oh, and food. And gloves and things—"

"Map and compass first. Get those, stow them in your pockets right away, and don't do anything else until you have them. And, Zeb?"

Zeb turned his head. Gideon kissed him, hard and desperate, and Zeb grabbed his shoulders and clung on, kissing him wildly with hungry, frightened, open-mouthed gulps that were close to sobs.

They held on to each other a moment longer in silence, shoulders heaving, until Gideon said, "We should go."

"Yes."

Gideon squeezed his hand. "We *will* get out of here. Together."

"What about Dash? And Bram?"

"There's damn all we can do about Dash now. If we come back with a pack of policemen, maybe they can search the place. Bram...ugh. Is there any chance at all of persuading him to scale a wall and walk twelve miles across a moor?"

"None. But if I leave him behind, what might happen to him?"

"I don't know. But I don't see what we can do to help him or anyone at all except get ourselves out and come back with the police."

"No. No, I suppose you're right."

Gideon squeezed his hand again. They rose and shuffled their stooped way out of the folly.

∽

Gideon headed off alone to look for a ladder. That made sense, since Zeb didn't know the servants' areas, the outbuildings and places where the work happened, and had no reason to be there with him. But he couldn't help thinking of the chauffeur's contemptuous face, and the nasty expression in the footman's eyes, and wondering what would happen if they caught Gideon poking around.

Hopefully, nobody would be there to catch him. Gideon was sensible, so if he felt splitting up was the right way to proceed, it probably was, even if Zeb felt raw and exposed.

He strode into the house repeating *Map and compass* to himself, and hurried up the stairs. Voices rose from the drawing room as he passed, including Bram's, which was a relief. If they'd trapped anyone in the crypt, it would be Hawley, who could probably do with a few hours locked away from whatever he was drinking.

Or maybe they had never intended to trap anyone in there at all, and Zeb had made an almighty, unforgivable fuss at what should have been a solemn moment.

He put that thought away with all the rest of the ones that said *You're making a fool of yourself* and *Imagination*. He'd let those thoughts persuade him to do as Wynn asked too often. From now on, he was going to listen to his fears.

Map and compass. He made it to Dash's room without seeing anyone. It was very cold and felt dead in the way of unused rooms, a film of dust settled on the mantel and the floor. The staff weren't even troubling to clean. It was very much as though they didn't expect him to come back.

Zeb went to the dressing table and stopped.

The compass was still there, a compact thing the size of a fob watch. So was a pocketknife, pearl-handled with Dash's initials embossed in silver. There was also a gun.

Zeb was positive that hadn't been there before. He'd have noticed. But there it was, an actual gun.

He didn't know anything at all about guns beyond that you pointed them and pulled the little stubby thing. He thought this was probably a revolver, mainly because it wasn't a rifle, but it might be a pistol, or an arquebus for all he knew. It was a *gun*.

Why the devil had Dash brought a gun to a house party? How had Zeb missed it? Should he take it? Was it loaded? He had no idea how one would check, and he wasn't about to start playing with it in case he set it off. He didn't want to carry a loaded gun; he'd probably shoot himself in the foot. An *unloaded* gun, on the other hand, which people didn't know was unloaded and thus would be frightened of anyway, and which one might use to wave at the gatekeeper and threaten him into unlocking the gate...

Zeb stood for a moment, thoughts flickering. Then he took what he needed of Colonel Dash's possessions, made himself pause to stow them carefully about his person, and hurried downstairs, his coat pockets heavy with stolen goods.

Map and compass, he reminded himself, and he had the compass, so now for the map. He headed to the library, hoping for an Ordnance Survey map or suchlike. Assuming Wynn had any such thing, and that he kept it in here rather than to hand in his study. But Wynn had grown up here, not to mention he looked like he'd barely left the house in years: he wouldn't need a map in his study. Zeb would search the library, and he *would* find what he needed because Gideon had given him this task and he couldn't fail.

He found atlases, but no local maps stuffed next to them or folded inside them, and no bound books with maps that could be torn out if one were a barbarian. He checked the desk next, going through the drawers. They held old account books and notebooks and bundles of paper that might have been Walter Wyckham's original manuscripts or laundry bills, he didn't care. No maps.

He had the sweaty feeling again, the one he got at work when there was a task with a deadline and it had started well but he'd gone wrong and lost time, and now everything was falling apart. He imagined Gideon outside, with an efficiently stolen ladder, waiting, waiting. *Breathe.*

There were plenty more drawers to check. The bookshelves started a bit below hip height; below them were long rows of cupboards, each topped with a wide drawer. The drawers looked like the kind of thing you pulled out in a museum to reveal pinned, dead insects. Maybe Walter Wyckham had collected butterflies, or beetles, or spiders.

Zeb pulled out the first drawer. It was full of paper, and

he ruffled through it with fingers that were quivery, if not quite shaky yet. It was deeds, legal things, all unreadable writing, no damned maps. He moved to the next drawer and pulled it open. That took a bit more force because it contained a Bible.

The sheer magnificence of the book stopped him in his tracks. It was a huge thing, fifteen inches by twenty at least, leather bound, very old, and its beauty put everything else out of his mind. He opened it carefully, marvelling at the feel of the ancient paper, and noting the impenetrable blackletter type. He wondered when it dated from. Was it Stuart? Might there be a date on the flyleaf?

He turned back to the beginning, feeling the soft weight of the oversized pages, and a piece of notepaper fluttered out. Zeb caught it and saw it was in Wynn's hand.

It had the number *28* at the top, underlined several times. Then there were a string of women's names, five in all, each with a number by it, and then *Wilfred–47, Mary–30*, followed by *Albert–49* and *Catherine–36*. That was Wynn's and Zeb's fathers and their wives, along with, he very much suspected, their ages at their deaths. Hawley's parents were there too, and so was Laura, her name written with care, along with her age at death, 38.

So the first set of names were probably Walter's five wives and their ages. Zeb glanced at the last name. *Constance–26*.

Twenty-six. The housemaid had been young when she married Walter, Zeb knew, but just nineteen? Had she lost her youth to that terrible room, scrawling on the walls?

Beneath that litany, Wynn had scribbled a lot more numbers. It looked like he'd added up all the ages, subtracted that total from 600, and divided what he got by 28 to reach a total of exactly 6. Under that he'd written, *6=1???*

Zeb had no idea what that was about. He turned the paper over and saw another list of names. *Bram–38. Elise–30. Hawley–34. Zebedee–28.* That last had an arrow pointing to it and an exclamation mark, and then Zeb's birthday, which was in January.

Wynn had added up those ages too, subtracted the sum from 200, divided the result by 6, and got a result of eleven and two thirds, after which he had written *61!!* in heavy pen with angry underlining, and then added, *Dash???*

Maybe it made sense if you knew what he was on about. Zeb put down the paper and looked back at the Bible's flyleaf. It bore a list of names and dates in various hands and inks, starting with Theophilus Wyckham, born 17th August 1698. Toward the bottom of the list was Walter Wyckham, 2nd December 1777 to 28th December 1855. It was the second of December today. Happy birthday, Walter.

Walter had written in his three sons with dates of

birth. Laura's name had been added in Wynn's hand to one side, as had Georgina's, her daughter. They were the only women's names listed. No wives or daughters allowed, and Zeb, Bram, and Hawley weren't in there either, as mere progeny of the younger sons. This was a list of inheritors.

Wynn was duly there: born 12th June 1855. *Six months to go*, Zeb thought nastily, then remembered Wynn had probably been lying about his supposed death at fifty. Unless he really believed in the Wyckham curse.

The Wyckham curse.

Zeb stared at the flyleaf, with its spidery writing and its missing people, who didn't matter because they were there only to feed the people who did matter, and at Walter's dates of birth and death. He'd outlived the supposed curse by twenty-eight years.

Zeb picked up the stray paper again and looked at the side headed 28, and the answer bloomed in his thoughts, understanding far outpacing words.

"Oh my God," he said aloud.

He needed to find Gideon. Wynn might be recreating their grandfather's literary atrocities, but that was just the method, not the goal. Zeb knew the goal now, and it changed everything.

He shut the Bible, slammed the drawer, and ran from the room.

twenty-two

EB STOPPED HIMSELF IN the hall, midfumble for his coat, as he realised he didn't actually know where Gideon would be hunting for ladders, and probably shouldn't come crashing in on him anyway.

Fear was thrumming through him, making him jittery, and perhaps he was good in a crisis, but they'd been in a crisis so long now that he could feel the drag of exhaustion pulling him down. *Think.*

Getting things together: that had been his role. Map and compass, but he hadn't found a map. Move on. Food: he'd take—steal—some food, and something to drink if he could find a bottle, and then as soon as he found Gideon, they could run like hell.

He wasn't sure where the staff areas were, but he made

his way through a couple of plausible corridors toward the back of the east wing, passing the bleak, empty anteroom where Elise's body had rested, until he came to a plain door and a corridor that had a kitchen sort of smell to it. There was a heavy door at the end, closed. Zeb headed towards it, keeping his ears pricked. He wanted to avoid people.

He eased the door open, just a fraction, and sound rushed through. It was Gideon's voice, sounding raw and panicky. "Let me go!"

"You were warned," said a deep, contemptuous voice. The chauffeur, Zeb thought through a wave of panic. "Chose the wrong side, didn't you?"

"What blasted side?" Gideon snarled. "Why the blazes are you doing this? Get off me!" There was the sound of a scuffle, a blow, a cry.

"Hang on to him. Not going to do that, *Mister* Grey," the chauffeur said with a sneer. "Wynn's got a need for you and he doesn't want Useless running away, so you're going to sit tight for a while. If I put him in the stables—"

"Don't be daft," said a male voice. "Useless will be looking for him, and he'll start outside. Let's shut this one up and put him...uh..."

"Stick him in the cellar," an unfamiliar woman said. "Keep him out of the way till the others are done with. Nobody will hear him down there. Well, except—"

"We're not doing that." It was a voice Zeb knew all too well. Rachel, the housemaid, except she didn't sound distressed or respectful or any of those things any more. She sounded, in fact, highly authoritative. "Come, Anna, that's not right. He hasn't done anything."

A man snorted. The first woman asked, sharply, "Then where do you suggest we put him?"

"The anteroom where they laid out Lady Macbeth," Rachel said. "Nobody will hear anything from there, or if they do, they'll think it's ghosts."

That got a general unkind laugh. Zeb felt his stomach plunge. He had passed the anteroom on his way here. They'd be coming out this way.

He retreated rapidly up the corridor, opened a side door with fumbling urgency, and revealed a storeroom into which he wedged himself. *Don't knock anything down. Pull the door closed. Don't sneeze. Don't breathe. Don't move.*

He wanted to move: he wanted to run and run and not look back. He could feel the twitch in his muscles, the unbearable torment of enforced stillness, and the urge for escape was near-overwhelming. He dug his nails into his palms, held himself rigid, and waited, heart thundering so loudly that it would surely be audible to anyone passing.

After a moment, he heard the squeal of hinges from the kitchen, and then the sound of feet: several pairs, one dragging. He let them pass, then he made himself wait, and wait, and wait some more, teeth gritted, his muscles jumping with the urge to break out and flee. It felt like his entire body was holding its breath.

The feet returned at last, two sets of heavy tread, and he heard the kitchen door shut. He gave it another agonizingly long moment, listening to the silence, pulse racing, and then, once he was absolutely sure the corridor was empty, he eased the door open with a long exhalation of relief and slid into the corridor.

Rachel was standing opposite, arms folded, waiting for him.

A man of action might have leapt at her, bound and gagged her with some handy twine and a handkerchief, and stashed her in the cupboard. Zeb just stared.

"Come on," she hissed almost soundlessly, jerking her head, and set off down the corridor, back towards the main part of the house. Zeb followed, utterly bewildered. They went through another set of heavy doors, and then she unlocked the anteroom door and gestured him in.

Gideon was inside, tied to a chair with a gag in his mouth. His face was marked dark by a blow, and his lips were bloody.

Zeb wasn't sure what he said. He just found himself on

his knees, fumbling desperately with the gag. Gideon was making urgent noises at him and Zeb crooned, "Wait, wait, I'll get you out, just wait—"

He pulled the gag free. Gideon coughed, choked, and said, "Get out of here, you fool!"

Zeb looked round to the door. The door of the room he'd run into, in which Rachel now stood with the key in her hand. He said, "Oh."

"I'm not locking you in," she said. "Unless you try to attack me. Don't do that." She shot a glance down the corridor, then stepped inside and mostly closed the door, keeping her hand to it. "Come on, get him free. Hurry."

"Er," Zeb said. "Are you helping us?"

"I'm helping *you*. Can you get him untied?"

Zeb groped for Dash's pocketknife. "Wait, wait—here. Uh, why are you helping?"

Rachel gave a mirthless sort of smile. "It hardly matters."

"No, it does. It truly does." Gideon's hands had been tied tightly together, then lashed to the chair. His wrists were already red and puffy and the knots looked horrible. Zeb set to sawing at the thick, tough twine. "Because I think I know what Wynn's doing. And if I'm right, that makes him frighteningly unhinged, and I don't think you ought to be here in a house with him. It's not safe for you."

Rachel actually laughed at that, an incredulous choke.

"Not safe for *me*?" she repeated. "Littlest Wyckham, you have no idea what's happening here."

"Probably I don't," Zeb agreed. "Could you tell me? And could you start with—what you said about my brother? Because he truly doesn't seem to remember doing it, you see, and maybe that's because he's losing his mind but—"

"Of course he didn't rape me," Rachel said, voice hard and cold. "That was Hawley."

Zeb looked up at her. She looked down at him.

"I'm sorry," he said. "I'm very, very sorry. But why did you say it was Bram?"

"Because a girl named Florence isn't here to say what your brother really did."

"Bram told me about her. Or, at least he said that he abandoned his expectant mistress when she had nowhere else to go, and she died trying to procure an abortion."

"Proud of that, is he?"

"I think he probably feels very guilty somewhere inside." A strand snapped. Zeb sawed away, concentrating on not cutting Gideon, his fingers cramping from his death grip on the knife. "Maybe quite deep. Did you know Florence?"

"Never met her in my life."

"I don't understand. Could you just tell me, please? Why are the staff helping Wynn to do all these horrible things to all of us? I can quite see that you would loathe Hawley, but the chauffeur, say—"

"Florence's lover," Gideon said suddenly. "Or brother, or father."

Rachel clapped her hands in ironic applause. "Very good, Mr. Grey. The chauffeur, Fenton, was her father. He threw her out in a fit of rage. The next day he was sorry, or sober, and he went looking for her, and if your brother had so much as given her a few pounds to tide her over, some indication of kindness, she might be alive now. But she was abandoned and afraid and she had vanished into London. She took the stuff that killed her before Fenton could track her down."

"Wait. Bram was absolutely wrong in what he did. But if her father *also* sent her away—"

"He changed his mind."

"Bram might have changed his mind in time!" Zeb snapped. "Why is he the only one to blame?"

"He isn't," Rachel said. "Fenton has been racked with guilt and remorse every day of the last ten years or so. Has your brother?"

"Regardless," Gideon said, in the tone he used to close down conversations. Possibly he felt Zeb should not be arguing with her right now, and possibly he was right. "That's the chauffeur. What about the others?"

Rachel contemplated Zeb for a few seconds longer,

then switched her gaze to Gideon. "Oh, it's all the same story, told a variety of ways. Anna, the cook, was an artist's model, as I was until Hawley left me afraid to be in the company of men. He called her his muse, made her promises, put a baby in her belly, and discarded her when his painting was done. Her husband came back from abroad, beat her, and left her. The child was stillborn; she turned to drink. Her whole life ruined because Hawley wanted inspiration, and she's far from the only one."

Gideon nodded slowly. "And the footmen?"

"Alfred's sweetheart was Mrs. Bram's lady's maid. Bram pawed her; Mrs. Bram caught him at it and dismissed her without a reference. She stole a pair of earrings on her way out, with an idea of compensation, and Mrs. Bram prosecuted. She's serving two years. Another life spoiled."

"Right. What about the other footman?"

Rachel smiled, in a way he hadn't seen before. "My husband."

"Oh, well, that's good," Zeb said. "I'm glad you have someone. That's nice. So all the staff hate my family, then. What about Dash? What did he do?"

"Wynn told you what he did. Colonel Dash ingratiated himself with a schoolgirl, his pretty young cousin. She was several months gone when she drowned herself."

Zeb stopped sawing and stared at her. Gideon said, "That was *Dash*? Why did Wynn not act before?"

"He only found out last year. He was going through some old exercise books of Georgina's that had been rotting in a chest and discovered one was a coded diary." She shrugged. "I quite agree he's unhinged. I suspect that discovery played a role in the unhinging."

"But that can't be right," Zeb said. "Because Jessamine is, or is supposed to be, Georgina's child. That would make Dash Jessamine's father, which he must have realised, but he offered her marriage. I heard him."

"Yes," Rachel said. "He did, didn't he. Wynn was quite angry about that."

"That was the night he disappeared," Gideon observed. "What happened to him?"

She gave him a cold smile. "You don't want me to answer that. Or do you? Do you intend to rescue him from the consequences he's avoided all these years? Do you think there is any other prospect of making him face those consequences?"

"I suppose there's no such prospect for any of you," Gideon said. "The police and the law courts don't do well with intimate crimes."

"Oh, there would be no justice at all." Rachel's every word was bitter as aloe. "Florence became Bram's mistress willingly enough—she was sixteen and wanted pretty dresses. It isn't illegal to turn one's pregnant mistress into the streets, and Mrs. Bram had every right to tell her husband to throw the harlot out. Georgina should have known better than to walk out with men, even her handsome Cousin Dash. Alfred's sweetheart stole the earrings, and that is a crime of property, which makes it important. Anna let Hawley seduce her in the first place, so she has no right at all to complain about the consequences. *I* didn't let him. I fought, just as a good woman is supposed to, but when I went to the police with the injuries he inflicted on me still showing, they heard that I was an artist's model, decided what that meant, and told me not to trouble them again."

"That is all wrong. Horribly wrong," Zeb said. The last bit of twine parted under the knife blade. He pulled at the entangling strands, and Gideon's hands were free. He shook them out, while Zeb moved to free his feet, teasing the knot undone with his fingernails. "And when there is no justice available, I quite understand why you would act yourselves. But what did I do? Who did I harm? Because, honestly, the only one I can think of is Gideon, and—"

"*No*," Gideon said, with force.

Rachel looked down at Zeb, face unreadable. "Wynn said you were as venal and cruel as the rest. He said you would do anything for the inheritance, that you would take vengeance on Bram and court Jessamine for her money, and especially that you'd panic when you realised your former lover was in the house. We were waiting to see what you'd do to keep him quiet."

"Were you," Gideon said tightly. "How kind."

She gave a tiny lift of her hands, which might have been interpreted as apology, or not. "Wynn said he had treated you appallingly and got you sacked as some sort of lovers' quarrel. You were resentful enough about him that I didn't question the story."

Gideon had gone rather white about the mouth, under the drying blood. "I might have been angry, as if it's any of your business. But Zeb did nothing to merit this and I never said he did."

"It's all right," Zeb said.

"No, it is not! You people put spiders in his room and scrawled on his walls, made him the object of his family's hate, and brought me into it to use against him—"

"We thought you would pose a threat to each other." She nodded at Zeb. "Jessamine would favour you; your brother would try to push you out of the way, as he did before; Hawley would see you as his main rival; and meanwhile you'd need to silence Mr. Grey, because he could so easily reveal your shameful secret—"

"We don't have a shameful secret," Zeb said. "Gideon and I have nothing to be ashamed of. Or perhaps I do.

Perhaps all of us Wyckhams are murderers, by act or proxy or inaction or just heredity. But Gideon has done nothing wrong, and this isn't fair to him."

"No," Rachel said. "I didn't think about that; none of us did. We expected the Wyckhams would grab for the inheritance with both hands and everything else would follow. But you didn't do it, and then you were kind to me. I told you that tale about your brother so you could use righteous retribution as your excuse—that's usually the last refuge of the scoundrel—and you didn't even do that. You simply asked me what I wanted you to do. And I thought, those *are* your true colours. Wynn lied."

"Yes, he does that," Zeb said. "He is dangerously deluded, and probably a murderer. Why the blazes are you all listening to him?"

"Because he offered us revenge we'll never get any other way, and a good chance we'll walk free. Mrs. Bram is already dealt with. Bram and Hawley will be soon. And Dash can rot. He deserves it. They all deserve it."

Zeb had been kneeling by Gideon. Now he sat abruptly back on the floor, as a child might, because he had the urge to cry like one. To be this utterly disregarded as a human being, treated as if his life didn't matter at all...

Rachel would know exactly how that felt. They all did. That was why they were doing it.

Gideon had bent to finish untying the knot himself.

He kicked his feet free, sat up, and put a hand on Zeb's shoulder. It was a small comfort. "Are you telling us this for a reason?"

"Yes," Rachel said. "It was wrong, bringing you two in. I want my vengeance, but not at this price. I told Wynn that yesterday but he said it was too late, and the others agreed. Some of them think you and Mr. Grey deserve it anyway, as—" She waved a hand between them.

Zeb had rather assumed that might be the case, because this house was very full of hate. All the same, he felt his stomach give a cold, fearful lurch, and put up his hand to meet Gideon's, still resting on his shoulder. "I'm glad you disagree, but what does that mean in practice?"

Rachel gave a twitch of a smile. "There's a delivery due today from the grocer."

"What?" Gideon demanded, sitting up straight and wincing at the movement. "When?"

"It could be any time, so you'll need to be there when he leaves. The gatekeeper's orders are not to let anyone out, but he probably won't stop you by force if you ask the grocer's man for a lift to town. But he will alert the house if he sees you waiting before the cart gets to the gate, so you can't just hang around there."

"There's nothing near the gate," Gideon said. "Empty land. Nowhere to hide."

"You'll have to work that out for yourselves. I'm going

to lock you in here and I'll warn you when the grocer's man arrives. He won't stay long because Wynn sacked the real cook, who he was sweet on, but he'll take a little while to unload and I'll keep him talking as long as I can. As soon as you hear my signal, head towards the gate. See if you can catch him on the drive. It's the best chance I can give you."

"But how will we get out if you're locking us in?"

Rachel went to the panelling and beckoned them to join her. She pressed a carved boss in the shape of a flower. There was a click, and the panel swung inwards, revealing a black rectangle of darkness.

"A secret passage," Gideon said, with profound resignation. "Of course. Where does it go?"

"The passage to the left takes you to a door that opens to the outside. There's a paraffin lamp and matches on the shelf inside."

"There are lots of passages, aren't there?" Zeb said. "Along my corridor, for footsteps?"

"Footsteps, eavesdropping, surprising appearances in Mrs. Bram's room. All very useful. Don't come out until you hear my signal, because if anyone catches you, I won't help again. And don't miss your chance at the gate, because there's nobody else coming for days."

"Thank you," Zeb said. "Truly, Rachel, thank you for this. And I am so very sorry for everything that was done to you." He took a deep breath. "But you're talking about *murder*. And Wynn is doing all this for a very strange reason, and you ought not trust him at all, so—will you come with us? I promise you will be safe with us, and I will do my best to help you afterwards if you need it."

"That's very sweet," Rachel said. "But I want to see Hawley Wyckham die."

"What if we go to the police? You could hang!"

"What will you tell the police about? Ghosts? Or the things your family did to earn this? What if Wynn tells them all about you and Mr. Grey, as I assure you he will?"

Zeb swallowed. "Bram is my *brother*. I can't just leave him to his death."

"He left Florence to hers. And it was not one of us who pushed Mrs. Bram down the stairs, by the way. But make your own choice."

She left on that. The key turned in the lock.

"Jesus Christ," Zeb said, and sat down hard on the chair. "Jesus."

Gideon dropped to one knee in front of him and held out his arms. Zeb folded forward into them and let himself be held and rocked for a few soothing moments. He needed it.

"What do I do?" he said into Gideon's shoulder. "Gideon, what do I *do*?"

"I don't know, love. I know what you've done."

"What?"

"Quite possibly saved our lives." Gideon kissed his hair. "If we survive this, it will be because you were good to her, you and that oversized heart of yours."

They hung on to one another for a moment, then Zeb pulled away. "I need to tell you, I worked out what Wynn's doing. His ultimate goal."

"On a scale of one to ten, where one represents normal, rational behaviour—"

"Twelve."

"Go on."

Zeb braced himself. "He's sacrificing us, the Wyckhams. Possibly to Satan?"

Gideon just shut his eyes. Zeb pressed on. "Remember the Wyckham curse, that we all die before we're fifty? Wynn told me that Walter had made a bargain—a deal with the devil—that he would live longer by exchanging his wives' and children's futures for his. Well, I found a paper with a list of Walter's wives and children and the ages they died at, and a lot of calculations in Wynn's hand. He was trying to work out how many years they had lost and Walter had gained. I mean, how many years past fifty Walter got for all the years under fifty the others *didn't* get, if you see what I mean. He calculated that Walter had an extra year of life for every six years lost by his relatives, but I didn't check his sums."

"I can see why you wouldn't trouble to."

"Well, no," Zeb said. "But on the other side of the paper he had all our ages—me, Elise, Hawley, Bram—and done the same sort of calculation, and he'd concluded he'd live to sixty-one if we all died now. He even had my birthday written down, I suppose because he didn't want me to get another year older. Is this making sense?"

"No, it really is not," Gideon said. "But I think I understand. He believes he's fated to die at fifty unless he makes the same imaginary bargain that Walter did, and he intends to kill you and steal your remaining years?"

"That's what I think."

"But he'll be fifty next year. If he wants to extend his own life, why didn't he start earlier, when everyone was younger?"

"Are you seriously applying logic to this?" Zeb asked. "Maybe he only developed his theory recently. Maybe he has to be the same age as Walter for it to work. Maybe the goblins are telling him what to do. How should I know?"

"Fair. Well, I suppose that explains why he's involved. I couldn't see why Wynn would care in the slightest that Bram abandoned his mistress but, of course, he doesn't. He brought these people together because what they wanted would help his goal."

"To kill the lot of us and get away with it. He wants it to look like we murdered each other, and failing that, he's got plenty of other people here to blame. Oh, that's what he wanted you for. An obvious scapegoat if he killed me."

"Very possibly," Gideon said thinly. "And he'll play the gentle, baffled recluse, hopelessly surrounded by people fighting over his money or pursuing their own schemes. Who'd believe a story about spiders and sacrifices and ghosts when there's such an obvious lot of motives about? Christ." He put both hands into his hair and gripped hard, as if he was trying to pull himself upright by main force. "It's ingenious, I suppose, but a score of twelve might be underrating this."

"There's something else," Zeb said. "It's possible I'm fraying at the seams now, but this all goes back to Walter, yes? Well, today is Walter's birthday. I can't feel that's a good thing."

Gideon considered that in silence. Then he said, "You asked what we're going to do. The answer is, wait for the signal and get out of here as though the hounds of hell are at our heels."

"What about Bram and Hawley?"

Gideon grimaced. "What can we do? There are two footmen and the chauffeur itching to mete out righteous retribution, and I don't think we'll get anywhere tangling with them. The chauffeur caught me trying to take a ladder from a shed and gave me a rather bad time before he dragged me back in here." He indicated his bruised face. "They're all strong and brutal and they really did not mind hurting me."

"Are you all right?"

"No. He punched me in the face and kicked me in the ribs when I fell. I didn't know if he was going to stop."

Zeb grabbed his hand. "Oh, God."

"I can't fight them. I don't know how. And unless you've taken up the study of jiujitsu in our time apart, nor can you."

Zeb thought about the gun. "Well—"

"We'd have no chance at all in a scrap, even with Bram and Hawley's aid, which we're not going to get, are we?"

"Hawley will be no use. I wouldn't trust him not to run to Wynn, thinking he's being clever; I'd rather leave him here. That's awful."

"No, it isn't," Gideon said grimly. "It's the calculation of necessity, and I think you need to apply it to Bram as well."

"I can't do that," Zeb said. "I can't. I have to try."

"Try what?"

"Talking to him."

"Zeb—"

"He's not Hawley. Hawley is a bad man but Bram could do better, I'm sure he could. I really think he feels guilty about poor Florence."

"And the maid he fondled? And what about Elise?"

"You don't know that was him. If it was your sister, or your brother-in-law—"

"To my knowledge, none of my family have ever driven another human being to their doom. If the best you can say of your brother is that he might not have murdered his wife—"

"He's my brother!" Zeb said, voice rising. Gideon shushed him urgently, and he switched to a hiss. "I promised our father that we'd stand together. Damn it, Gideon, I have to try, can't you see?"

"No!" Gideon's voice was strangled by his attempt to shout quietly. "I *can't* see! He's treated you like dirt for years, and we need to be in here waiting for this blasted signal, not risking missing it because you've wandered off for a chat with a brother who's never thought twice about you! What if he takes it badly? What if he tells Wynn we're planning to make a run for it? Please, Zeb, *think*."

"I have thought. I need to warn my brother, so I'm going to go and find him. Look, there's no reason *I* can't move round the house; I'm not supposed to be locked up. I'll be back as soon as I can. And if I'm not back when Rachel signals, don't wait. Go anyway."

"No. Zeb—"

"I've got to try," Zeb said. "I'm sorry. I love you. But I have to."

He pushed himself to his feet. He didn't want to look

at Gideon's bruised, hurt, angry face; he didn't dare ask for a kiss in case it was refused.

"I'll be back soon," he said again, and went to the secret passage.

Behind him, Gideon said, "Zeb, please. Don't." Zeb didn't turn round.

twenty-three

THE SECRET PASSAGE WAS horrible beyond words. It was narrow. It was dank and dark, and mostly it was *cobwebbed*, with swags of old dusty web draped in sheets from every beam. Zeb could sense the mindless eight-eyed gaze of spiders, hear the rustle and click of angular legs, feel the sticky cling of a strand of web or the horrible brush of a touch. He wanted to run, to drop the lamp and get out of here before he found himself trapped in the bowels of this hellish house under a mound of chittering mandibles—

His imagination would be the death of him.

He forced himself onward, primarily by fixing his gaze on the circle of light the lamp cast on the floor and keeping his head down. It was all right while he had the light. He refused to acknowledge anything moving in the corner of his eye, whether spiders or shadows.

The passage led up a flight of rickety stairs, where the prospect of a plank giving way underfoot momentarily distracted him from the thought of spiders, and found himself faced with a rough wooden panel in the wall. It was secured at eye height with a catch, and lower down with a latch. Both had clearly been used recently because there were no webs attached, a fact for which Zeb was deeply grateful.

He listened a moment to be sure he couldn't hear anyone, and stepped out into what proved to be Elise's bedroom. It still smelled of her face-powder and perfume, and grief hit him like a slap in the face.

He hadn't been fond of her; she hadn't invited it. But she had been *alive*. She had applied cosmetics and put on clothes and gone about the business of living. She had smiled, and he'd seen the woman she might have been. And now she was dead and cold, and it was all so terribly wrong.

Zeb took a moment to recover himself, eyes shut, breathing hard. He went to see if Bram was in the room next door, which would have made everything a lot easier, and thus was not the case. Then he headed out to find his brother.

Gideon had told him this was a bad idea but he really

hadn't needed to. It was a terrible idea, one that nagged at every muscle in his body to turn round and go back and skulk with Gideon until they had a chance to get out.

If he didn't try, though. If he saved himself and left Bram behind without even trying...

Gideon had said *a brother that never thought twice about you*, but Bram had been kind sometimes. He'd played card games with seven-year-old Zeb when he had been at home with nothing better to do, and rarely mocked his fear of spiders. It wasn't much, perhaps, and it was a long time ago, and since then Bram had stabbed him in the back, told lies about him, and set his life on a far harder path.

But none of that merited a death sentence. Not even his betrayal of Florence did that, terrible wrong though it was. Bram unquestionably needed to take a damned hard look at his life, and if they got out of this, if Zeb got him out of this, then he would have a lot of words for his brother.

If they got out. Bram wasn't going to make the escape easier. Zeb still had to try.

He didn't encounter anyone as he came to the landing at the top of the stairs. The house was quiet, unpleasantly so.

He made his way downstairs feeling horribly exposed, spine prickling with the possibility of a push even though there was nobody around. He couldn't hear voices from anywhere, or see anyone. It felt like a tomb.

Where might Bram be?

He made his way to the library, and his brother was indeed there, sitting in the chair where he'd been—Christ, it was only this morning. He looked even worse than before, wreathed in smoke.

Zeb shut the door. "Bram."

Bram glanced around and away. He didn't launch into a diatribe about Zeb's behaviour in dumping Elise's body on the ground. That was worrying in itself.

"Bram," Zeb said again, and then didn't know what else to say. "Are you all right? Would you at least speak to me?"

Bram stared, silent, and Zeb had a sudden horrible memory of the scene in *The Monastery* where the heroine begged for information from a servant who finally opened his mouth to reveal his tongue had been cut out. "Bram!" he yelped.

"What, damn you?"

"Oh, thank God. I mean—Listen, I'm just going to say this. Wynn is trying to kill us. He wants us, all the Wyckhams, dead."

"Nonsense."

"Listen to me," Zeb snapped. "I don't have time to explain, so I need you to trust me. On Father's life, Bram, we have to go. We have to get out of this house and we don't have long to do it, so come with me, because if you stay I don't think you'll be alive tomorrow. You aren't going to inherit. Wynn's used that to lure you here, and to make us turn on each other, and at the end of it, he's going to enjoy his wealth for many more years, and we'll be dead."

"Dead," Bram said.

"Like Florence. Remember Florence? Her father is here, and he wants you dead for what you did. You have to come with me. I will get you out of here, but come *now*."

"Florence is dead," Bram repeated, musing. "And Elise. She killed her, you know. Elise killed Florence, and Florence killed Elise. Florence stood at the bottom of the stairs, and Elise told her to go away. And then Elise stood at the top of the stairs, and Florence sent *her* away. I felt her."

"Felt her how?"

"Her spirit impelled me." Bram moved his hands as he spoke, a tiny gesture like a push.

Zeb couldn't respond. He stared at his brother, feeling an odd numbness in his face and fingers.

Gideon tried to tell you...

"It is for the best," Bram said, voice a starveling version of his usual pomposity. "I am free now and can give Jessamine the protection of my name. The inheritance was promised to me, and Elise stood in my way. It is all for the best."

Zeb considered one last appeal. *If you ever cared about me*, perhaps, or *By the vow we made at Father's deathbed...*

But he'd be wasting his breath, as perhaps he had always been wasting his breath. And now he needed to get back to Gideon, and leave everyone in this house to the hell they'd helped build for themselves and each other.

"Goodbye, Bram," he said, because he couldn't think of anything better, and headed to the door. He was two steps away when it opened.

"Ah, Zebedee," said Wynn.

"Excuse me." Zeb took a step sideways, poised to run, and stopped when he saw one of the footmen looming behind Wynn, blocking most of the door.

"No, I don't think so," Wynn said. "You have done enough harm. Bram, I came to warn you. Your brother is dangerous. He wants to kill you."

"Oh, rubbish," Zeb said. "Come home with your drawers torn and say you found the money. You're lying," he added for clarity.

"Bram." Wynn's voice was compelling. "You know he has been trying to steal your inheritance all along. First your father's money, now the Wyckham fortune. You know how envious he is. And now he has got you alone. Thank God I found you."

Bram looked at Zeb, his eyes clearing a little for the first time in their conversation, as if he was actually bothering to pay attention. "You," he said.

"Oh, stop it," Zeb snapped. "We've been talking for a while with absolutely no homicide, and what would I kill you with anyway, a pen? A hardback edition of a Walter Wyckham novel?"

"Or the gun you have on your person," Wynn said, the note of triumph clear in his voice. "Look, Bram, you will see—"

Zeb stood up, pulled out the sides of his coat, and flapped them, then pulled them higher so his gun-free waist could be seen. He opened the front of the coat. "What gun?"

"You have it," Wynn said. "You took it."

"No, I did not. Because someone who goes around with a gun is someone who wants to hurt or threaten people, and I don't." *And also I can spot a bear trap when one is set for me, you smug prick.*

"Of course you have it," Wynn said, sounding just a touch off-balance. "It isn't there."

The gong boomed in the hall. Zeb glanced at the clock. It was barely twelve, which was early for lunchtime—

The signal. Oh God, that must be Rachel's signal. He had to go.

"What was that?" Wynn said, with a frown.

"I have no idea where your gun is, Wynn. You should be more careful." Zeb needed Wynn not to pay attention to the gong, and even more, he needed to get out of here. "I expect Hawley took it."

"Hawley?"

"Why not? He doesn't mind hurting people. And you've made him pretty desperate, haven't you? I don't know what you've been giving him—oh, is it in those ghastly cigarettes?" He glanced back at Bram, recognizing the vagueness in his face. "You've got them both smoking it. Clever. Anyway, he's not making much sense, so if someone's running around with the gun you left lying about, it's probably him."

The footman's expression hardened menacingly. Zeb might have felt guilty, but he needed to get back to Gideon now, *now*, and everything else was secondary.

"Yes," Wynn said. "Yes, that will be it. Hawley has it. And I don't know where Jessamine is. She has changed her mind, Bram, she no longer wants this foolish engagement to Hawley. If he has taken her somewhere secluded—if he thinks to compromise her and force her into marriage, so he can steal your inheritance—"

"The swine." Bram rose heavily to his feet. "I will not have it. He has no right."

"Save her. You will have it all, if you find him and save her."

"Don't listen, Bram," Zeb said. "He's trying to make us all fight, and you're falling for it."

Wynn shot him a nasty look. "You are a coward. Bram will play the man's part here. Find Hawley, Bram. Take the poker. You can't trust him. Don't give him a chance."

Bram picked up the poker. Zeb said, hopelessly, "Don't."

He might as well not have spoken. Bram walked out of the room like an automaton. Wynn went with him. Zeb made to go too, and found the footman in his way. As he tried to get round, Jessamine stepped into the room. Bram must have walked right past her.

She looked at Zeb, a little smile curving her lips, and he had no idea how he'd ever seen the innocent schoolgirl.

"Please," he said. "Let us go. Whatever you're doing, Wynn's doing—I just want to leave. I don't want the money."

"Don't you?" she said. "I do. Lock him in."

"No!" Zeb yelped. He tried to rush forward, and the footman pushed him back, a sharp, hard shove not to his shoulder but to his face. The shock of it along with the force sent Zeb stumbling back.

"Nothing personal, Cousin Zeb," Jessamine said, and shut the door. He heard the scrape of a key in the lock.

No.

He rattled the door handle, then tugged. It didn't budge.

He thought about kicking it in, but the doorjamb was on the wrong side, the door looked like oak, and he'd never kicked in a door in his life. Of all the useful skills not to have.

"Hey!" he shouted. "Let me out!"

Nobody answered. That wasn't really a surprise.

Window. Zeb ran to it and stopped dead, because he noticed for the first time that it wasn't a sash window. It was divided into twelve panes, all in one large frame. It didn't bloody open.

He could break it. He could take the chair and put it through the window, smashing out the glass and woodwork until he'd made a hole he could escape through. And Wynn's vengeful staff would hear him do it, because they could hardly not, and they would come out after him, and if Gideon was taking the opportunity to escape that Zeb had thrown away for his stupid, greedy, murdering big brother, they'd catch him too.

Not the window, then.

Zeb was aware of his heart beating a little too fast, the odd clarity of crisis battling with the dragging sensation of oncoming exhaustion because the last days had just been too damned much, and he was fast running out of steam. He exhaled hard and turned to the wall. This house was a Swiss cheese of secret passages on Rachel's account: there would surely be one in the library. And most of the walls were covered in bookcases, so—

He went to the painting of Walter Wyckham, hanging in the only free wall space, and examined the panelling around it. There was a row of carved bosses like the one Rachel had used; he pressed them in order and the third one clicked.

Nothing happened. He pushed the panel, working out where the concealed door must be, and felt a tiny bit of give, but it wouldn't open, no matter how hard he pushed.

It must be latched on the other side, like the door in Elise's room had been. It was latched, and there was no other spot in this damned room for another secret door, and now he was out of ideas, out of energy, out of time.

Despair swamped him, washing the strength from his legs. He sat on the nearest chair and put his face in his hands.

If he broke the window, he'd be caught, and Gideon with him. But if he stayed here and waited for Wynn to come back with his twisted plans and angry men—well, it was Zeb they wanted. Gideon could get away if he had the sense to run, if he wasn't waiting for Zeb to come back. If Zeb hadn't ruined them both, this time for good.

"Please go, Gideon," he said aloud, voice scratchy. "Please be going. Please, please, please have gone without me, *please*."

There was a quiet scrape. The panelling swung open, revealing a dark space and a tall form in it.

"Not a chance," Gideon said.

Zeb wasn't sure what he responded. He wasn't sure of anything except that somehow he was on his feet, in Gideon's arms, holding on because Gideon was here, not escaping, and that was terribly right and even more terribly wrong.

Gideon gave him an ungentle shake. "Zeb! We have to hurry. Here, put this on."

He scooped up a coat he'd dropped on the floor and thrust something into Zeb's arms once he had it on. "Don't lose this. Quick, now, and whatever you do, stay quiet."

He gestured Zeb into the passage and shut the door behind them. It was instantly, horribly dark. Zeb stumbled and put his free hand out, right into a dusty, sticky mass that rustled against his skin. *Cobweb.* He tried to swallow his instinctive noise of horror, batting the filth from him.

"Zeb!" A hand grabbed his. "I have you. I'll take you. Just follow me and stay quiet. *Please.*"

I can't. I can't.

You have to.

Zeb didn't think he could speak, but he squeezed Gideon's hand. "Thank you," Gideon said softly, and led them, feeling his way, Zeb gripping his fingers. It smelled like spiders in here. It would be full of spiders and he couldn't see and they could be landing on him in the dark and he wouldn't know...

There are people out there who are going to kill you. We are not going to fuss about fucking spiders.

He couldn't help fussing about fucking spiders. He put every scrap of willpower he had left into the acts of breathing, walking, and holding Gideon's hand like a lifeline. *I will not scream. If I scream they will catch us so I won't, I won't, I won't...*

Eternity passed, and then at last there was a click, and light, and they lurched out into the anteroom where Gideon had been imprisoned. Zeb released his hand with a gasp of relief, and brushed frantically at his shoulders.

"You did it," Gideon breathed. "Only a few feet more and then we're out."

Zeb set his teeth. "Lead on."

Gideon opened the other panel and they plunged into the passage. It was just a few steps this time, then Gideon opened the door, and they were outside Lackaday House, in the fresh breathable air of a cold, grey-bright winter day. It felt as though he'd been airless for the whole terrible time he'd been here.

Gideon set off at speed. Zeb hurried to match his stride and realised within seconds that something was wrong.

"Gideon? Are you all right?"

"My ribs hurt like blazes."

"Oh hell. Can you walk this fast?"

"I'll run if I have to," Gideon said through his teeth. "We have definitely outstayed our welcome."

He was marching down the curving path to the follies, breath steaming in the cold air. "Shouldn't we head to the main drive?" Zeb said.

"When we're out of eyeshot of the house."

That was logical, even if Zeb wanted to run to the gate in the straightest possible line. He matched Gideon's brisk pace and ducked round to his painful side, got his shoulder under Gideon's, took a bit of his weight.

"Thanks," Gideon said on a breath. They were walking at a speed that couldn't be called running but was uncomfortably brisk. "Didn't go well with Bram?"

"You were right. He killed Elise." Zeb had to stop there a second, pressing his lips together against the wave of grief and anger. "He said Florence's ghost made him do it."

"God."

"He wasn't in his right mind. Wynn's been drugging him, and scaring him out of his wits, and it was all Florence this and Elise that. But even so...he was still going after the inheritance. That was what mattered to him. In the end, it was all that mattered to him." The words were desolate in the moorland air.

"Yes," Gideon said. "That's what he chose. And if there

was ever anything to be done about it, it wasn't by you, and it wasn't now."

They walked for a moment in the silence you got when there was nothing else to say. Gideon steered them down a side path. "Let's head to the damned drive. Ow."

"You shouldn't have been running around the house," Zeb said, his voice wobbling with gratitude that Gideon had done exactly that. "How were you there?"

"I had a look around the room while I was waiting for you and found another secret passage which I realised must lead towards the hall. I'd noticed earlier that you'd left your satchel with the coats there, and I suspected you might not remember. So I thought I'd try to get it."

"My—" Zeb belatedly noticed what he was holding. His satchel, reassuringly thick with paper. "Wait. You went out there just to get my manuscript? You saved my *book*?"

"Well," Gideon said, sounding a touch embarrassed. "You write them, and I'll look after them?"

Zeb couldn't find words. Gideon gave him a quick smile. "And we couldn't abandon the new Faraway Meadow. Imagine what my nieces would say. Anyway, I had started heading back after the gong, and I thought I heard you shout, so I came to listen."

"Thank you," Zeb said raggedly. "Jessamine locked me in. I couldn't get out, and—and I thought, if you didn't go, if you waited for me and you missed the chance to escape because of me—"

"Of course I didn't go. I made you a promise, remember? A concrete and specific promise that you can mark as kept, and to which you can refer back as evidence when you're wondering about future promises."

"Well, you shouldn't have!"

"But I did, because I love you," Gideon said. "You lit up my life when you asked if you could buy me a drink, and when the light went away—I can't do that again. I am with you and that is all there is to it, even if it means staying in this hellhole. Although, in the name of all that's holy, can we not."

"Amen," Zeb said. "And I knew you wouldn't go without me, really. That's why I was so upset. Because I knew."

"Good," Gideon said softly. "Then—Oh *shit*!"

Zeb didn't know what he meant for a moment, and then he saw it. Far too far ahead of them, well out of hailing distance, a horse-drawn cart, heading up the drive, towards the gate.

"*Run*," they said together.

Zeb hadn't run any sort of distance in a very long time. He set off at a spanking pace, far too fast, because his legs started to hurt within a few steps. It was so cold that every dragged-in breath felt like broken glass in his lungs. His shoes were utterly inadequate and dangerously slippery, his satchel and overcoat felt like they weighed as much as himself again, and this was a nightmare where you ran and ran without ever getting any nearer your goal.

Gideon had hurt, perhaps cracked, ribs, and he was still charging on though his breath heaved and sobbed. Zeb put his head down, and forced his thighs to move, tasting something like iron in his mouth. Something like blood.

Blood. Wynn. Bram. Hawley.

Run.

"Can't," Gideon gasped. "Can't. You go."

The cart wasn't so far ahead now, but the gate was in sight, too, and the gatekeeper might emerge any moment. Zeb looked over his shoulder, grabbed Gideon's hand, and said, "Motor. They're coming."

He could feel the pulse of shock. Gideon made a panicked noise and sprinted with a last burst of energy, long legs covering the ground, accelerating away. Zeb pounded after him, trying to catch up and failing, blood roaring in his ears, and then Gideon stopped running and doubled over, hands on knees, and Zeb thought, *No, no, no, you can't give up now,* and took just a few more frantic paces before he realised the cart had stopped too.

The carter was twisted round in his seat, looking at them both oddly. Zeb could hardly blame him.

"Lift," he managed through whoops as he attempted to suck in oxygen from air that seemed very short of the stuff. "Town?"

"In a hurry, are 'ee?" the grocer's man enquired.

"Row," Zeb explained. "Mr. Wyckham. Awful man."

That would have to do it, because he was going to throw up if he did anything but breathe for a while. Gideon straightened a bit to add, "Very disobliging chauffeur," which was more syllables than Zeb could imagine uttering in one go ever again.

"That's a nasty bit of work," the grocer's man agreed, with a darkling look. "Both on 'em, come to that. Sacked my young lady for nothing, that Wynn Wyckham did. You may as well hop on. Be a bit chilly, so there's an old blanket in the back if you want. Mind, you've warmed yourselves up nicely." He chortled. "Aye, warmed yourselves nicely, you have!"

Zeb helped Gideon get into the cart with a push, and then couldn't make his unwilling thighs do the necessary climb. Gideon looked down at him and said quietly, "If I tell you we're being chased, would that help?"

"Sorry," Zeb said. "Worked, though."

"Swine." Gideon pulled him up. "We're in," he told the driver, who was still chuckling at his own witticism. "Might just lie down to catch my breath. Shall we go?"

They hunkered down in the cart, concealed by its

wooden sides. Zeb took Gideon's hand, cold and sweaty, and felt long fingers lace through his.

They trundled on to the gate with agonizing slowness considering how fast the cart had seemed to go before, and stopped again. It would take time for the gatekeeper to go through the lengthy palaver of opening the gate. They'd just have to wait, and keep still. Again.

Zeb stared at the sky. He wondered if he could hear the motor-car in pursuit, or if it was the blood still roaring in his ears. He wondered what was happening back at Lackaday House, and what they would do when they reached town. He wondered if Gideon might like to find a place together in London, or what he might feel about living in the countryside instead, and everything except whether the gate might not open, because he could not bear to think about that.

He could feel Gideon's pulse in his fingers, thudding against Zeb's. If the gatekeeper kept them here and sent to the house for help...

The gate screeched and squealed, agonisingly slow. They stood for aeons longer and then finally, finally, the cart jogged into motion. Gideon let out a long, silent breath and whispered on the edge of hearing, "Still us."

Zeb squeezed his fingers. Gideon squeezed back. The cart drove slowly, ploddingly, into the moor, jolting their way to freedom, and behind them the gates of Lackaday House screamed one last time as they shut.

epilogue

At the coroner's inquest into the tragic events at Lackaday House, Wynn Wyckham and his staff testified that Elise Wyckham's death was the act of her husband, Bram; that, in the course of a confrontation the following day, Bram Wyckham was fatally shot by Elise's former lover, his cousin Hawley; and that Hawley Wyckham jumped off the roof rather than face justice.

Zebedee Wyckham attempted to interrupt the proceedings several times and was eventually removed from the hearing by order of the coroner, who had his bizarre and implausible accusations struck from the record. No blame was attached to Wynn as the unfortunate host of the disastrous party.

After the tragedy, Wynn Wyckham became more

reclusive than before. However, local acquaintances noted that a Miss Jessamine Evans appeared to have taken up residence at Lackaday House.

A few months later, on the evening before Wynn's fiftieth birthday, the acetylene gas plant exploded and Lackaday House burned to the ground. Wynn's charred remains were recovered from the ruins, with the coroner noting it was unclear what had prevented him fleeing the house. A disused well in a cellar was also discovered to hold a badly decayed human body, identified by clothing as Colonel Wyckham Dash.

Jessamine Evans's body was not found, but due to the fierce blaze, she was presumed dead. An expensively dressed woman of her description carrying nearly fifteen thousand pounds in cash and jewels travelled on a cross-Atlantic steamer not long afterwards and disappeared in the United States, but no connection was ever established.

Zeb Wyckham inherited the remaining Wyckham fortune by default. He immediately had the full sum put into a trust to be repatriated to the islands where Walter Wyckham had owned plantations, administered by his live-in personal secretary and business manager, Gideon Grey.

Zeb went on to have a forty-year writing career, publishing some thirty children's books as Zinnia Waters, and a number of adult books under his own name, including the hugely successful Barnaby Black adventure series. A Buzzfeed listicle of 17 Surprisingly Queer Olden Days Books cited *The Black Agency* at #2, calling it "great fun and gay as a box of frogs."

Walter Wyckham's average rating on Goodreads is 2.3★. The top-rated text review for *The Monastery* reads, in full, "Boring."

author's note

I owe more gratitude than I can say to my ADHD readers on this book: Bethany Witham, Kylie Mulligan, MJ, and Roxie Noir. All of them gave me their time, advice, and experience with incredible generosity. I hope I have done justice to their grace and care in the portrayal of Zeb. Any mistakes or infelicities are, of course, mine. Deep gratitude to Marcela Bolívar for the wonderful cover art, and to the Sourcebooks design team for making it all look perfect.

As ever, I am reliant on my invaluable first readers, Lis Paice and May Peterson, patiently sifting the wheat from my chaff, and my marvellous agent, Courtney Miller-Callihan.

Huge thanks to Mary Altman and Gretchen Stelter at Sourcebooks for insightful criticism, supportive edits, and (most importantly) laughing at my jokes.

Some doctors, in particular paediatricians, had started to note and describe what we now call ADHD at the time this book is set, but it was not formally recognised as a neurodevelopmental condition until the 1960s.

If you're curious about the stories with evil patterns, they are "The Yellow Wallpaper" by Charlotte Perkins Gilman, to which this book pays tribute, and MR James's "The Diary of Mr. Poynter" (scary curtains) (no, really).

Many UK institutions, such as the National Trust, are moving towards acknowledging how much of our cultural heritage was built on slavery. Walter Wyckham was loosely inspired by William Beckford—plantation owner, Gothic novelist, massive creep, and builder of houses that fell down—who was at one point the richest commoner in England off the backs of enslaved people until he blew the lot building houses that fell down. Uncollapsed remnants of his construction fetish survive at Beckford's Tower in Bath; his book *Vathek* is equally poorly structured.

Some readers may be aware I turned fifty while writing this book. That has nothing to do with anything, and I have no idea why you're bringing it up like this.

Hungry for more?
Enjoy this glimpse into the world of *The Secret Lives of Country Gentlemen*, available now.

February 1810

KENT WAS STILL THERE.

Gareth had tumbled into the Three Ducks with his lungs burning from walking too fast in the cold night air, his face instantly reddening as the warm fug of the taproom assailed him. He didn't even know why he'd hurried: he was over two hours late and he'd told himself the whole way that Kent would have left already. If the situation were reversed, Gareth would have decided his lover for the night wasn't coming and left cursing the man's name. He'd fully expected Kent to do the same or, even more likely, find another warm body to go upstairs with.

He'd come anyway because...well, *because,* that was all. Because it was rude to miss an appointment, because he had nowhere else he wanted to go, because he hoped against hope that just this one thing might not be taken from him today.

And there Kent was, unmissable, the only man in a room crowded with men. He was sitting with a mug of ale and his feet up on a stool, chatting to the landlord without a care in the world. Then he looked round at the door and smiled, and the sight of him took Gareth's remaining breath.

The landlord slouched away as Gareth came to the table. "I'm so sorry I'm late."

"Watcher, London." *What cheer,* Gareth had worked out that phrase meant: Kent's version of *good evening.* Gareth would have been furious in his place, but the smile in Kent's warm golden-brown eyes looked entirely real. "Thought you weren't coming."

"I didn't mean to keep you waiting so long." *Thank you for staying,* Gareth wanted to say.

Kent waved a hand before he could go on, dismissing his failure to appear as though it didn't matter at all. "You look fraped. Everything all right?"

Gareth didn't know what *fraped* meant, but he had no doubt he looked it. "Not really. No. It's been rather a bad day. Terrible, really."

"Here, sit down. I'll get you a drink and you can tell me about it." He rose from his seat.

"No, don't." Gareth regretted the words as he spoke them. He would have liked very much to have a drink with Kent, to pour out what had happened and the bewildering uncertainty that now surrounded him. Except that if he tried to explain anything he'd have to explain everything, and he didn't want to do that. To present himself as a pitiable object, an unwanted thing, to easily confident Kent who didn't look like he'd been rejected in his life, then to watch him be repelled by the stench of failure, as people always were—No.

Anyway, Gareth had better ideas of how to spend the evening than brooding about his dismal situation. He had the rest of his life for that. "It doesn't matter. Could we go upstairs?"

Kent's thick brows angled. "In a hurry?"

"It's late. And I was looking forward to seeing you."

Kent frowned, just a little. Gareth probably didn't seem a particularly desirable prospect, sweaty and flustered as he was. Fraped, even. He reached for Kent's mug of ale, watching those glowing brown eyes watching him, and took a long, deliberate swallow.

"Thirsty?"

"In need," Gareth agreed, and dragged the back of his hand over his mouth in a meaningful fashion.

Kent's lips curved. "Better?"

"Getting there."

"Suppose we might as well go up, en."

The Three Ducks made the back room and the dark covered courtyard available for illicit fumbling and spending. Gareth knew the spaces well, having come here many times over the years. He'd always assumed the upstairs room was private, but Kent, who he'd never seen in here prior to this week, apparently had the privilege of using it. Perhaps he was an old friend of the landlord. Or perhaps it was just that smile of his, that wide, irresistible grin that sluiced you in happy anticipation and confidence and sheer joy of living. Gareth had gone down poleaxed at the first flash of that smile. He wasn't surprised the Ducks' taciturn landlord couldn't resist it either.

They crashed into the upstairs room together, already kissing wildly. Kent was strong, with broad shoulders and taut muscle, several inches under Gareth's height but a lot more solid, and he moved with all the confidence of his smile. He planted a hand on Gareth's arse, pulling him close, and Gareth sank into the sensation with a flood of relief.

Fingers grasping, lips and tongues locking, the press of thigh against thigh—Gareth got both hands into Kent's long, loose curls, the strands so thick and strong by comparison to his own flyaway hair. He held on hard as Kent kissed him, and felt Kent's smile against his mouth.

"London," Kent murmured. "I want you bare."

Gareth let go with a touch of reluctance: he liked Kent's hair. But Kent liked him undressed, so he stood as Kent pulled first coat then waistcoat off his shoulders; raised his arms obediently as Kent tugged his shirt over his head.

He'd worn trousers and shoes partly because the Three Ducks was not a place to dress well, partly because Kent dressed like a working man, and mostly because they came off easily. He kicked off his shoes, inhaled as Kent unfastened the buttons at his waist, and bent to peel off his stockings.

And there he was, exposed to Kent's gaze in the golden lamplight.

It had felt very odd the first time he'd stood naked like this under Kent's scrutiny. He'd never been fully bare with a lover before Kent. Surreptitious fumblings in dark corners didn't come with the luxury of time, or of more undressing than necessary. And he had no idea why Kent liked to look at him so much. Gareth was nothing special: tall but thin, pale and uninteresting. He wouldn't have noticed himself in a crowd, whereas a man could look at Kent's firm, fit body and that outrageous smile for hours.

Yet there was no mistaking the heat in Kent's eyes when he stood back and examined Gareth, and the frank appreciation tingled like a touch on his skin.

"Hearts alive, you're a pretty one," Kent said, voice a little deeper than usual. "Ah, London."

Gareth breathed the feeling in: naked, exposed, offering every inch of himself up and waiting for Kent's touch. His prick was stiff at the thought. "Christ," he said. "I love it when you look at me."

"Makes two of us."

Kent moved forward, slid his hand over Gareth's chest. It was narrower and far less impressive than Kent's own broad muscles, but Kent didn't seem to mind. His fingertips were light. Gareth quivered under the feathery touch as it roamed his skin, and couldn't help a gasp as Kent's hand finally closed around his jutting prick.

"Eager," Kent murmured. "You ready for me, London?"

"Whenever you are." Kent was still fully clad. "If you're joining me, that is."

"Oh, I'll be doing that."

Kent was smiling. Gareth smiled back, and his heart was pounding every bit as hard as the blood in his groin.

He'd only come into the Ducks last week for a drink with like-minded company. Of course he'd have taken a bit of pleasure if any offer came his way, but he'd have been perfectly happy with a mug of ale and a chance to breathe out from another day. He'd looked around to see who he knew—and then he'd seen *him*.

A working man, by his dress, in a long dark leather

coat. Tawny brown skin; thick, wavy black hair loose to his shoulders; a faint shadow of black beard; a generous mouth. He was talking to a pretty youth of very similar colouring, and as Gareth watched, he had thrown his head back and laughed.

Yes, Gareth had watched. Stared, even. Very well, he'd gaped like a hopeless fool, but one didn't see a man, a smile, like that every day. He'd still been looking when, unexpectedly, the man had glanced over, and their eyes met.

Gareth had looked away at once, embarrassed and annoyed at himself for the needy display. He'd carefully stared into the opposite corner of the room to mark his lack of interest, until a throat was cleared close to him, and he realised someone was standing by his chair. Not just someone. *Him.*

"Watcher," he'd said. Gareth's cheeks instantly flamed because he'd unquestionably been watching, but the man went on without a pause, "Wondered if you might be wanting company."

That was bewildering. Was he being mocked for gawping so obviously?

The man gave him a quizzical look. "Did I startle you? You look like a sighted hare."

Gareth had no idea what that meant and it sounded oddly bucolic for a London alehouse, especially in that country accent, with broad vowels and a roll to the 'r'. It didn't matter, because the man, this man, was *talking* to him.

He managed a smile that he hoped didn't look too idiotish. "I beg your pardon, I was in a brown study. I'd love company, if you'd like to join me."

The man took a stool. "I will, en. What's your name?"

Gareth winced. "Uh. Um, I don't usually, here—for discretion, you know—"

"No names? Got you, beg pardon. I'm Kentish."

"Well, hello, Kentish," Gareth said, pure instinct. At least part of his brain was still working.

The man's eyes crinkled responsively. "*From* Kent. I meant, we're friendlier down there."

"I don't know. Londoners can be quite friendly, in the right circumstances."

"I bet you can." He smiled, and the dazzling force of it close up rocked Gareth in his seat. "You're London, then? Nice to meet you, London."

Gareth smiled back, hopelessly enthralled. "You too, Kent."

They'd left the question of names there; they'd had better things to do. Kent had obtained the luxury of the upstairs room—private, comfortable, no unexpected puddles of stale beer, drain-water, or worse—in about five minutes, and Gareth had been naked for him two minutes after that. Naked and delighting in it, as though Kent's physical confidence and frank enjoyment were contagious.

They *were* contagious. He rejoiced in his own body and in Gareth's. He laughed, he set out to please them both without shame, or fear, or second thoughts, and Gareth, who was usually consumed by shame and fear and second thoughts, all but forgot them in Kent's company. They'd met every night since and it had been the most joyous week of his life, this unexpected, gleeful, frank pleasure. Kent's admiring looks, his capable fingers and strong arms. His smile.

Gareth stood now, bare and erect, as Kent stroked and kissed him till his prick was leaking and his knees were weak. He undressed Kent with shaking fingers, in awe of the magnificent solid muscle, loving the rich look of Kent's warm brown skin against his own city pallor. He went to his knees on the bed, and cried aloud as Kent held his shoulder and fucked him with little urgent whispers—"You're lovely, London, so lovely"—and when it was over he buried his face in the rough mattress to hide his sudden urge to weep.

Kent's arm came over his waist. "You all right?"

"Yes. It's—I'm very well."

Kent stroked Gareth's spine. "You've a nice back. Nice arse, come to that."

"Well, you certainly came to it."

Kent chuckled. "So I did."

Gareth stretched luxuriously. Kent's breath came hot against his back in an exhalation. "London?"

"Mmm?"

"I've got to go."

Gareth's stomach plunged. "Already?" he said, and hated the plaintive note he heard in his own voice. "Sorry. Of course. It was my fault for being late."

Kent gave him a little squeeze. "Not right now. I meant I'm going home."

Gareth's eyes snapped open. He stared at the wall. The heat of rutting was fading from his skin and he felt quite suddenly sore, and sticky, and stupid. "To Kent?"

"To Kent. I've finished my business here, and I've a lot to do there that won't wait."

Of course he did. Of course he was going back. Gareth could feel his cheeks heating, not so much at Kent's words as at his own foolishness in not anticipating this. He'd lived in a continuous present of *see you tomorrow* without thinking about when it would end—how had he not thought about when it would end?—and of course that wouldn't carry on. Of course Kent had been planning to walk away all along.

"Yes, of course you must. Have a safe journey. It was good to know you."

The words were well enough, but the tone sounded horribly false in his own ears. Kent, lying against his back, went still, and then took hold of Gareth's shoulder and tugged until he was forced to roll over and face him. "Good to know me? What's that mean?"

"Well...goodbye? Isn't that what you were saying?"

"I was saying I've got to get home. Doesn't mean I can't come back. I have business here, regular-like. I'll be back in April, reckon." He brushed a finger over Gareth's cheek. "Wondered if you'd care to meet again."

Gareth's chest clenched tight. "Meet? What do you mean? How?"

"The usual way? You tell me your name and how I reach you. I write you a note and say I'll be here on such-and-such a day. You turn up. I turn up. Maybe we make a bit more time for a drink and a talk first. Have a bite to eat." He cocked an eyebrow, lips half smiling, eyes full of easy confidence: a man who absolutely expected his week-long lover to be waiting for him in two- or three-months' time.

The enraging thing was, Gareth wanted to. He could already imagine the heady anticipation as April approached, the thrill of unfolding a note with shaking fingers and walking into the Ducks to the greeting of "Watcher, London"...

That was easy to imagine. Fantasies always were. But

he could also imagine the slow-dawning realisation as April ticked into May and no note came, or ever would, because Gareth might have amused Kent for a week but that meant nothing. He wouldn't write; he wouldn't come, and Gareth didn't wait for anyone any more.

about the author

KJ Charles spent twenty years as an editor in British publishing before fleeing the scene to become a full-time historical romance novelist. She has written more than twenty-five novels since then, and her books have been translated into eight languages. She lives in London.

Website: kjcharleswriter.com
Bluesky: @kjcharleswriter.com